I0522477

the

LOST

PHOTOGRAPHS

the
LOST
PHOTOGRAPHS

RICHARD IRA CARROLL

Sojourn Publishing, LLC

The Lost Photographs
Second Edition
Copyright © 2018 by *Richard Ira Carroll.*

Paperback ISBN: 978-1-62747-144-2
eBook ISBN: 978-1-62747-138-1

All rights reserved.
No part of this publication may be reproduced, distributed, or transmitted in any form or by any means, including photocopying, recording, or other electronic or mechanical methods, without the prior written permission of the publisher, except in the case of brief quotations embodied in critical reviews and certain other noncommercial uses permitted by copyright law.

This novel is a work of fiction. Names, descriptions, entities, and incidents included in the story are the products of the author's imagination. Any resemblance to actual persons, events, and entities is entirely coincidental.
The opinions expressed by the author are not necessarily those of Sojourn Publishing, LLC.

Published by: Sojourn Publishing , LLC
Printed in the United States of America

Praise for "The Lost Photographs"

"I like this novel very much . . . it is a slam-bang adventure story that is quite well-written, moving along from one action-packed scene to another. It is also a sweet love story that takes its good old time to come to a denouement, as all good love stories should.

"And . . . it's a rollicking good time between two males who have been friends for a long, long time. I especially like the easy dialogue Richard has created between these two guys - it is believable and amusing. I predict a possible best seller." — Bill Worth, editor, and author of "Outwitting Multiple Sclerosis:" How Forgiveness Helped Me Heal My Brain By Changing My Mind" and the novels "House of the Sun: A Metaphysical Novel of Maui" and "The Hidden Life of Jesus Christ: A Memoir."

* * * * *

"The best things about this book are the minute but not tedious descriptions of the engineering allowing the search through the ice. I often schedule chunks of time for edit work; *Photographs* kept me reading on past my deadlines. This is what Stephen King calls "the gotta." *Gotta stay up an extra half hour to finish this. Gotta see how they get out of this one.* It's probably the single most important attribute a work of fiction can have, and *Photographs* succeeds admirably." — Idony Lisle, Style Editor

* * * * *

I loved the plot, action and the characters in The Lost Photographs. I am really looking forward to Richard Carroll's next book. — Tom P.

* * * * *

This book has a little of everything, except offensive, gratuitous sex or gore. Action, mystery, romance, relationships, all underscored by the author's hypothesis of what could have happened to the lost evidence of the remnants of Noah's Ark. Interesting! — Amazon Customer

* * * * *

This book is incredible from start to finish. Historical information intertwined in a novel that becomes so real and detailed that you feel as though you are a part of the story. Mr. Carroll's writing and descriptions create within the mind of the reader the moods and scenes that enable this story to flow from one page to another. If you are interested in history, suspense, adventure, or just good old fashion reading, sit back and enjoy this book: — Dan C.

* * * * *

An epic adventure with friendships, a hint of romance, as well as a search transcending many decades to discover Noah's Ark. —Angie L.

ACKNOWLEDGMENT

Without the help of my best friend, Yvonne, who is also my lovely wife, this story would never have been told.

I thank her for challenging me to write this story, which was locked in my mind for years.

Historical Notes

Russian soldiers have claimed that in 1916 during an unusually hot summer, a pilot in the Russian Imperial Air Force spotted a large wooden vessel protruding from a frozen lake in a glacier high up on Mount Ararat in Turkey. Other flights from Russia supposedly confirmed the discovery.

The Czar of Russia, Nicholas II, sent two army engineering companies up the very difficult and dangerous mountain to investigate.

When the soldiers returned, they said they had reached the vessel and determined it had to be the actual ark of Noah. They claimed to have found cages and animal pens inside. The measurements of the vessel matched the ratio of the length, width, and height as shown in cubits in the Bible. They took many photographs, some showing Russian soldiers standing on the ark.

All the information, drawings, artist sketches, wood samples, and photographs were sent to the Czar. There is a rumor that the Czar and his household were fascinated by the discovery. Unfortunately, all the information regarding the expedition was lost or destroyed during the ensuing Russian Revolution and was never seen again.

Soon after, the Czar and his family, including his daughter, Anastasia, were murdered. All that remains is the testimony from the soldiers who were a part of the expedition. The testimonies were recorded many years later when it was safe to do so.

This story and many other stories of persons who claim they have personally seen and touched Noah's ark on Mount Ararat in Turkey can be found in public libraries and on the Internet. This novel, "The Lost Photographs," is based on those stories.

Prologue

3000 BC

Startled, the bearded man woke from a restless sleep, knowing something was dreadfully wrong.

The storm had been raging for three days now. Exhaustion had consumed him when he finally laid down to rest. A foreboding darkness filled the cold, confining space as the rain pounded on the deck and the wind howled across the wood planking above.

Alarmed, Noah, the man God chose to start mankind anew, realized the ship was not moving. In a storm like this the vessel should still be rolling back and forth violently.

The forty days and forty nights of constant heavy rain had passed followed by a period of sunshine. But the local storm they were experiencing now was frightening. Noah prayed the rain would only last a few days.

The problem they were facing now was the receding water as it refilled the massive aquifers of the earth and evaporated into the atmosphere.

Suddenly the roof hatch above him sprung open, allowing the rain to pour in. A burst of lightning illuminated the opening and drew his attention to his youngest son rushing down the ladder.

The young man was hysterical. Trying to catch his breath, he uttered, "The stern has settled on a rock shelf. We can't dislodge it! If we don't do something right now, we are either going to capsize or a hole will be torn in the bottom!"

Noah jumped up from his skin-covered mattress stuffed with straw. He could feel the deck under his feet sloping sharply toward the bow and a heavy list to the port side. A sickening groan of wood grinding on stone pierced the night's silence. He was already fully clothed.

Neither he nor his sons had slept in days, only resting when fatigue set in. He quickly slipped his sandals on and clambered up the ladder.

The commotion had awakened the rest of the family sleeping in the communal living space just below the roof hatch. The women were hysterical as they rose from their beds, slipping their robes over their nightclothes. Quickly, they also ascended to the roof deck above.

Against the black skyline, he could see his other two sons struggling with a long, heavy wooden pole. He headed up the steep incline to the stern of the ship. The women, already drenched by heavy rain, and his son trailed closely behind with only intermittent flashes of lightning lighting their way. The lightning was followed by the loudest, most terrifying claps of thunder they had ever heard.

His two oldest sons had already secured a chain to the parapet wall of the wooden ship on the stern near the starboard side. A myriad of noises resounded from the decks below. The multitude of animals had sensed imminent danger. Their screeches, roars, and howls were adding to the panic.

In the pouring rain, they put the pole through the loop in the chain, extending the short end over to the rock wall, leaving the longest part of the pole parallel to the deck to use as a leverage bar.

They all heaved together, including the women. The chain became taut. The short end of the pole bit into the rock wall. The extreme pressure bent the long pole almost to the breaking point, but the weight of the large vessel was pressing too hard on the rock shelf below to break free. Finally, exhausted and realizing their efforts were in vain, they let the long pole rest on the deck.

His full head of hair and trimmed beard blew in the wind. His muscular body stood taller than each of his three full-grown sons. He looked at his wife standing beside him, with trust in her dark eyes. They had loved each other since they were very young. He knew there was no land they could swim to except for the jagged rock peak, and it was too steep to climb. They could only cling to the rocks until they perished. Noah was afraid — afraid for his family, afraid for the animals, but most of all he was afraid he could not complete the task the Lord had asked him to perform. Noah knew the creator of heaven and earth was all powerful, but he also knew he and his family were only men and women. Men, women, and animals could easily die.

They were all wet and cold as they stood in the almost constant barrage of lightning, thunder, and heavy rain. As his family looked anxiously at him, he gazed up at the sky for just a moment. Then looking at their anxious faces, he said, "We've only one chance, and we must act quickly. We must move all the heavy animals to the bow to shift the weight off the stern."

The four men rushed down the ladder from the roof and ran through the living quarters out to the ramp and passageway and down to the lower deck where the largest animals were caged. He turned to his sons and said, "First, calm the animals that are frightened and pacing in their cages."

Then he directed the women to stay in the living quarters.

All at once the Ark lurched to the port side. Empty wooden feed boxes, pitchforks, wooden shovels, and everything loose started to slide to the left. Only the starboard side of the stern was hung up on the rock shelf. As the water receded, the bow sank lower, and the vessel tilted even more to the port side. They were afraid the vessel would capsize.

His two oldest sons had moved the two elephants out of their cages and were leading them down the passageway in the center of the craft toward the bow. The elephants balked at going down that passageway. They were loudly trumpeting and trying to turn around to go back up to the stern where it was higher.

Suddenly the ship groaned, and heavy timbers inside cracked with a sickening sound. The great vessel rolled hard again to port. The two elephants were sent sprawling to the passageway wall. The wall cracked under the weight but miraculously didn't break. Most of the other animals were thrown to the floor as pandemonium erupted. On the deck above, the cage housing two Bengal tigers snapped loose from its mounting and crashed against a beam, shattering the cage and releasing the tigers.

The two oldest sons landed between the two elephants but luckily not under them.

"It's going to completely roll over!" his youngest son screamed above the clatter.

Above the chaos of the animals and creaking beams, they could hear something else happening. Something dreadful was taking place. Water was pouring in around the huge door on the port side. That sound was a great shock to all of them. The weight of this additional water would surely cause the craft to sink or capsize.

There was not much light on this deck. An occasional lightning flash came through from the ventilation system high above in the roof. Some light came from the oil lamps wildly swinging from the chains above.

Inching his way to his two oldest sons, who were struggling with the elephants, he urged, "Come on, boys. Let's get them back on their feet and walk them down single file in that trough between the wall base and the floor."

Heartened by their father's calm demeanor, finally they were moving the animals slowly down to the lower bow. Behind them came his youngest son leading the two rhinos, each slipping and sliding.

After securing many of the heaviest animals in the bow, the ship had still not broken free. Water kept pouring in at the bottom of the great door.

In desperation, he cupped his hands and shouted above the noise, "Continue bringing all the heavy animals — hippos, horses, cattle — to the bow. If the ark does capsize, save yourselves. Take deep breaths, and swim down to the louvers to get out. I'm going up to help the women escape the vessel if we capsize."

He pulled himself up the incline by grabbing the cage bars. The oil lamps hanging from the chains were now swinging at a forty-five-degree angle.

Entering the doorway to the living quarters, he saw all four terrified women with their arms around each other, clinging to the large center support pole, crying hysterically. Two Bengal tigers were lapping up molasses that had spilled onto the floor. The snarling tigers looked up and carefully watched him.

Then his eyes went to the provisions that had fallen from the cupboards. Clay pots containing much of their food supplies were already shattered on the floor. He carefully slipped past the tigers, trying to get to the women who were crying out to him. Then the vessel seemed to actually lunge forward causing it to tilt even further over to the port side. Suddenly without warning the wood beneath his feet began to shutter and shake. Soon the vibration was radiating through the entire Ark. Noah was sure the planking on the bottom was being torn completely apart. Just then the high stern of the ark dropped and the massive vessel began to violently roll upright, and then it swung far over to starboard. A shift back to port followed, with the stern plunging down and the bow shooting up. The violent action caused the timbers to shriek and groan with loud popping and cracking. The animals were again tossed violently about. The tigers in the living quarters bounded out the door and down to the level where their cage was.

The violent action continued until at last they started to float level once again.

The storm began to subside; the animals began to calm down. The exhausted family praised the Lord and gave him thanks. They at last were safe again.

Although they did not know where they were, in time, the ark finally came to rest on the slopes of Mount Ararat.

There it became encased in the great ice cap.

* * * * *

Once about every fifteen to twenty years, usually in August after an unusually hot summer when some of the ice melts, men have claimed to have seen it with their own eyes. Some claim they have entered the ancient vessel and examined the animal cages inside. Some even swear they stood on top of the ark of Noah, and had their photographs taken. But those photographs have all been lost. They are now appropriately named, "The Lost Photographs."

xv

Part One

Chapter One

A small farm north of Moscow, Russia Fall, 1915

The orange glow of the sun, now low in the late afternoon sky, cast long shadows on the dried corn stocks left in the fields. A cool breeze moved the fall autumn leaves up against the base of the barn.

With the door closed, the barn was quite dark. Twelve-year-old Jelena Malavski was hiding behind several tall stacks of wooden crates, trying desperately to control her heavy breathing. Even though it was cool in the barn, she could feel her body sweating under her long cotton dress. If he got any closer, she knew he would hear her breathing.

Her eyes searched the dark barn trying to quickly find another place to hide. She wished she wasn't wearing these big, heavy, leather shoes. She could move much quieter in her bare feet, but it would take too long to unlace them.

The sweat on her forehead matted her auburn hair, framing the delicate features of her olive complexion. There was panic in her dark eyes as they darted about, scanning the immediate area.

Then she heard his footsteps. He was just on the other side of the crates. She thought of trying to get into one of the horse stalls lining one wall, but the stalls had no doors. If he left the crates and walked past the stalls, he would see her. If only she was more familiar with this barn. Never had she been in a barn this big before; it was huge.

Jelena looked above her to the roof. There was a cupola way up high with wooden louver slats letting in a little bit of light. Above the horse stalls was a loft where hay for the horses and cattle would soon be stored. There just had to be some place in this barn where she could hide, and he wouldn't be able to find her.

A chill went up her spine as she heard him speak. "I know you're in here, Jelena."

His voice was close now. She had no choice; she had to leave. She crawled along the stalls as quickly and quietly as she could, thankful that the floor here was soft dirt. Maybe he wouldn't hear her. She knew he was probably on the other side of the crates by now, right where she had just been, so he probably couldn't see her. Then she saw it, a door on the other side of the last horse stall. The door was standing partially open. *Can I slip into the room beyond the door without him seeing me?*

Hurriedly, she rounded the end of the last stall and slipped through the door, being careful not to move it in case the hinges made a creaking sound. Inside, the room was fairly large and was full of sacked grain and corn. On one wall was a ladder leading to the loft, which served as a roof for the room. Some sunlight shone down from the louvered cupola above and fell directly on the open access to the loft, creating a little more light. She started to climb the ladder to the loft, but then changed her mind. She looked around for a better place to hide. Quietly she crouched down and hid between the wall and a large pile of grain sacks. She was afraid to move.

Just as she started to believe that he was not going to find her and hopefully give up and leave, she heard the door creak open. Gasping, Jelena froze, hoping he hadn't heard her. She was trembling, and her breathing was shallow.

Suddenly, he towered over her. He reached down and grabbed her by the arm.

Jelena screamed in surprise and then started to laugh.

Yuri was already laughing hard. They both laughed till tears came to their eyes.

"I've never seen anyone as surprised as you were, Jelena."

"You scared me!" she replied, still giggling.

"By the way, you're it," Yuri said and they laughed some more.

They sat down on a low stack of grain, exhausted. Jelena looked at Yuri with admiration as he said, "Next time we play hide-and-seek, it will be your turn to look for me. And I know a place where you'll never find me."

"Yes, but it's your barn. I've never been in your new barn before. You have to give me a chance to find a better hiding place, too."

Jelena watched Yuri, who stood up and was now leaning against a stack of grain, still chuckling. She thought Yuri was the nicest and most handsome boy she had ever seen. He was slim and tall with a shock of light brown hair, which covered his forehead and was clipped off just above his blue eyes. It seemed to Jelena that he was always happy and smiling or laughing. He was popular at the school they both attended.

They were almost the same age; Yuri was a few months older. She loved the times they could play together. As she watched him, she thought how lucky she was that Yuri Pavaloski and his father and mother had moved onto this farm two years ago. This farm was about half a kilometer from the farm where Jelena, her mother, father, and grandmother lived.

Jelena glanced at the dirt as they talked. Surprised, she pointed down and exclaimed, "Look, Yuri. What is that?"

"What, Jelena?"

"Those lines in the dirt by your feet."

They both got down on their hands and knees to examine the fine dirt on the floor. There were strange lines in the dirt, one extending about two thirds of a meter before it turned ninety degrees and ran under a sack of corn. The other end did the same.

Yuri was just as puzzled as Jelena for a few seconds. "Oh, I know what it is." Getting to his feet, he stammered, "But you're not supposed to know about it. No one is."

"About what, Yuri? What is it?""Well" — Yuri hesitated — "wait a minute, Jelena. My dad's back in Moscow, but I want to be sure my mom's not home yet."

As he started out the door, Jelena trailed right after him. "I'm going with you. This room has got me scared." She caught up with Yuri and walked close to him. She felt safe with him.

Yuri went out the door of the barn with Jelena right on his heels. He stopped and looked for his mother's buggy. Then he turned, and as they walked back into the barn, he said, "Okay, I'll show you what it is, but first you have to promise never to tell a soul what I'm going to show you. Okay?"

"I promise, Yuri. But if you don't want to show me, that's okay," she blurted as she tried to keep up with Yuri's long strides. "You don't have to."

"No, I want to show you. It's just that my dad told me never to tell anyone about this, not even my uncles or cousins. But since you're my best friend, Jelena, I know I can trust you."

She felt thrilled Yuri would tell her she was his best friend.

Jelena watched Yuri as he moved the bags of feed that covered the lines. When the bags were moved, she saw that the strange trench in the fine dirt formed a square.

Yuri stepped out the door. Jelena started to follow him, but he came right back with a shovel. She watched, puzzled, as Yuri began scraping away the dirt. Under four or five inches of dirt, she could see a wood floor. Then Yuri began prying up a loose section of the floor. It was an access door. Jelena immediately spied a room below—a secret room!

Yuri descended into the dark hole on the horizontal boards attached to the wall. The boards made a ladder just like the one to the loft.

Soon he appeared at the bottom of the hole, his face illuminated by the lantern he was holding. "Come on down, Jelena."

She hesitated a few seconds. Then she slowly crept down through the opening.

Yuri held the lantern up while she surveyed the room. It was a little smaller than the feed storage room above. She noted the walls were red brick, as was the floor, while the ceiling was made of large wood beams and heavy wood planking. Jelena could smell the new wood that was used for the ceiling, which also formed the floor above. She glanced at Yuri. He was taller than she was, but the roof was still much higher. "A man could stand up in here," she remarked.

"Yes, even my dad can stand up in here. After the carpenters finished building the barn, I helped my dad build this secret room. We didn't mortar in the bricks on the floor so moisture could drain away."

Jelena nodded.

"Mom and I are the only ones who know we built it. My dad told my mom and me that we may need a place to hide some day if war ever comes to this part of the world, and he's afraid it will. We are going to store some canned food and water down here if he thinks war is getting close."

Jelena looked up in surprise. "Your dad thinks there is going to be a war?"

Yuri quickly added, "But that may never happen. I was supposed to keep the door to the feed storage room closed. You weren't supposed to be in that room."

"I'm sorry," Jelena said.

"No, it's my fault for leaving the door open. We put roofing paper on top of the floor before we covered it with dirt. I guess we didn't think about the dirt filtering down in the cracks around the access door. But let me show you how the room works.

"My dad is really a smart guy," Yuri said proudly. "He thinks of everything. Just watch this. If my mom and I had to hide in here, I could go up the ladder, grab the wood access door, and close the opening from the inside." Yuri pointed over to one corner. "See that wooden chute?"

Jelena looked.

"It goes up through the room above and up high in the loft, bringing in fresh air. It looks like part of the wall in the storage room above, but here is the best part. See this rope that goes up in the chute?"

She turned to where Yuri was pointing and saw a heavy rope hanging down inside the wooden chute.

"After we are safe inside and have food and water in here, I will pull this rope and a big pile of straw will fall down from the loft above. It will cover the top of the wooden access door. It really works," he said excitedly. "My dad and I have tested it several times. If someone comes into the room, they would just see feed sacks. If they look behind the feed sacks, they will just see a big pile of straw."

"Wow!" Jelena responded. "Your dad really is smart."

"Yeah, he really is."

The next few moments were spent exploring the room and its meager furnishings. Looking around nervously, Yuri whispered, "Well, we had better get out of here before my mom comes home."

After putting the lantern out, they climbed back up out of the hole. Yuri looked at Jelena and told her, "Maybe you'd better go home now.

My mom will be home soon. I'll close this up and put strips of roofing paper over the cracks before I cover it up with dirt. Also I'll make sure the feed sacks cover the whole door."

Yuri turned to Jelena, put his hands on both of her shoulders, and said, "Please don't ever tell anyone, Jelena."

She placed her hands over his and, looking into his blue eyes, promised, "I never will tell anyone, Yuri. Never!"

Jelena walked down the gravel road to her small farmhouse. She kissed her mother and gently hugged her grandmother. She told them about Yuri's huge new barn and how much fun they had playing hide and seek. She never mentioned the secret room. She knew she never would. She had promised.

After she did her chores, helped cook supper, and washed the dishes, she went to her room. She lit her lamp on the old vanity and brushed her long chestnut-colored hair. Her reflection in the faded round mirror on the wall revealed her olive-tone skin, deep brown eyes, and high cheek bones.

Jelena blew out her lamp and crawled into a cold bed covered with a patchwork quilt her grandmother had made. Soon she was toasty warm and comfortable. Her bed was near the only window in the room. As she lay there looking at the stars, she started thinking about the secret room and the strange lines in the dirt that had revealed its location. *What if a war or some other calamity does occur and just Yuri and I had to stay down in the secret room?* The notion of the two of them alone together in the secret room was exciting. She felt happy when she was with Yuri, no matter what the circumstance.

Soon Jelena was asleep.

As the months went by, when Jelena and Yuri were not in school, doing their chores, or working on their parents' farm, they continued to spend their spare time together. Yuri built a rope swing in a tree on his farm, and Jelena loved it when he would push her in the swing. They often played in the barn, but they never went into the feed storage room again. They never even mentioned the secret room until one day nearly two years later.

Chapter Two

The year was 1917, and Yuri and Jelena were both fourteen years old.

Yuri was breathless when he knocked on Jelena's door that Saturday morning. He arrived earlier than usual. As Jelena finished her breakfast, she noticed he was fidgeting and acting strangely. No sooner had she cleared the table than Yuri grabbed her coat from the hook by the kitchen door and helped her put it on. As soon as they were on her porch, he said, "Ask your mother if you can come over to my house. I've got something I really want to show you. It's really important!"

Instead of walking down the road to the corner like they usually did, Yuri cut across the road, across the drainage ditch, through the barbed-wire fence, and headed across the field toward his big barn.

"It's faster this way," he said as she followed, sometimes jogging to match the pace he set.

It was a cool, windy day. The sky was dark and cloudy. It started to rain, and they sprinted the last few yards to the shelter of the barn.

"Here." Yuri smiled, handing her one end of a towel so she could wipe the raindrops off her face. "It's clean."

The barn smelled like horses. Jelena was surprised to see a matched team of Percherons munching hay in two of the four stalls.

Yuri said, "They belong to my uncle. He uses them to plow and plant our farm when my dad is in Moscow, like he is now. My uncle has been teaching me how to handle them.

"My mom took the buggy to my grandmother's farm early this morning. Grandmother is very ill. I'm going tomorrow to see her."

Yuri took Jelena by the hand and led her across the barn toward the feed storage room. When he opened the door, she hesitated.

"It's okay, Jelena. Come on in. I really want you to see this."

"See what, Yuri?"

"I'll show you," he replied.

As he entered the room, the feed bags were stacked aside. The dirt that covered the access door was in a pile, and the access door was leaning against the wall exposing the hole that led to the secret room. Suddenly the room grew a little darker, and Jelena could hear the rain pounding on the roof. Then lightning flashed through the cupola, followed by thunder. She had heard her father say barns were sometimes struck by lightning and burned to the ground.

The horses were nervously stomping and neighing in their stalls. They didn't like the storm, either.

Yuri tugged on the sleeve of her coat. "Don't be afraid. Let's go down. I've got something special I want to show you."

Jelena remembered how mysterious and exciting the secret room had been the first and only time Yuri had taken her down there, but this time she was apprehensive. She didn't want to go down into that dank hole. Cobwebs lined the opening, and who knew what else might be down there. Besides, she was not even supposed to know the room existed.

Lighting a lantern, Yuri turned to face her as she backed away. "Just like a girl! Scaredy cat!" he taunted as he went down the ladder.

"Am not!" she shouted back. Swallowing the lump in her throat, she stepped onto the first rung of the ladder leading into the abyss below. By the time she felt the floor of the lower room with her foot, Yuri was already on his knees over in the far corner. He had a screwdriver and was using it to lift out one of the bricks in the floor. After he got the first one out, the rest were easy. He removed about ten bricks.

Under the bricks was a folded, rather thick, waterproof rain cover. Jelena knew it was from the army because it was brown khaki-colored. Under the cover was a wooden box. Yuri lifted the box out of the hole, and she saw another rain cover under the box.

As Yuri pulled the lid up and off, he exclaimed, "Look at this!"

There was a bundle of large photographs. They were wrapped in a cloth with a piece of some kind of linen between each picture. As he laid them out on the floor and lifted the lantern, she could see they were pictures of a very large wooden boat. The front of the boat was sticking out of the ice. Each of the pictures was taken from a different direction. One picture showed several smiling soldiers standing on top of the boat. "When my father developed these pictures for the army, he made himself this extra set."

Jelena knew Yuri's father was in charge of the photo development department at the army base just outside Moscow. He was an officer with a very important job and lots of responsibility. He was always bringing pictures home — pictures of soldiers, big guns on wheels pulled by horses, sometimes truckloads of soldiers. She would see them all around their house. She had only seen his father a few times. He wasn't home very much, and when he was, he and Yuri would be busy working on the barn or shearing the sheep.

"No one knows my father has them. He says they are pictures of the ark of Noah from Mount Ararat."

Jelena looked at each picture carefully. They were large black-and-white photographs. She touched Yuri's arm and stared at him in amazement. "You mean Noah's ark from the Bible?"

"Yes," Yuri replied emphatically, "from the Bible."

Jelena's eyes were transfixed on Yuri as he rattled off the series of events leading to these photographs of the ark.

"That's what my father told my mother," Yuri said excitedly, his bright blue eyes sparkling in the lantern's dim light. "Last night my father came home from Moscow again. After supper, he told me it was time I went to bed. He came into my room and told me good night, like he sometimes does when he has to leave again the next day. He said he would probably not be back for quite a while but when he came back he would take me hunting with him. He said he was sorry he was sending me to bed early, but he had some important things to talk over with my mother about the running of the farm, and he had to get up real early the next morning to go back to the base.

"I fell asleep for a little while. Then I woke up and could hear them talking at the kitchen table. You know the door to my bedroom opens right up into the kitchen. Anytime I want to hear what they're talking about, like just before my birthday, I get out of bed and sneak over and put my ear close to the door. I can hear almost everything they say, so that's what I did last night."

Intrigued, Jelena leaned forward, briefly forgetting the eerie feeling she had in this musty room.

"Once I heard my mother say, 'Just a minute. I want to make sure Yuri is asleep.' I heard her chair scrape across the wood floor. I ran to my bed and quickly jumped in and pretended to be asleep. Mother opened the door and came in with the coal-oil lamp. She looked at me and then tiptoed back out and closed the door.

"As soon as the door closed, I got up, being really careful not to step on the floor where it always creaks. I put my ear up to the door, and I could hear them talking again. My father said a lot had happened since he was last home. He said about six months ago, they started hearing stories about a pilot flying over Mount Ararat in eastern Turkey. He had spotted an ancient vessel partly covered in a glacier.

"He must have written about this in a letter because mother said, 'Yes, you wrote to us and told us about it in your letter.' Then he asked her if she had told me about it. Mother said no because she didn't want to fill my head with nonsense and rumors. My father said, 'Good, because many things have changed in the last few months — and not for the better, I'm afraid. There are rumors of a revolution, possibly even a civil war.'"

A shiver went up Jelena's spine. She suddenly felt closed in by the brick walls of this chilly room. Something about Yuri's words frightened her, but she didn't understand why.

Yuri continued spilling out the words quickly, as though he had to hurry to tell her everything before someone found them. "He told my mother I may be better off not knowing. Father said the Czar, Nicholas II, had ordered two engineering companies from his base to go down to Mount Ararat to climb the mountain and report back to him their findings.

"Father said Mount Ararat was a very difficult mountain to climb. It had high winds that could blow you right off the mountain and areas of shale rock on steep slopes. Big rocks were always sliding and tumbling down. And the final challenge was the ice and glacier.

"My father told my mother that he knew all of this because he had sent five of his best photographers on the expedition with the very latest in cameras and film. He had interviewed four of them when they returned nearly two months later. One man was killed when he fell into a deep crevasse while crossing the ice." Yuri paused to catch his breath. His voice softened and lowered. "Father seemed very upset because the one who was killed was one of his best friends. I think I heard my father cry, something I've never heard before."

Feeling his sadness, Jelena gently touched Yuri on the arm.

Then Yuri continued, "Anyway, my father said they had actually found the ark. Some of the ice had melted, and part of it was sticking out of the ice. Father said he and the photographers who took the pictures developed only one set just as he was ordered to do and turned them over to his superior officer."

Jelena was fascinated by the story Yuri was telling.

"Father said everyone on the entire base was talking about it. The soldiers who were on the expedition and actually saw the ark were like heroes, and everyone was quizzing them about what they saw. They were more than willing to tell everyone. They all agreed it had to be Noah's ark. The engineers had measured it as best they could since most of it was still buried in ice and water. But the width and height matched what the Bible said. They reported large rooms inside and also small cages with old rusted iron bars still partially intact. They brought back samples of the old wood. It had been hand-hewn with wooden pegs to hold the joints together."

Yuri paused. "I'm trying to remember everything father told mother." He thought for a second and added, "Oh yes, he also said none of the photos of the inside of the ark where they used a powdered flash to take pictures of the cages turned out. It was almost impossible to tell what the pictures were showing. He said he was sure he would have to answer for that sooner or later, but the pictures taken outside of the ark were really good."

Yuri hesitated for a minute and then pressed on. "My father would never travel that entire distance home and then go right back unless it was really important, like maybe me or my mother or his mother was sick or something. It is just too far. I knew it had to be serious so even though it was late and I was tired because they had been talking for such a long time, I kept my ear to the door and listened.

"Father then said he was working in the photo lab late the night following the day they developed the photos of the ark. He was all alone, and he decided to take just five of the best negatives of the pictures taken of the ark and make one copy of each. After all, he was the officer in charge of all the military photos. So he took the negatives from the vault and quickly made one copy of each of the five and hurriedly put the negatives back. He dried the prints and put them in his desk. After locking his desk drawer, he started to leave the lab. Just as he got to the door, a high-ranking security officer with two security guards knocked on the glass window. This, father said, was very unusual. It was after eleven at night, and he had never seen the security officer or the security guards before. He said the officer was polite but asked him why he was working so late. Father explained what he was doing and showed him the report he had just written and dated that day. The officer asked him where he kept the negatives from the ark expedition. He had father bring them out of the vault. The officer showed a paper from the general in charge of the base authorizing him to take the negatives.

"As he walked to the door, the officer turned to my father and asked, 'How many copies of these have been printed?'

'Just one set, sir, as I was ordered,' my father told him.

"'Are you positive of that, Captain Pavaloski?'"

"'Yes, of course, I'm sure.'"

Yuri continued, "I'm sure my father, since he was in charge of all the base photography and had made extra copies of army things before, didn't think any harm would come from him making a copy. But now he was afraid to admit he had made himself a copy, so he had to tell a little white lie and said he hadn't made any other copies."

"I don't blame him," Jelena said.

"Neither do I, Besides, since it's such an important thing to find, wouldn't they show all the Russian people and anyone else who would be interested in what had been discovered?"

"I'm sure they will," Jelena nodded. "What else did your father tell your mother?"

"Well, he said none of the soldiers who were on the expedition had been allowed to leave the base for any reason since they had returned from the expedition. The very next day the commanding officer of the base was replaced by another general that my father said he had never heard of before. He said everyone was brought in to assembly halls all over the base and given the same orders. They were to never talk about the expedition to Mount Ararat. If anyone was to speak about anything they saw or heard, even to their families after they were allowed to leave the base, they would be court-martialed and could be shot."

"But why?" Jelena gasped.

"I don't know, but please don't ever tell anyone about any of this, Jelena. I don't want my father to get in trouble. I probably should not even have told you, but you're my best friend. You always have been my best friend, and I just had to tell you about it."

"Thank you for trusting me, Yuri. You're my best friend too," Jelena whispered. "And you know I'll never tell anyone, not even my mother."

Proceeding, Yuri said, "My father told my mother he brought those five pictures home with him. I could hear him unwrapping them and showing them to my mother. She was really excited at first to see them, but then she told him she was afraid and said maybe they should just burn them. But my father said no. They should be saved and someday shown to the world. He said they could bury them under the floor here in the shelter. No one knew he had them, and no one knew about the secret shelter he had built. So I heard them get a lantern and come out here to the barn. I wanted to see the pictures, so I came out early this morning, climbed down, and saw where he had lifted up the bricks. I knew that's where he had hidden them, but I didn't dig them up until you were here to see them with me. I didn't want to dig them up twice."

Yuri and Jelena carefully wrapped the pictures up and put them back just like Yuri's father had them. Yuri smiled at Jelena. It would be their secret.

Part Two

Chapter Three

Africa
Present Day

Archaeologist Dr. Matthew Lane shined his flashlight toward the space up ahead, which appeared large enough to stand up in. "At last!" he yelled back to Jim Morgan, who was a few yards behind him. Both men were crawling on their hands and knees.

"At last what?" Jim shouted. "I don't see anything."

Matt didn't reply immediately. He just crawled faster toward the large room he could now see at the end of the tunnel.

Matt was thirty-one years old. His face was tawny from having spent so much time outdoors in the sun. Although he was clean shaven, there was stubbly evidence of a heavy beard. Complementing his strong jaw was a nearly perpetual smile. But his most striking feature was his eyes. They were blue-green and seemed to draw you into his soul, as the Caribbean waters draw you to the sea.

Pausing to catch his breath, Matt turned his head and shined the light back on Jim. "You okay?"

The good-looking, young archaeologist who had been Matt's best friend since seventh grade, hollered, "You mean other than my knees wearing out? Yeah, I'm okay."

Matt wiped his brow with his handkerchief and continued to shine his flashlight back on the floor of the narrow tunnel in front of Jim.

Jim is an impeccable dresser, Matt mused, *but not today*. He laughed out loud as he watched Jim, closer now, crawling in his sweaty khaki-colored pants and shirt. The tunnel they were crawling through was cool, but sweat was beading on Jim's forehead under his black, curly hair and dripping into his dark-brown eyes. He was only thirty years old, with a dark complexion inherited from his Italian mother and French father.

Finally Jim caught up with Matt. "Give me a minute to get some rocks out of my boot. I can't believe you can crawl faster than I," Jim groaned.

"Those daily workouts you put me through at the gym must be paying off. Lean, mean, muscle machines — that's us!"

Ignoring Matt's taunting remarks, Jim was lacing up his boot. "What did you see up ahead?"

"It looks like this tunnel opens up into a room — maybe *the room.*" Matt's voice cracked with excitement as the suspense mounted.

As soon as Jim was ready, Matt turned and they resumed crawling on their hands and knees on the sandstone floor of the tunnel.

As they entered the large room and started to stand up, Jim warned Matt, "Watch your head, bro. The roof in here may not accommodate your bod." Matt's six-foot-two-inch frame sometimes made spelunking difficult, but that's what he and Jim loved to do.

Matt stood up carefully, shining his flashlight on the rough rock ceiling above. Then with a laugh, he said, "You'd better watch your own head. You're only one inch shorter than I am."

As they stretched out their aching arms and legs, Matt remarked, "Look at the walls. This is a natural tunnel and cave. A little stone chiseling was done in the tunnel to enlarge it. This *has* to be the burial chamber."

It was a long area. The floor was not flat and smooth as were most Egyptian burial chambers. Instead, it was cluttered with large, jagged rocks.

"They must have been in a big hurry. The chamber was never completely finished," Jim observed.

Matt and Jim moved farther into the cave, continuing to search the walls and floor with their flashlights. Suddenly, they both saw it.

"Just as Ira predicted," Matt said. In the far corner of the room was a low stone burial box with some hieroglyphics carved into the lid. It was not huge like an Egyptian sarcophagus. It was not ornate, just a box big enough for a man to be buried in.

The lid was only about four inches thick. Matt wiped a layer of dirt off the top and tried to interpret what it said. "I can understand only part of this, but I think our ancient African king is in this burial box."

It took some effort before they finally got the lid off. They shined their lights inside. There lay the skeleton of a man who had been quite tall. His arms were crossed with his hands up to his shoulders. Then Matt's flashlight caught the green reflection of a beautifully carved jade mask covering the skull.

"Look at those eyes," Jim exclaimed. The eyes in the mask were large, bright, transparent stones. They sparkled with an array of colors under Matt's flashlight.

Matt looked at them closely. "These stones are a matched pair of very large diamonds. They don't find diamonds this big today, I have never seen uncut diamonds reflect that much color. These would be worth a fortune in today's market."

The cave smelled musty, but Matt smelled something else. Suspicious and afraid of what he might find, he slowly stood up and turned his flashlight around the rest of the area. There were some large slabs of rock in the cave. Matt moved closer to them.

What he saw caused his heart to skip a beat.

Behind the large sandstone rocks were the unmistakable signs of a lair. Suddenly, he understood. "Oh no," he uttered under his breath. The area was littered with old animal bones. *Maybe several lions live here*, he thought. That's what he had smelled.

He quickly came back to Jim. "Did you ever read the book of Daniel?" Matt whispered to Jim, who was squatting down by the burial box, busy photographing everything with both a still camera and a video camera. His flashlight was propped up on a rock so that the light shined into the box.

Jim turned toward Matt's light, "I remember someone threw him in a lion's den." Jim stopped abruptly and slowly stood up. "Don't tell me..."

"Okay, I won't tell you, but in case you really want to know, we are inside a lion's den. Let's get this recorded and get out of here."

Jim jumped up and followed Matt to the corner. He saw what Matt had discovered. "Great," he exclaimed, exasperated. Hurriedly, he went back to the box. "I'm almost done here. I assume we're taking the mask. What about the beads? They used to be on a necklace around his neck, but the leather they were strung on fell apart a long time ago. Now they're all loose around the skeleton."

"Unless you see some diamonds or rubies down among the bones," Matt replied as he hurriedly packed up the camera equipment, "just leave them. I doubt that you will find any diamonds from a necklace. I don't think they had tools that would drill a hole through a diamond when this old boy died. He's been here several hundred years."

"No, the beads are all jade."

"We'll take the mask though," Matt told Jim. "We'll turn it over to the curator of the museum in Nairobi. Otherwise it may turn up in the wrong hands."

Matt came over and held the light and watched Jim as he carefully lifted the jade mask off the skull of the ancient African king. It was stuck at first, but, with a tug, it came off, revealing a complete human skull with a thin layer of dry, dark skin attached to the forehead. Most of his teeth were still intact.

Matt remarked, "He wasn't very old."

"No, he wasn't."

Matt quickly took a few pictures of the skull. "If anyone out in the bush saw us enter this cave, this priceless artifact will disappear. With the map we used to get here, the museum can put the mask back and seal the cave entrance if they choose. I'd love to gather up all the jade beads, but if we don't want mama lion and papa lion to catch us like Goldilocks, I think we'd better rush back out of here, like right now."

They had just put the lid back on the burial box when they heard a noise in the tunnel. Both men froze. It wasn't a growl, but something or someone was definitely there.

Jim went down on one knee and shined his light back into the dark tunnel. He couldn't see anything.

Matt started shining his light on the floor behind them.

Jim whispered over his shoulder to Matt, "If you're looking for another way out, there isn't any."

"I know there isn't any, I was looking for this."

Jim turned and saw Matt had an ancient reed torch in his hand. "I saw this lying on the floor back in the corner when we first came in. It dried up and fell out of its holder a long time ago. It won't have any oil left in it, but if it doesn't fall apart in my hands, the reeds should still burn. Is that cigarette lighter still in the pack?"

"Here," Jim said, handing it to him.

The only weapons the men had were the hunting knives on their belts. They purchased these before they rented the helicopter. They wanted to buy a gun but knew there was too much red tape for a noncitizen to buy a gun.

Jim had his knife in one hand and a flashlight in the other. Matt had the dried-up reed torch in one hand and the cigarette lighter in the other. Jim kept his light shining back in the tunnel.

Suddenly, with a loud roar, a huge lion's head appeared in the light. Her yellow eyes lit up from Jim's flashlight shining on her snarling, growling face. She came through the tunnel fast and then stopped at the entrance to the big room, letting out a bloodcurdling roar.

Both men were shaking, but Jim kept his light in the lion's eyes. He tightened his grip on his knife. Matt was right beside Jim, ready to light the torch.

"She's not leaving," Matt spoke softly, "so let's back up and let her come in."

Jim was already backing up. As soon as they retreated, the lion roared and darted in and turned to their left side. She stopped at the bones and started sniffing the ground. Then she made a quick turn toward them, curled her lips in a snarl, and squatted in a lunging position.

"Get behind me, Jim," Matt instructed. "She's ready to attack."

Matt held the flame of the lighter to the dried torch in his hand. It flared up into a ball of flame just as the lion pounced toward Matt. He instinctively shoved the ball of fire in the lion's face. The animal turned quickly and ran to the back of the cave.

Matt still had the torch in his hand, but its life was nearly spent. There was no oil or animal fat to keep it burning much longer.

Both men moved quickly to the entrance of the tunnel. Jim was ahead of Matt. He reached down and picked up the small pack with the cameras and the mask and shoved Matt into the tunnel ahead of him. Matt dropped the slightly burning torch at the tunnel entrance.

Matt had his flashlight on now, crawling as fast as he could on his hands and knees. He knew the lioness didn't want any part of that flame and figured she probably would not follow them until the last of the fire had died out completely, but that would be soon. Jim kept turning the flashlight behind him to be sure she wasn't coming.

At last they saw light up ahead. Knowing they had to be close to the entrance, Jim joked, "It's my turn to be in front, Matt. Don't you think?"

"Okay, If you think you can pass me in this tunnel at the speed I'm crawling, go for it. You can be the one to face her boyfriend if we meet him coming in for a visit."

They were joking like they always did, both believing they were probably out of danger, but then they heard something that sent shivers up their spines: a loud growl back in the tunnel … and then another. She was closer now. The fire was out, and she was coming after them. They crawled faster. Suddenly Matt stopped, and Jim ran into him.

At the bright sunlit entrance, a large yellow mane appeared. In the center of the mane was the huge face of a large male African lion. Matt couldn't believe what he was seeing.

Jim was panicked, but before he could protest, he saw why Matt had stopped so abruptly. The big male was coming into the tunnel. Suddenly the male lion saw Matt in the tunnel. He was just as surprised as Matt.

The men were frozen, daring not to move. Behind them the lioness let out a blood-curdling roar. She was almost on top of them.

The male at the entrance seemed confused. He had heard the roar of the female coming toward them, so he let out a loud, deep-throated roar. Both Jim and Matt were petrified. Caught between two wild killers, they didn't know what to do. Paralyzed, they knew they could easily die right here. Their hearts were pounding in their chests, and they were dripping with sweat.

Then Matt could hardly believe what he saw. The big male backed out of the tunnel. Matt couldn't see where the lion went. Knowing the lioness must be right on Jim, Matt started crawling again as fast as he could for the entrance.

Just as they reached the entrance, the female caught up with Jim, and with a deafening roar, she took a swipe at his legs with her huge claws, catching his pant leg and boot. The lioness could have easily killed Jim, but she stopped her attack as Matt and Jim scrambled to their feet and ran for the helicopter.

They didn't dare look back until they were in the cockpit and Matt was flipping switches to start the engine.

When they looked back at the entrance in a cloud of dry dust, they saw three very large, very agitated lions, two females and one huge male. All three were pacing back and forth, watching the helicopter and growling.

As the engine began to roar and the choppers blades began to cut the air, all three ran down the hill, turned ninety degrees at the bottom, and disappeared into the bush.

Matt and Jim just sat there in shock with the engine running, trying to catch their breath.

"Wow!" Matt finally said. "Do you believe that?" As he began to regain his composure, he joked, "I don't think she was very happy about us being in her den." His thick brown hair was matted from the sweat on his forehead, and his blue-green eyes flashed with excitement.

"I don't blame her," Jim replied. "I wouldn't be very happy if I came home and found her in my den, either," he said, laughing. "Actually, I was really afraid we weren't going to get out of that one." As he spoke, he was examining his slashed pant leg and leather boot.

"Man," Matt exclaimed as he saw the damage the lioness had done. "Did she do that to you?"

"Yes, she did that to me! Next time it's my turn to be in front," Jim said, laughing again.

"Are you okay? Did she draw blood?"

"No. I don't think so." Jim pulled his boot off and examined his leg. "But she tried. Look at this shredded pant leg, and the slashes are almost through the upper leather of my boot."

"Let's count ourselves very lucky, Jim. That could've turned out to be a whole lot different."

"Yeah, one more time we lived to tell about it."

"My guess is they had recently had a big meal, because if they had been hungry, we might not be here discussing what happened. I think you have a major problem now though, Jim," Matt said seriously.

Jim gave Matt a questioning look.

"Just how are you going to explain those pants to your tailor?"

They both broke out laughing. The shock was wearing off.

"You were right about her having a boyfriend." Jim said, laughing, "Wow, wasn't he a big guy!"

"As a matter of fact, that is probably what saved us. That big male started to bring another girlfriend into the cave, but when he heard how mad she already was, he decided he had better not come in."

Soon they were laughing so hard tears came to their eyes as they flew out over the plains of Africa.

Chapter Four

A few days later
University Archaeological Department
Washington, D.C.

Ira Jensen greeted Matt and Jim warmly. "Help yourselves to coffee and some rolls."

"You know Jim and I never turn down an invitation like that," Matt said as he headed for the tray of caramel rolls.

Matt really liked his boss. With an amused look on his face, Matt watched the fifty-six-year-old Ira as he poured himself a cup of coffee. Although he was only five foot six inches tall and had a small frame, the slightly balding Ira had earned Matt's admiration as an intelligent humanitarian and an accomplished archaeologist. He was highly respected as the head of the archaeological department at the university, and he worked closely with the Museum of Natural History.

Matt and Jim were always kidding Ira about one thing or another, and he was quick to respond and enjoyed playing a practical joke on them. Today, however, they were serious as they waited to hear if their find was significant.

Ira moved around the large oak desk to settle into his high-back, leather chair. Matt and Jim listened carefully to their boss as he praised them for being able to find the African king's tomb. "I've seen the pictures and video. Wow! How thrilling that must've been, and what about the lions you encountered? What were they doing in that cave? That's very unusual."

"Yes, it is," Matt replied, "very unusual. They actually had a den in there. Some lions do have dens. The two man-eating lions back in the late eighteen hundreds, the Tsavo lions, apparently had a den. It's said they killed and ate one hundred and forty people."

"I think we met their descendants," Jim interjected with a laugh. "When I felt her hot breath on the back of my neck, I was afraid I was going to be her supper."

They all chuckled.

"What about the mask, Ira? Were the eyes really uncut diamonds?" Matt asked.

"Oh yes, the mask is priceless, and thanks to you two finding the tomb, we are going to be allowed to display the mask in our museum in just a few months for a whole year," Ira responded proudly. "I'm just so glad neither of you got hurt."

"So are we!" Matt and Jim replied in unison.

"The mountain was almost exactly where your map indicated it would be, Ira. How do you come up with these maps?" Matt questioned.

"Oh, I have my sources." Ira grinned broadly. "But my map only indicated a rock wall at the base of a small mountain where there was carved an epitaph of an ancient African king. The man who sold me the map had exhausted his resources to no avail. He couldn't find the burial chamber. That's why he sold me the map. How did you two discover it?"

"Oh we had a special tool, Ira, and you paid for it." A sly smirk crept across Matt's face. "You'll find out when you get our list of expenses. But believe me, we could never have found the opening without it."

A hint of apprehension was exhibited by Ira's demeanor as he leaned forward in his chair. "And what was this tool I paid for, Matt?"

"One day rental of a small helicopter!"

"I see," stammered Ira, pretending to be concerned. He knew the trip was worth every penny they had spent.

"We carefully examined the rock wall as we hiked the whole area around the hieroglyphics. There was not a hint of an opening. So we drove back to the city, rented a helicopter, and flew over the mountain. With a stroke of luck, Jim spotted the top of a huge round boulder with heavy brush growing all around the base of it. We were looking for a boulder that might have been rolled to block a tunnel entrance. Hovering over it, we could tell it had been chiseled to make it round. We landed and climbed back up to it. Under the heavy brush, water had eroded a hole along one side. We crawled back into the hole, and it opened up into a tunnel. Anyway," Matt said, "hovering in a chopper to search the terrain below is one heck of a tool, Ira. Believe me when I repeat, we would never have found the opening without it."

"Well," Ira conceded, "the revenue we'll receive when we're allowed to display the jade mask at the Museum of Natural History will more than pay the expense of the trip — even with the helicopter rental!"

As Jim answered some of Ira's questions, Matt remembered how he and Jim had come to be there. *Both of our families lived in the same upper middle class neighborhood here in D.C., and neither of us had any siblings. Maybe that's why we've always felt like brothers and have always been there for each other.*

A veil of sadness clouded Matt's eyes as he recalled the tragic day Jim's parents were killed in an automobile accident by a drunk driver when he was only sixteen. *Luckily, he was adopted by his aunt Jenny and uncle Jake Morgan, who lived just a few blocks away from us. The large settlement in a trust fund Jim received when he was twenty-one hardly made up for that loss!*

We were really lucky, Matt thought, *escaping from the lions. I hope we can always be that lucky.*

Matt knew he and Jim would now be eager for their next adventure, anything from searching for ancient artifacts to hunting for buried treasure.

Little did they realize it was already waiting for them, and it would be the most exciting adventure of their lives. As Matt and Jim prepared to leave, Ira motioned for them to remain seated. "Before you go, I received this letter in this morning's mail. It was addressed to the university with our address here in D.C."

Ira passed the letter across the desk to Matt, who took the letter out of the envelope and read it aloud.

Dear Sir:

My name is Ronald Kempson, and for many years I was a teacher of archaeology.

I'd lost track of two of my former students but was recently informed that they do field research for your museum. I'm looking for Dr. Matthew Lane and James Morgan. If they are employed at your museum, please inform them I've come across something that's related to our "common search" that I believe they would be interested in.

Please have them call my assistant at 410-555-8820 to arrange a meeting as soon as possible.

Sincerely,

Dr. Ronald A. Kempson, Archaeologist

Matt and Jim looked at each other. Then Matt exclaimed, "Noah's ark!"

"Yes, yes!" Jim shouted. "That's got to be it. Professor Kempson was as excited about anything pertaining to Noah's ark as we were," Jim told Ira, who was listening intently. "When Matt and I were taking archaeology classes from Professor Kempson, sometimes on Friday evenings after class, the three of us would meet for pizza and discuss Noah's ark —"

Ira interrupted, "Excuse me, but why would you need more than one or two meetings to discuss all there is to know about Noah's ark? I mean, I think you could easily discuss everything about Noah's ark in … two hours."

Matt retorted, "Ira, do you have any idea just how many people claim to have actually seen the ark? How many books have been written about it? How many people claim to have even been inside the ark? Taken pictures of it?"

"Well, yes, I guess I'm somewhat familiar with that."

"Well, we used to bring the books to the pizza parlor and research the stories."

"Then you two really believe the ark exists today?"

"Absolutely!" Jim emphatically replied.

"There's just too much evidence to be ignored," Matt added.

"Please correct me if I'm wrong, guys," Ira quizzed, "but didn't you two actually climb Mount Ararat a few years ago looking for the ark?"

"Yes, we did," Matt admitted.

"And did you find it?" Ira said a little sarcastically.

Matt grinned. "No, but the conditions weren't right. The summer we went up, it was too cold. The ice that hides the ark didn't melt enough that year to expose any of it. That only happens about once every fifteen to twenty years. The American astronaut, James Irwin, believed it was on Mount Ararat, and he and his team didn't find it, but he still believed it was up there on that mountain. Unfortunately, he passed away before he could go back and search for it in a warmer year."

"But wait a minute," Ira again questioned. "I remember reading a while back that an expedition found the ark, and it wasn't even on Mount Ararat."

"They have never proven that what they found was actually the ark," Jim rebutted. "What looked like petrified wood has not proven to actually be petrified wood at all. Many scientists believe it was just rock that looked like wood. They also couldn't find a single man-made joint or intersection where two separate pieces of wood were joined together."

Matt continued, "Jim and I have read all the reports, and we don't believe what they found was Noah's ark. We both firmly believe the ark is buried in the glacier on Mount Ararat. And if it has been preserved in ice all these centuries, it could still be in good enough condition to be recognized as a vessel, especially if ice is inside the ark. Then the weight of the ice outside would not have crushed the hull. Jim and I have studied the 1955 film showing Fernand Navarro removing a large plank from the ice while his son, Raphael, held the camera and filmed it. We reviewed the film several times, and we don't believe the film was a fake."

"But how could the ark have gotten up to the top of Mount Ararat when scientists claim there's not enough water on the earth to cover all the mountains?"

"Well," Matt said, "there are many things about the ark story that sound almost unbelievable, but these questions can be answered if you really think about it with a non-prejudiced mind and you really have faith the story is true. For example, no one really knows where the ark was built. It was assumed that Noah built the ark somewhere in Mesopotamia. The mountains in that area are not extremely high. The Bible says the waters prevailed fifteen cubits upward and the mountains were covered. The Bible doesn't say the water covered Mount Everest. In addition to that, geologists tell of mountains rising and falling over thousands of years. Most of the people who say they have actually seen the ark indicate it is between thirteen thousand and fourteen thousand feet above sea level. Maybe the ark was deposited on Mount Ararat five thousand to six thousand years ago, and as the mountain pushed slowly higher, the ark rose with it. The Bible says it rained forty days and forty nights all over the earth, which would empty all the earth's atmospheric water. The polar ice caps probably melted, and the Bible says God opened all the fountains of the great deep, which could mean all the aquifers of the world were emptied. I think that would be enough to put the ark that high. But if that isn't high enough, maybe God used a huge tsunami to boost it to its present level. I really don't know how it was accomplished, but I believe it was done, and I don't believe any magic was involved."

"Then how could all the animals have fit into that ark? In fact, how could they even build a wooden boat that big?"

Matt replied, "First of all, we agree with many others who don't believe every separate breed of dog, cat, antelope, and many other species were in the ark. They, in most cases, descended from a common ancestor, so only the core animals were on the ark. The different varieties we have today are descendants from the original animals. For example, many of the hundreds of different types of dogs and cats we have today are a product of breeding and evolution.

"During one of our discussions in the pizza parlor, Jim, the professor, and I put ourselves in Noah's place and really thought about how we would go about the task God had given him. How could we accomplish what Noah was able to do? Now, we know Noah must've been a brilliant man, and he had the Creator of the entire universe guiding him. He could've done anything. He and his sons could have located some iron ore. From that, they could have made tools and iron plates to hold the main timbers together. So to answer your question, it would not have been easy, but it was not impossible."

Ira stood and walked around the room behind his desk in deep thought. Then looking to Matt and Jim, he said, "Well, I guess when you consider all that, plus the fact that we know ice would have preserved the wood, I would urge you to go see what the professor has discovered."

Matt and Jim needed no encouragement. There was never a doubt that they would immediately visit the professor.

Chapter Five

The Jaguar headed north out of Washington, D.C., toward Maryland. About an hour later, Jim left the main highway and traveled through a pristine forest before turning onto the long, paved road leading to the estate of Professor Kempson. The grounds were covered with blue spruce, all uniform in size. The quiet of the country was in direct contrast to the hustle and bustle of D.C. Winter was just winding down, and the days were sunny, but it still got quite chilly after the sun went down.

Matt and Jim pulled into the circular drive at approximately 5:30 p.m. The house itself was a large, ranch-style home, probably built in the late seventies. Matt and Jim had never been there before. Matt knew the professor's wife had died about twenty years ago in her early forties. Professor Kempson never had any children, and he never remarried. As a diversion from his grief, he totally immersed himself in his passion for archaeology. Therefore, it was no surprise when the invitation to spend the night had been extended to Matt and Jim.

Alfred Simon, the professor's butler, was there to greet them as they drove up. He took their luggage and brought them into the great room where a fire burned brightly in the huge marble fireplace. The room itself was spacious with mahogany-paneled walls and leather furniture, cobalt-blue accents — a gentleman's retreat.

Alfred said, "The professor will join you shortly," and left to take their suitcases to their respective rooms.

Matt walked around the room looking at the paintings on the wall and the pictures on the grand piano. A massive, lighted étagère displaying some very intriguing artifacts caught his attention. "Jim, come and look at this."

The whir of an electric motor caused them to turn toward the doorway. At that moment, the professor entered the room on a three-wheeled electric cart. He drove right up to Matt and Jim and exclaimed with a robust laugh, "Well, I see you boys have discovered 'the death mask.' That's the original image of an ancient king who died over two thousand five hundred years ago."

Greeting both of them with a hearty handshake, he said, "It's wonderful to see you again. It's been quite a few years since you were young 'pups' in my class. I really want to thank both of you for driving all the way up here. What can I get you to drink?"

He maneuvered to the corner bar and fixed drinks for all three of them. "We'll have a chat and get reacquainted before dinner, and after dinner, we can discuss the wonderful world of archaeology."

As they talked, Matt studied the professor, a fairly large man in his sixties, now bald on top but with a neatly trimmed gray beard.

Professor Kempson explained, "I was in a climbing accident about four years ago and injured my lower spine. That's what put me in this motorized machine. I'm not paralyzed, so I can stand and walk, but slowly and not very far."

In spite of the injury, Matt observed, *he has not lost his outgoing, friendly personality, still possessing a zest for life.*

The next hour passed quickly as they caught up on the status of their lives.

"Let me show you around the place before it gets too dark." Professor Kempson led them through the single-story, beautiful home and grounds as the sun quickly disappeared below the horizon. After dinner, they went back into the great room where they were served coffee. The warmth of the fire felt great, as the outside evening air was turning damp and cold.

Easing his scooter closer to his guests, the professor confessed, "Boys, I'll have to admit I kind of took advantage of a unique situation just to visit with you two again after — what has it been? — eight years since we've seen each other?"

Matt agreed, "It's been far too long."

"I have a niece and her husband who check on me from time to time, and of course, Alice, my cook, and Alfred do almost everything for me. They live on the property full time. But I just really miss talking about archaeology with my friends and colleagues. I hope I haven't inconvenienced you fellows by bringing you all the way up here."

Matt and Jim assured him they were glad he invited them. They were just as excited to see him again as he was to see them.

They were seated comfortably in front of the fireplace with the light of the fire adding to the mystery of their visit. Finally the professor began, "Let me tell you a story. About seven years ago, I was in Iran searching for two stone tablets. They had been unearthed in an ancient tomb of a king found in the buried ruins of the ancient biblical city of Nimrod, the name given to the great-grandson of Noah. The city had been located and partially excavated in about 1846. The lost city of Nimrod is on the banks of the Tigris River. Hundreds of stone tablets were found in the ruins, many broken but some still intact. Most of the tablets were shipped to the British Museum in the mid-1800s, but the two I was looking for were taken away by workers in the tomb. I've not yet found the tablets, but I'm getting close. However, in my search, I was led to a young Iranian man who possessed an old map on crumbling parchment. It had been in his family's care for generations. After several meetings, I was convinced it was genuine, so I bought the map for the equivalent of one thousand dollars and considered it a bargain."

Matt and Jim were listening intently to every word because they loved the intriguing mystery of archaeology. They knew treasure maps were often fakes and seldom led to any treasure. However, they also knew the professor could not easily be fooled.

"The map shows the location of a cave. It's high up on one of the many canyons that carry rainwater down to the Tigris River. I had the parchment ink dated, and I was told it was over five hundred years old."

The professor then backed his electric cart up a few feet, pulled open a flat plan drawer, took out a piece of drawing paper about eighteen inches by twenty-four inches, brought it over to the coffee table, and laid it in front of Matt and Jim. Using a remote control, Dr. Kempson turned up the lighting in the room. "This is a large photocopy of the original that is in my vault, which I will show you later."

Matt and Jim looked at the map showing the winding Tigris River. It revealed numerous canyons leading to the river and some significant rock formations. Then they saw an X marked where the cave was.

"What is this word by the X?" Matt asked.

"That is what got me so excited," Professor Kempson replied with a sparkle in his eyes. "That, my friends, is the Farsi word for *ark*."

Matt was astounded. He stared at the professor "What do you think the word *ark* means at this location? And correct me if I'm wrong, but both the Euphrates River and the Tigris River run through Iraq."

"Iraq?" Jim repeated. "That's right. They do, in fact. They come almost together in, of all places, Baghdad."

"Yes, but remember, the war in Iraq is much different now. Let me explain a little more," Professor Kempson interjected.

"First, I know the word *ark* might represent anything. I don't really know what it could mean, but I'm betting there is something of interest in that cave. Second, I know where the cave is. I've been there. It would take someone who's never been there months of looking even if they had this map, and they still may never find it. But with the map I bought and comparing it with my notes at home here, I've almost pinpointed the cave's exact location. Third, I've got great contacts in Iraq. I've been in touch with the curator of the museum in Baghdad, and we've made a deal."

"What kind of a deal?" Matt asked skeptically.

"They will allow someone to go in and search for whatever there may be to find. That individual can catalog and photograph, but they don't get to keep any of the artifacts. There is only one little problem."

"And what is that?" Matt asked.

"I don't know what's in the cave."

"Wait a minute. You said you've been there. Why don't you know what's in the cave?"

Professor Kempson responded, "Many years ago, I was with another archaeologist. You wouldn't know him, and he has since passed away. But we, with an Iraqi guide, took a boat trip down parts of the Tigris River. We spotted this cave and pulled our boat ashore. The cave doesn't face west looking out over the valley. It's up one of the canyons. If you stood in the cave and looked outside, you would see the other wall of the canyon in front of you. If you look to your left, you would see the Tigris River and much of the flat plains between the Tigris River and the Euphrates River, which is about one hundred miles west. The cave is high up on the side of the cliff, probably one hundred feet up from the canyon floor and fifty to sixty feet down from the plateau above. The cliff slopes outward, up to the cave where the water flowing down from the canyon has eroded away the face, making it even more difficult to climb from the base because you're not lying on the rock; you're always hanging from it. The best way to get in that cave now would be to lower yourself down from the top, and that's also difficult because you would have to swing yourself until you could get a toehold on the fairly narrow ledge. The cave seemed shallow, maybe only eight to ten feet deep."

"Wow," Jim said. "That sounds almost impossible to get into."

"Yes," Matt agreed. "If the cave is only eight to ten feet deep, what could it contain that would make it worth the effort?"

"Well," the professor said, "the cave wasn't always that hard to reach from the canyon floor. A ten-foot ladder might have been all you would've needed. Centuries of water washing down the canyon have greatly lowered the canyon floor. I studied the cave with my binoculars, and on one side of the entrance, I swear, boys, that rock has been carved. I'm sure it has some kind of a picture scribed on it. I'm hoping it's a picture of a vessel. I couldn't tell what it was through the binoculars, but I know it was carved."

"A boat?" Jim asked.

"Yes, an ark to be exact. The area below that cave between the Tigris River and the Euphrates River is ancient Mesopotamia. It is considered the cradle of civilization. Many believe it is where the Garden of Eden was. And there is evidence that, at one time, a large forest was in that area. I think the cave used to be much deeper. Maybe some of the face has fallen away into the canyon. That cave would've been a perfect place to observe and carve into the stone wall a picture of crazy Noah building his huge vessel. I know it's a long shot, but I'm sure something is carved on a smooth rock surface on the west wall of that cave. This map I obtained much later has the word *ark*. It must mean something."

The professor's dialogue was becoming more intense, and he spoke rapidly. "I tried to make notes of where the cave was by sketching landmarks around it, thinking one day I might be able to go back and examine the carving on the wall to see what it meant. I had all but forgotten about it until the map came into my possession. So between the map and my notes plus the notes of my friend, I'm sure I can take a modern map of the area and mark it close enough so that you could locate the cave, even though I have never been inside it. That is, if you are at all interested."

"If we are interested?" Matt was ecstatic from the mere thought of the adventure. "Of course! You know we are interested."

Jim was already bent over the table, looking closely at the map. "I'm sure you've found your guinea pigs, Professor. But, of course, you knew we would be anxious to do this when you wrote the letter, didn't you?"

"Well, I had a pretty good idea you would go for it, but I could never be sure. I sincerely hoped you would. But before you guys sign on, I want you to consider the dangers involved. Americans are still aiding in the fight against ISIS in Iraq, and it's not going to be easy getting into that cave. Also, the carving on that wall might just say, 'Ali loves Krista.' It might be a wild goose chase!"

Matt assured Professor Kempson, "We've been on dangerous missions before, and sometimes they turned out to be nothing."

Impetuously interrupting, Jim added, "Call us a little crazy, but that's what we do. We seem to thrive on adventure and danger. We always try to prepare ourselves for the dangerous part first, doing our homework before we go."

The professor later took them into his temperature- and humidity-controlled walk-in vault, where he had the original parchment stored, and showed it to Matt and Jim. Yearningly, the professor said, "I wish I were going with you. I had planned a few years earlier to explore the cave myself, but then the war started. Then I got hurt. I finally realized I would have to give the quest to someone else, and since I have no children and my favorite students were you two, I hoped you would be interested."

After breakfast the next day, Matt and Jim thanked the professor for giving them the opportunity to do the exploring for him. Matt promised, "If we find anything of interest, Professor, the story about how we found it from your diligent research will be told."

"I'm so happy you've decided to go. I'll contact my colleague in Bagdad and arrange for you to be met at the airport." The professor pulled himself up from his motorized cart and, with tears in his eyes, gave them each a big bear hug. "Even if you find nothing, be careful. Return safely, and come back and tell me about your adventure." They assured him they would.

Chapter Six

Three weeks later

As the military plane made a sharp bank to start lining up with the runway at the base just outside Baghdad, Matt was intently watching out the window. He was excited about what he and Jim might find in that cave but was also concerned about the dangers of being in Iraq. The war against ISIS was still going on.

Nervously, he ran his fingers through his thick, wavy hair, now dyed a darker shade of brown. Neither he nor Jim had shaved in three weeks other than to trim their beards. With their dark beards and khaki clothes, Matt hoped they would blend in and not look conspicuous.

As Matt felt his heavy stubble, he looked at Jim asleep in the seat next to him. Even though he knew Jim was tough and smart and could easily take care of himself, Matt had always looked upon Jim as the little brother he never had. Matt had always been the leader, and Jim had followed him wherever he went. It was a great relationship.

A bit of fear crept into Matt thoughts. *I hope I'll never lead us into a situation where Jim would be seriously injured or even killed. I could never live with that.*

Then Matt thought about his conversation on the phone a few days previous with the curator of the Baghdad Museum who was providing their visas and transportation and assigning military guards for them. The curator said he was looking forward to meeting them.

This was the last leg of the trip. They had spent the last three weeks trying to learn more of the Arabic language. It was a difficult language, but they could now manage a few common phrases, although not enough to carry on a conversation. Another task had been brushing up on their climbing techniques, and each carried a bag with all their needed climbing equipment.

As the plane touched down, Jim woke up and stretched. Matt grinned and asked, "Are you ready for this, partner?"

"I guess I'm as ready as I will ever be." Jim put a khaki hat over his wavy shock of ebony hair and smiled broadly at Matt.

They both stood up when the plane came to a stop. There were only a handful of Iraqi military men on the plane besides Matt and Jim.

Matt donned his khaki hat and sunglasses to hide his ultramarine eyes. Leaning over, he whispered to Jim, "Let the adventure begin."

They laughed as they sauntered out of the plane, but both men knew full well their luck traveling in dangerous parts of the world might just run out someday. They hoped it wouldn't be in Iraq.

Right now, the excitement of possibly finding some tangible evidence that could prove the story of Noah's ark was really true fueled the resolve they would need to overcome the dangers.

The air was extremely hot and dry as Matt and Jim disembarked the plane. Upon entering the terminal, they were approached by two Iraqi soldiers. Introducing themselves in broken English, the soldiers stated they had been directed to assist them through customs and immigration and drive them to the museum of Bagdad. After verifying their credentials, Matt and Jim retrieved their luggage and were directed to a waiting van. As soon as Matt and Jim had taken their seats in the rear, the two soldiers climbed in beside the driver, rifles resting on their laps. The driver eased into the congested traffic and took a route leading into the heart of the city, arriving at the museum an hour later.

The soldiers escorted Matt and Jim to the curator's office, a large ostentatious room. Here they were greeted by the curator, a rotund man probably in his fifties, Matt guessed. He was impeccably dressed in a black suit, and his large hands were adorned with diamond and gold rings. "My name is Ahmad Lafta, but please address me as Ahmad." His English was excellent, indicative of years of formal education.

The soft-spoken host offered them tea, pita bread, and meat and cheese, a welcome respite after their long flight. After they had eaten and pleasantries were exchanged, Ahmad quickly dove into the reason for their visit and the rules to be followed. "Gentlemen, I must warn you. Please be very careful while you are here in our country. It can be very dangerous for you."

Matt nodded and replied, "We plan to keep a low profile."

"I realize you must be suffering from jet lag after your long flight. I can only sympathize with you, but the sooner you accomplish your mission and leave the country, the better."

Then Ahmad asked if he could see the map that Professor Kempson had sent with Matt and Jim. Matt spread the map out in front of them. "It doesn't pinpoint the exact location, but as the professor told us, if we search the canyons in the exact area he highlighted on the map, with a helicopter we should be able to find the cave."

The area was about 120 kilometers north of Baghdad on the east bank of the Tigris River. A note on the map told them to search the canyons, and they would find the cave high above the canyon floor.

Ahmad cautioned them, "Remember, you can measure, catalog, videotape, and photograph anything you might find. But you must leave everything exactly as you find it. That was my agreement with Professor Kempson. This entire region has been searched and excavated thoroughly since the early eighteen hundreds. Wonderful archaeological treasures have been found. Ancient biblical cities have been unearthed. If there was anything in some cave in that location, I'm sure it was taken out many years ago, but I promised my old friend Professor Kempson I would allow you a day or two to search."

It was getting late in the afternoon when their business was concluded. "I have booked a two-bedroom suite for you at a hotel not far from the air base."

Ahmad then formally introduced them to the two Iraqi soldiers who had escorted them from the airport. "These two men have been assigned to accompany you in a military helicopter up the Tigris River in search of the cave. Also, they will be in the suite next door to yours and will be acting as your guards and guides the entire time you are in Iraq. They are excellent members of the Iraqi military, and they can be trusted."

Both soldiers smiled at the words of praise.

As Ahmad ushered Matt and Jim out to the van, he placed his hands on their shoulders. "Please don't get your hopes up, gentlemen. I really don't think you will find anything."

As the van sped through the city streets to the hotel, Matt and Jim stared at the devastation from the war. They saw burned-out automobiles sitting along some of the streets, while others had been towed to vacant lots and left. Burned American Humvees and American army trucks reminded them of the role the United States played in the war. Every block had badly damaged buildings — just rubble, having been hit with bombs or rockets.

Several of the buildings were being rebuilt. Crews were working on water mains and trying to get water back to the fire hydrants. Matt quietly told Jim, "It's going to take years to completely rebuild the city, but the Iraqis are a very resourceful people. I have no doubt the city will someday be even better than it was before the war.

They finally arrived at the hotel. It was new, built after the war, to accommodate visitors and potential investors in the revival of the war-torn country. The two Iraqi soldiers went to the front desk, confirmed their arrival, and obtained room keys. Matt and Jim waited by the elevators, trying not to be conspicuous or to draw attention to themselves.

Their suite was on the sixth floor. It was quite large with two separate bedrooms, each with its own bath. There was a living room complete with couch, chairs, coffee table, and two reading lamps on end tables. One wall of the living room had a countertop with coffee pot, coffee, and a small refrigerator. There was also a small balcony with a great view of part of the city.

Matt and Jim would've enjoyed going to the restaurant they had seen off the lobby for dinner, but they didn't want take a chance on being recognized as Americans, so Matt had the senior Iraqi soldier order dinner delivered to their room.

* * * * *

By nine o'clock the next morning, they were flying north above the Tigris River in an Iraqi-owned, American-built Bell 205UH-1 Iroquois

Huey. It was much more helicopter than they needed and could carry one pilot plus twelve fully armed troops.

Matt was in the seat opposite the pilot. "I've flown Bell helicopters before but never this model," he told the pilot.

The young pilot was an officer equal to a lieutenant in the army. He was quite friendly and spoke fairly good English. Eager to please, he explained the controls and even let Matt fly for a while. "Good. Very good … for first time," he praised Matt.

Jim keyed his microphone and said, "Don't forget your promise to teach me to fly one of these choppers, Matt."

"Just as soon as we get back home," Matt replied.

Soon they were approaching the area indicated on the map. Most of the country was arid, but close to the river it was green, and there were small patches being farmed. They also flew over fishing boats on the river. The canyons on the east side of the river in some areas looked steep, rocky, narrow, and treacherous.

After a short time, they spotted a cave up one of the canyons just as the professor had described. Matt pointed to the cave and, through the mike on his helmet, told the pilot, "That's where we want to go."

The ravine was so narrow they couldn't fly the helicopter very far up the canyon. They could only view the entrance from an awkward angle as the helicopter hovered over the river. They could not even get as good a look as the professor had, since he had hiked part way up the canyon when he viewed the cave with his binoculars.

The pilot shrugged his shoulders and replied, "No good. Not safe."

The rocks on the east bank of the river would not allow a helicopter to sit down, and if they landed on the flat land west of the river, they would be too far away to see anything. The river was too wide and deep to cross without a boat. The walls on both sides of the deep, narrow, rock-strewn canyon sloped toward each other as they rose up where the water had carved them over the centuries. Like the professor had said, the canyon was actually wider at the bottom than it was at the top. The opposite wall of the canyon was another fifty feet higher than the approximately one-hundred-and-sixty-foot cliff where the cave was, so dropping the climbers down on a cable from the helicopter wouldn't work.

Matt gestured to the pilot and pointed to the mesa on top of the cliff. "We'll have to sit down up there and rappel down."

After hovering over the river and picking out a landmark on the rock wall opposite the cave, they rose to the top of the cliff and landed.

Matt and Jim immediately jumped out and started looking for a place to tie off their ropes. They positioned themselves directly across from the rock outcropping they were using as a reference point. Soon they were rigged, each on his own rope. The plateau was strewn with fairly large boulders. They had no trouble finding rocks on which to tie the ropes.

Matt said, "I think we'd better hurry. This American-built helicopter hovering over the area and then landing up here has probably aroused the curiosity of the fishermen and farmers and who knows who else. They might climb up here to investigate, and they may not be too friendly. I'm guessing we might only have a few hours before they decide to have a closer look, so let's not waste any time."

Matt and Jim quickly connected their safety harnesses onto their ropes and slowly walked backward over the edge.

"Be careful," Matt warned Jim.

Jim grinned back. "I'm always careful. You be careful. You know you're not as young as you used to be."

"You're right. So save your strength. You might have to pull me back up." They both laughed.

They were about six feet apart as they descended. The walls sloped away from them, and soon their feet no longer touched the cliff. Now they had to lower themselves straight down by paying out their ropes.

They had judged the location accurately and were nearly centered in front of the entrance. The cave was only about ten feet wide and about six to seven feet deep, even shallower than Professor Kempson had judged. As they stopped their descent in front of the cave about sixty feet down, they could see why the cave was so shallow. They couldn't have seen it from the ground, but the entrance had collapsed, and broken rock formed the back wall, not solid rock. Dangling from the rope, they were a good eight feet from reaching the ledge they wanted to be standing on.

Jim threw the end of a short rope to Matt. "No sense both of us expending all that energy. I'll swing in and then pull you in."

Jim lowered himself down another five feet, almost level with the floor of the shallow cave and started swinging back and forth toward the entrance.

Matt felt helpless as he watched Jim trying to grab something solid with each swing. Rocks would crumble beneath him, and the backswing would jerk him off solid footing every time. Matt called out, "Be careful, bro. Don't let go of your main rope at the wrong time. Wait till you get a good grip on the rock. It's a long way down!"

Anxious moments passed before Jim got his feet on the ledge and stood safely at the entrance of the cave. Quickly he positioned himself and began pulling on the short rope he had given Matt. Soon the adventurers were standing side by side on the ledge, grinning and pumped with adrenaline.

Turning, they started exploring the cave. Immediately their attention was drawn to the carved flat rock near the entrance that Professor Kempson had seen with his binoculars. They had been too distanced from it and on too steep an angle to see it from the helicopter and, later, too busy to notice it when they were suspended from the ropes. The etching had been badly weathered, so it was hard to actually see anything on the rock face.

Excitedly, Matt dumped some water from his canteen on his handkerchief and began to wash a little of the dirt off the face of the carving. A faint impression appeared, and Matt saw the profile of an animal. After closer inspection, he discerned it could be a lion with a large mane.

Jim was hastily cleaning the next portion of rock. "Matt, here's a giraffe!"

The etchings started about three feet up from the floor and were carved into the side of the flat, western wall of the cave.

Matt and Jim were both down on their knees to make better use of the light. The rock was hard, but still the weather had eroded some of the carvings. As they scrutinized the carvings, they could see that there were other animals above the lion and giraffe, maybe a kangaroo, and another might have been an ostrich. They were so badly weathered, though, they were hard to decipher. All the animals were facing the same way, toward the inside of the cave. The engravings continued behind the rubble that had once been the roof of the cave.

"I can't wait to see what they are looking at," Matt said as he and Jim hurriedly started removing the large stones and dropping them into the canyon below. It took both of them to roll some of the larger pieces to the edge. Feverishly they worked to remove the rubble.

Stopping momentarily to rest, Jim noted, "Kangaroos have never been native to this part of the world, Matt."

"You're right. Many of the carved animals are not native to this area, but we don't know how old this carving is."

Piercing the solitude of the cave, the static of Matt's walkie-talkie interrupted their conversation. Matt grabbed it and moved closer to the edge.

The soldier in charge spoke, asking how they were doing. He was obviously getting nervous waiting on top of the cliff surrounded by large boulders.

Matt didn't tell him about finding the carvings. Instead he replied, "We have to move a lot of rubble to get into the cave. Please be patient a while longer."

Returning to Jim, Matt said, "We'll have to hurry. He's getting anxious up there. Also if someone with a handheld rocket launcher takes out the chopper, we're done for!" They started working even faster.

After a while, the pilot, who spoke a little better English, called. "I assume you are still working to get into the cave."

Matt answered, "Yes, we are okay and proceeding with our work."

"Very good," he replied. "I should warn you. It's getting dark and cold up here. A storm is blowing in. We may have to lift off and fly away to avoid heavy rain or possibly hail." He added, with a chuckle in his voice, "Don't worry if we leave. We will return when the storm is over."

"I understand. Just don't forget about us."

They continued to remove rocks, and finally they had a hole at the top big enough to crawl into. But the rubble still covered the carving on the wall, so they pushed on, taking away only the rocks on the side where the carving was to save time. After another hour, their efforts were rewarded, and the carving was finally uncovered. This area had not been exposed to centuries of weather and was easier to see clearly.

The storm was moving closer, and it was now becoming very cloudy and dark outside. They turned their flashlights on the carving. There were more animals, all facing the same direction. Both men were close to the wall, their eyes following the beams of their flashlights.

Suddenly Jim shouted. "Look! There is the ark or at least most of it with braces holding it upright. All the animals are looking at the ark."

Matt and Jim couldn't believe they were actually looking at a carving of the ark being built. As they stepped back and looked at the whole picture, it took their breath away.

"This is unreal!" Jim cried in disbelief. "The man carved what he was looking at — the ark with the animals gathering around it!"

They both stared at it. Moving closer again, Matt commented, "The ark is not quite complete. Just past the open door in the side, the stone is smooth. It's not quite finished."

Jim also noticed one animal close to the ark had only the head carved. "Why did he stop carving? Was he behind in his work and just chiseling from memory when the flood hit?"

Matt was trembling with excitement. "Wow! What a wonderful artifact! It's almost too good to be true."

Matt and Jim studied the picture chiseled in the rock for a few minutes. Then Matt said, "Jim, I would love to believe that right down below us is where the ark of Noah was actually built, but ... we need a little more proof."

"What do you mean?"

"Skeptics may say that some sculptor was just carving the story of Noah and the flood. I'm not sure anyone can date when this carving was actually made. Let's explore the inside of the cave and try to find something that will date this carving. We've been here this long, so we may as well take a chance and search some more. We won't get another opportunity to come back here."

By now it was raining hard, and they heard the helicopter engine start. It was leaving. The soldier was on the walkie-talkie again. There was too much static for them to understand what he said. Matt tried to call back but got no answer.

As a precaution, Matt and Jim pulled the approximate one hundred feet of rope up from below and tied their harnesses to a rock, just in case someone above found and cut their ropes. If that happened, they could at least rappel down to the canyon floor below.

Water was rushing down the canyon below them. The lightning and thunder crashed loudly. Matt and Jim were safe in the cave for now but hoped the helicopter and three Iraqis were away from the lightning strikes and the worst of the storm. Matt attempted several times again to call them but got only static.

Voicing his concerns to Jim, Matt said, "If anyone was climbing up the hills to check out the helicopter, this should have slowed them down. And with the helicopter leaving, they might just turn around and go back down."

"Unless they saw us rappelling into the cave."

Matt nodded. "Let's hope not."

They turned on their flashlights and went back into the cave. It was quite large inside, and the roof was much higher inside than at the entrance. It was easily thirty feet wide and forty feet deep. From the color of the rock at the top of the cave, they could see the roof had broken loose and fallen down long ago. It was full of fractures and looked like more could come down at any time.

There were signs the cave had once been full of water. Evidence of smoke on the ceiling showed someone had built fires, but there was no smoke on the ceiling where the collapse had occurred. They found a pile of very old animal bones in one corner. They didn't find any pottery, but they did discover two stones that had been used to grind corn or wheat. Someone had lived here.

Jim went outside to check on the weather. The storm was beginning to let up. However, the canyon below was a torrent of rushing water. *No way to escape by lowering ourselves down now.*

Moving back into the cave, he got out their cameras. They took pictures and videos of everything in the cave. They were packing up their cameras, getting ready to leave, when Matt spotted something strange protruding from under the remaining pile of rocks that had fallen from the roof. They both bent down, and there in the beam of the flashlights were the bones of a human foot. Carefully removing the rocks, they found a complete skeleton, intact, lying on its face. The skull had a fracture and a hole in it, and some other bones were broken. Under the skeleton was a tool, a hard stone with a sharp edge.

"Jim, I think we've got our proof. I believe this is the stone carver. I'll bet a chunk of the ceiling came down on him just as he was finishing his work and killed him."

"But if the cave was blocked when he was killed, how come whoever made the map wrote the Iranian word for *ark* on the map? All he could have seen was what we saw before we moved all those rocks. They would have only seen the animal carvings."

Matt kept talking. "My guess is five thousand to six thousand years ago this cave was occupied by a man who made his living carving stone. He probably moved here to carve a record of Noah and his sons building the ark. He was carving what he saw when the animals were gathering around the ark. That could have been months or only days before the flood. The carving doesn't show animals walking up the ramp into the ark. It just shows them gathering around the ark. I believe some rocks fell from the roof of the cave and killed him, but all the rocks we moved didn't fall at one time. A person could still get in the cave. If the floodwaters were in the cave for many months, they could've washed most everything out. Probably about five hundred years ago some Iranian found the cave, made the map, and maybe even took any stone tool he might have found and left. He probably never even found the skeleton. The sculptor would surely have had a stone hammer and a variety of stone-carving tools. Sometime after that, more of the roof came down and completely blocked the entrance."

"Sounds like a good theory to me."

"We have all the pictures we can take, but just in case some of the wrong people get into this cave and destroy or steal the skeleton before the museum people can get here, let's take one small bone back to the Baghdad Museum for date testing. I'll take a chance that the curator will be glad we did since we are turning it over to him. They will probably be back tomorrow for the rest of the skeleton. I'll bet the bone is over five thousand years old," Matt said.

It had finally stopped raining. They looked at the canyon below, and there was still a gusher of angry water rushing down the canyon to the Tigris River.

As they hurriedly gathered their gear again, Jim laughingly said, "I hope we don't get left in this cave. We could get mighty hungry before the water in the canyon slows down enough to get out that way. We might be as skinny as our friend over there."

"Hopefully we won't get that pale and thin."

They tried to call the chopper again but still only got static. Moving to the entrance of the cave, they watched and waited for at least a half hour.

At last, they heard the helicopter fly over and land above them. They tried to call on the two-way radio again but got no response. Shortly after, Matt felt a tug on his rope. At the same time, the radio came to life, and he heard the pilot say, "We're back. Are you all right?"

Both of them sighed in relief. Jim answered with his usual sense of humor, "Lost all track of time! Is dinner ready?"

Quickly Matt and Jim started the strenuous task of ascension with all their gear, including a piece of the wrist bone from the skeleton, pulling themselves up sixty-five feet to the top. Halfway up, Jim breathlessly said, "Matt…we've got … to get back … to the gym. This is harder … to do … than I remembered."

"I'm not having any trouble," Matt lied. "Maybe you're just putting on a little extra weight."

"What did you say?" Jim asked. "You were breathing … so hard … I couldn't understand you." They both chuckled.

Continuing the strenuous ascent, they worked their way up the cliff as fast as their aching muscles would allow. It was urgent that they get out of there quickly. They had been in the cave a long time, and even though it had been raining, some unfriendly persons could be waiting for them.

It was getting late. The Iraqi soldiers and the pilot helped pull them up over the edge. They gathered their gear, coiled the ropes, and put everything in their bags. All the grass and rocks on top were still wet from the rain, and the sun was low in the west. The pilot and the Iraqi sergeant were checking something that had gotten wet on the chopper. The other soldier was keeping watch on the rocks to the rear.

Matt took just a minute to look out across the Tigris River below them and across the flat plain between the Tigris and the Euphrates rivers. The Euphrates was too far away to see, but he knew it was out there west of them.

"What a sight!" Jim commented as he hurried past Matt.

"Yes, isn't it?" Matt replied. "Just think of the history of this valley. The huge forest where Noah and his sons harvested the wood for the ark was right below us. Centuries before that, the Garden of Eden might have been down there too."

"Yes, with Adam and Eve."

Both men were so excited about what they had found in the cave, they couldn't wait to find out the age of the bone. That would be the proof they needed. They lingered at the edge of the cliff just a few seconds longer before returning to the group. Matt and Jim jumped into the helicopter as the pilot was closing the engine cowling. Meanwhile, the other soldier, who had been standing guard, got in next to Jim on the right side of the helicopter.

The pilot and the sergeant, who had been helping him, were standing next to the helicopter engrossed in conversation. Anxious to get back to the museum with their discovery, Matt leaned forward and called out, "Let's get going. We have a long ride back."

The pilot had just taken his seat when, without warning, a bullet coming from the rocks behind the helicopter pierced the pilot's shoulder, and a second bullet hit him in the thigh. Small caliber bullets pelted the helicopter. Instinctively, the sergeant slammed the door shut to keep the pilot from getting hit again. He turned and started firing back toward the rocks, but the next bullet wounded him, and he went down.

Without hesitation, Matt grabbed two AK-47s from a rack behind him and four extra magazines. Tossing one weapon plus extra ammo to Jim, he leapt out the door. Immediately crouching behind a large rock, Matt started returning fire. The area was alive with zinging bullets and a barrage of ricocheting lead and rock chips flying over his head. He was pinned down.

Meanwhile, Jim and the Iraqi corporal managed to get out the right rear door and help the wounded sergeant into the chopper. Then dropping to their knees behind a stone outcropping on their side of the helicopter, they unleashed a volley of shots toward the boulders concealing the assailants.

Matt shouted, "There are about ten men shooting at us! They don't have large caliber guns, but if they hit a vital part of the chopper, we've had it!"

It will only be a matter of time before we are overtaken. I have to get to the pilot's seat on the other side of the helicopter and fly us out of here!

Looking under the helicopter, he yelled, "Jim, cover me!"

"Okay, Matt, we're ready, but stay low!"

Jim and the corporal started to lay down heavy fire toward the large rocks behind the chopper. Zigzagging, Matt sprinted around the front of the helicopter, hoping to dodge the enemies' bullets. As he ran, he got off some rounds, but his clip was almost empty as he opened the door.

Matt slid in and quickly started flipping switches to start the engine. The badly wounded pilot was slumped down, holding his shoulder and trying to stop the bleeding. "You fly," were his last words before losing consciousness.

As soon as the engine reached high RPMs and the rotors were up to speed, Matt slipped another magazine in his gun, opened his door, and shouted, "Come on! Get in!"

Jim and the Iraqi ran for the right rear door as Matt blanketed the area with gunfire to shield them. Just as they slammed the rear door shut, Matt dropped his AK-47 and tilted the blades. They lifted off.

Banking hard to the left, they could hear bullets hitting the sides of the helicopter. Jim slid the left door open and started firing at their assailants while Matt dropped the chopper down off the cliff to the valley below and out of range of fire.

As Matt watched the canyon floor coming up fast, he pulled harder on the controls. This helicopter was a lot heavier than any he had flown before. He would have to adjust for that. His eyes were darting between the fast-moving terrain under him and his instruments, alert for trouble if the engine had been hit. He flew low and nudged the big machine faster and faster, heading south toward Baghdad.

Matt grabbed the mike and handed it over his shoulder to the corporal and shouted, "Call the base! Tell them what happened!"

Matt could hear Jim shouting for the corporal to hand him the first aid kit. Both the pilot in the seat beside Matt and the sergeant in the seat with Jim were badly wounded and losing a lot of blood.

Matt was wary as he pushed the chopper to its limits. The river, the fishing boats, the fields — all flashed in front of him and disappeared under the chopper. He knew if Jim couldn't get the bleeding stopped, one or both of the Iraqis could die en route. He had to fly fast.

Matt glanced beside him and saw Jim was struggling with the pilot, trying to get a tourniquet tied. The Iraqi corporal was jabbering into the mike. Matt could only hope the base understood their desperate situation.

Matt continually scanned his instruments for any sign of a problem. Suddenly he noticed he was losing oil pressure.

He had been afraid a bullet might have hit the engine, and now he was sure of it.

Jim was busy grabbing bandages and tourniquets out of the first-aid kits. Doing the best he could to help the two wounded Iraqis, he shouted at Matt, "The pilot is still losing blood, and I think he's going into shock! Sarge, here, has been hit in the back of the leg. I wish this first-aid kit contained morphine because these guys are in real pain, but there isn't any. So hurry, partner!"

Matt watched as the temperature gauge went up, and the oil pressure slowly went down. He turned and ordered the corporal, who was helping Jim, "Tell the base we are losing oil pressure but we can't stop now. Be sure they have an ambulance waiting and are prepared to treat these men for a large loss of blood."

The corporal quickly got on the radio and relayed Matt's message to the base. "I ask them to inform curator at museum what happening," he reported to Matt. "A ambulance waiting for us."

Matt had just started flying over the populated city of Baghdad on the way to the base when the engine began to run rough. Then he smelled smoke, like hot oil burning. Looking up, he saw flames shooting out of the engine compartment. Trickles of sweat streaked Matt's dusty face as adrenaline surged through his body. He couldn't set down in the middle of the city. He had to keep this giant in the air.

"Hang in there, guys," he encouraged.

The corporal radioed the base again. He was almost hysterical as he pleaded for their assistance. "I don't want to die!"

The engine was now really running rough, and heavy smoke filled the cabin, setting off the alarm. Matt knew if the engine froze suddenly, they were done for. They would fall out of the sky like a rock!

Matt lowered his altitude to just above the trees and skirted around the higher buildings in the city, searching for a vacant lot or any place to set down. No such luck. Just houses, power lines, narrow streets. He had to keep pushing the chopper to try to reach the base.

They could all now feel the heat radiating from the fire in the engine compartment above their heads. Matt had already used the extinguisher, but it failed to put out the hot oil fire. With so much smoke, Matt could barely see where he was going. Finally on the horizon about a mile in front of them was the base. *Maybe we can make it!*

Two alarms were shrieking inside the cockpit. Thick smoke was billowing throughout the entire aircraft. Everyone was choking on the smoke, which was bringing tears to their eyes. They were almost to the perimeter fence about thirty feet above the ground when the engine died. The rotor was still turning but was quickly slowing down.

Matt shouted, "Prepare for a hard landing!"

Everyone braced themselves as best they could. Barely clearing the perimeter fence, the chopper hit hard, and a flurry of paper and metal ricocheted about the cockpit. The rotor blades struck the dirt in front of them, and the skids collapsed on impact. The belly of the craft slid across the sparse weeds and grass, finally careening to a stop.

The doors flew open. Jim jumped out and single-handedly pulled the pilot out and dragged him away from the wreckage. Matt helped the corporal get the wounded sergeant out and away from the chopper. Flames were now rolling out and engulfing the engine cowling. The base fire trucks pulled up with sirens blaring. Firemen sprang to action, and, within moments, they had put foam on the hot engine compartment, saving the helicopter. The engine was lost, but Matt knew that the helicopter would probably be flying again soon.

Right behind the fire trucks came the ambulance with lights flashing and sirens screaming. The medical personnel moved quickly to stabilize and treat the wounded men.

As the Iraqi army medics were getting the wounded pilot and sergeant ready to transport, Matt, Jim, and the Iraqi corporal quietly stood by. The sergeant looked up and, laboring for breath, murmured, "Jim good … with first aid. Stopped bleeding … or would die."

Downplaying the compliment, Jim called attention to the role of the other soldier. "I'm sure the corporal here would have made sure that didn't happen."

The pilot who had been in and out of consciousness gave Matt a thumbs-up and managed to utter three words: "*Good flying, ace.*"

The corporal told Matt, "We lucky you fly helicopter. We not know how to fly," gesturing to the sergeant. "Pilot no — not awake."

The sergeant added, "Whoever attacked us would kill us all. You save us. Thank you!"

As the medics put the men in the ambulance, Matt and Jim wished them a speedy recovery.

Even though it was now almost dark, there were lights from all the vehicles surrounding the shot-up helicopter. The three men examined the chopper and all the shots it had taken.

The van had been waiting for them when they landed. They got in and were whisked directly to the museum, and though it was very late, the curator, Ahmad, was there to meet them. Ahmad was gravely concerned for them and wanted a firsthand, detailed report concerning the attack and subsequent firefight. He had just heard from the base hospital. The pilot and soldier both had serious wounds but would recover. The patients were telling the hospital staff what had transpired. The curator smiled at them.

"The wounded men spoke very highly of all three of you. They said you two archaeologists acted like soldiers."

Then he said, "Corporal, I'd now like to hear your version of exactly what happened. Maybe we can determine who it was that attacked you."

The corporal related the entire story, including all the details. As he concluded his story, he said the two Americans had acted more like professional military soldiers than any archaeologists he could imagine. Grinning, he added, "Lucky for me, you both fighters!"

Matt and Jim each shook the hand of the smiling young Iraqi. "Corporal," Matt said, "you stayed cool and did a great job."

Feeling the time was right, Matt addressed Ahmad, "Would you now like to see what we found in the cave?"

The curator had a bewildered look on his face. He had assumed they had not found anything, at least nothing significant in the cave. The corporal was also eager to hear what they might have found. Up to this point, Matt and Jim never had a chance to tell anyone what they had discovered.

They showed the curator, the corporal, and two of the curator's assistants all the evidence: the photos, the video, and the bone they had brought back for date testing. Silence enveloped the room. Ahmad was absolutely astounded at what they had discovered. He was speechless.

Ahmad ordered meals delivered to his office. Matt, Jim, and the corporal had not eaten since early morning and realized how famished they were.

Meanwhile, the curator and his assistants duplicated all the pictures and video. Ahmad promised, "I will let you know the age of the bone and any other information we learn about the discovery as soon as the results are in. I have made arrangements to have a heavily armed team at the site tomorrow before anyone else can go into the cave."

Chapter Seven

"**G**ood evening, Matt."

"Good evening or good morning, Ahmad." Matt laughed. "We've been anxiously waiting for your call."

"I understand Jim Morgan and Dr. Jensen are there with you."

"Yes, they are here with me, Ahmad. We're in Dr. Jensen's office gathered around his desk on the speakerphone."

"Then greetings to you all, and thank you for staying up late to receive my call. I have just sent you a fax. It's the result of the carbon dating and the findings of a forensic panel here in Baghdad. Have you received it yet?"

"Just a moment, Ahmad," Matt said.

Ira ran to the fax room and returned, reading the report. His face lit up with a huge grin. "Wonderful! This is wonderful news."

Matt spoke into the receiver, "Yes, we have the fax, and Dr. Jensen is reading it now."

"I will stay on the line. You will be pleased with the findings."

Ira read,

My dear friends,

I am pleased, excited, and happy to inform you that the panel of forensic scientists here in Baghdad has traveled to the cave. They have spent many hours examining the contents. The results of their investigation were released to me today. I have paraphrased the report, which I will fax later.

The skeleton is the remains of a male. He was approximately forty years old when he died. Cause of death was a fractured skull. Some vertebrae in the neck were crushed at the same time. The most likely cause was the collapse of part of the rock ceiling in the cave. The entire skeleton has been brought to Baghdad. The radiocarbon tests indicate the bones are approximately 5,620 years old. The panel also concluded that more of the ceiling had fallen in on the skeleton, fracturing the dried bones at various times over the past years.

Also, there was evidence that the cave had been completely filled with water at one time.

Congratulations, my good friends.

I will send a copy of the formal report to your office later today.

Ahmad

Matt, Jim, and Ira were ecstatic with the great news.

"Fantastic news, Ahmad," Matt declared, with Jim and Ira chiming in. "This is the news we have been hoping for."

Ahmad agreed. "Yes, it is wonderful news, especially for our country. Thank you so much for discovering it. And, Matt, everyone I have spoken to, including members of the forensic panel here in Baghdad, agrees that the circumstantial evidence does, indeed, indicate the stone carver had probably been making a record of what he was observing in the valley below when he was killed by falling rocks from the ceiling of the cave.

"There is some talk here now about arranging with the owners of the farmland where the ark was built to carefully examine and perhaps do some excavation to search for artifacts in the area."

"I hope they do just that," Matt approved. "It would be wonderful if they could find even more evidence to substantiate what we found."

Ahmad carried on, "The cave has been secured, and the carving is being guarded around the clock. It's too early to know how to handle the site where the wonderful engravings are. But, I can assure you, it will be handled properly."

"I'm sure it will," Matt replied.

They had all previously agreed that if the results of the tests were positive, Ira would arrange a news conference to inform the world of the discovery. Ira said he would set it up soon.

After they thanked Ahmad and said good-bye, Matt hung up. They cheered and high-fived each other. Now, if someone could just locate the ark on Ararat.

* * * * *

Washington, D.C.
One week later

Matt knew he was arriving a half hour early for the news conference Ira had scheduled. He hadn't expected anyone to be there yet. As he entered the lobby of the auditorium where the conference was to be held, he was amazed and pleased to see Ira chatting with Professor Kempson and, of all people, Ahmad, the curator of the Iraq Museum in Baghdad.

The door behind him opened, and there was Jim.

"Hi, Matt. Wow, look who's here!"

"I know," said Matt. "What a surprise."

Matt and Jim quickly crossed the room and warmly greeted the professor and the curator.

"Ira, how did you put this all together?" Matt complimented his boss. "This is really great."

"I knew you and Jim were really disappointed when we learned neither of these gentlemen could be here. When we received word later that both would be attending, I told my staff to keep it secret. I thought it would be a nice surprise."

"It's a great surprise," Matt marveled. "These men played such an important part in the discovery. It would be a shame if they were not here when we announced it to the public. At this point, only a few people know about the discovery. Even the reporters, who I see are now coming in, are in the dark."

Someone tapped Matt on the shoulder. Turning, Matt was face-to-face with the two Iraqi soldiers who were with them in Baghdad. Surprised, Matt and Jim greeted the two soldiers warmly, genuinely excited to see them. They started to introduce them to the professor and Ira but found they had all met earlier in Ira's office. The sergeant was on crutches, but that didn't seem to diminish his enthusiasm about being in America.

Ahmad explained, "The pilot really wanted to come with us, and I had authority to bring him along, but the doctor said he was not well enough to make the trip. He sends his greetings."

Soon all the curious reporters were in their seats in the auditorium. They were whispering amongst themselves, inquiring if anyone knew what was going to be announced. No one knew.

Ira stepped to the microphone and welcomed all the reporters, thanked them for coming, and began by saying, "Gentlemen and ladies, today I have an announcement to make that, we believe, will be of great interest to everyone, especially to biblical scholars. We believe these men seated behind me have discovered proof, or at least circumstantial evidence, that Noah's ark was actually built and where the construction of the ark took place."

The entire audience of news reporters was in an uproar.

During the next hour, Matt introduced each man who had participated in the discovery and told the entire story, showing the photos and video on a large screen. Ira provided each reporter with a packet containing photos and the Iraqi panel's report.

The curator expounded about the discovery Jim and Matt had found in Iraq, the actual birthplace of the ark.

After the formal announcement, the excited reporters personally interviewed everybody involved. The two Iraqi soldiers were eager to tell their story, and all the networks were excited about the human-interest twist they lent. The story became embellished as the Iraqi sergeant expounded, "They were all around us! Bullets, grenades, smoke! Many attackers — maybe twenty or more!" His arms flailed about as he pantomimed the battle. Matt smiled as he watched the two soldiers bask in their moment of glory.

Matt made sure the professor got the credit he deserved. "If it hadn't been for the diligent research of Professor Kempson, we would never have made the discovery," he emphasized in an interview on a morning TV show.

Congratulations came in from all around the world.

Matt and Jim bought civilian clothes for the two Iraqi soldiers, took them sightseeing, and went for a night out on the town before they had to leave for Baghdad. The sergeant and corporal enjoyed themselves, and the four of them partied till dawn.

A popular magazine featured Jim and Matt on the cover with the photos of the carving showing the ark in the background: "New Discovery — Noah's Ark: Myth or Real?"

The tabloids published a story that exaggerated the attack on the helicopter, calling Matt and Jim heroes for saving the Iraqi soldiers who were supposed to be protecting them.

Matt was outraged. "I'm glad the sergeant and corporal were back in Baghdad when this hit the news stands. It's unfair to our friends, the Iraqi soldiers. They fought right beside us to fend off the attackers. I hope they never see a copy."

Colored pictures of Matt and Jim, the cave, the carving, and even the skeleton of the sculptor were printed in magazines around the world.

The photos of the cave, the carving, the sculpturing tool, the skeleton, and the testimony of the carbon dating convinced all but a few skeptics that the story in the Bible about Noah's ark was probably true.

Jim and Matt were recognized wherever they went. Television networks were jousting for personal interviews. Jim enjoyed the notoriety at first, but soon both he and Matt were looking for some peace and quiet and a return to normal life.

Chapter Eight

Matt had just finished his special presentation to the large class on religious antiquities. Everyone in the audience knew that just a couple of months ago he and archaeologist James Morgan had brought back proof that Noah's ark had actually been built in ancient Mesopotamia, now modern-day Iraq. The whole world had seen the pictures and heard the story of their adventure there, including the fight for their lives with Dr. Lane shooting at the attackers and then flying the Iraqi helicopter and James Morgan battling their attackers and administering first aid to the wounded, saving the lives of two Iraqi soldiers.

Matt was just closing his talk. "As you all know, I love studying religions and searching for artifacts. I'm sure that those of you who decide on that type of career will find it very rewarding."

Matt was one of the most popular speakers on archaeology and religious antiquities in the D.C. area. Many of the young women in his audience were captivated by his handsome features and tried to catch his eye.

As Matt gathered his notes and prepared to leave, he noticed no one in the audience had risen to leave.

A young lady stood up and said rather nervously, "Doctor Lane, before we leave" — she turned toward the audience — "I believe I speak for most of us here. Could you please tell us more about Noah's ark? I mean, do you really believe it is actually up on Mount Ararat?"

Matt smiled and replied, "Noah's ark is one of my favorite subjects, as you might have guessed."

The audience chuckled.

"Yes, I still firmly believe that Noah's ark ended up on Mount Ararat. I am convinced it is still partially intact, buried under the ice somewhere above the Ahora Gorge. Someday, perhaps in late August when the summer has been exceedingly warm, it may be partially sticking out of the ice, and someone will find it. That would turn the scientific community upside down."

The audience chuckled as Matt grinned.

Matt looked at his watch and said, "I have a few minutes. I'd be more than happy to answer questions if you like."

Immediately, several hands shot up, and Matt proceeded to answer questions.

After fifteen minutes, hands were still going up. Matt pointed at a young lady who asked, "Could dinosaurs fit into the ark?" Several people in the audience laughed.

"Excellent question," Matt replied. "Dinosaurs would never have been in the ark. Dinosaurs had all lived and died before man was created. Also whales, sharks, and fish, of course, could all swim so they wouldn't have been in the ark either.

"There would have been an abundance of floating logs and branches where animals that swam but also needed to rest could have taken refuge. Seals, walruses, and polar bears, for example, could have survived outside the ark."

Then Matt pointed to a young man who had a skeptical look on his face. "Doctor Lane, surely you don't believe the ark story could really have happened. I mean, getting all those huge, wild animals into one wooden ship and feeding them for months is hard enough to believe, but how could they have gone to foreign countries and brought back all those animals? They probably didn't even know many of the animals existed. It just seems impossible."

Matt answered with a smile. "A few years back, I felt the same way you feel. When I was in college, I and two of my friends discovered something that completely changed our way of thinking about the ark story." The audience was quiet, listening to every word. "If you look up the story of Noah's ark in the book of Genesis, you will find that God told Noah something that made the task a whole lot easier."

"What was that?" the young man asked.

"God told Noah, 'The animals you are to save will come to you.'"

Silence permeated the auditorium.

"Wow!" many in the audience whispered.

"Yes, wow!" Matt said. "That made Noah's task a whole lot easier."

"Yes, it would have," the young man replied with a smile.

"Just imagine," Matt continued, "a few years before the ark was completed, strange animals may have started appearing in the forest around the ark. Our assumption was that the offspring of these exotic animals would be the ones selected to go into the ark. Remember, they only needed two animals from each species. They could have selected these animals carefully just after they were weaned. They would have taken only baby elephants, rhinos, hippos, buffalo and such, not fully grown animals. One full-grown male African elephant can weigh over twelve thousand pounds; a young elephant calf would weigh a fraction of that. These young animals would not only weigh less and take up less space. They would also eat less, drink less, and produce much less waste. They would also be a lot easier to handle than their full-grown parents. I would much rather have a baby tiger by the tail than his mama!"

The audience laughed and nodded in agreement.

"Those two things alone—God gathering all the animals and the animals starting the journey when they were small—started to convince me and my colleagues that the ark story could have really happened.

"My two archaeologist friends and I spent a lot of time studying about the ark. We determined that the ark would have needed a well-designed ramp and passage system to allow easy access to every animal. They probably had rope and pulley systems to move feed through the vessel. They also would have had to bring all the animal waste up to the one great door in the side of the ship for disposal, which was probably not the most fun job on the ship."

Chuckles rippled through the audience.

"For fresh water, we determined they could have shaped the roof of the ark so it sloped to the sidewall to trap rain water. This water could have been diverted with wooden chutes and water stops down to each deck and stored in large wooden barrels. The excess water would have simply flowed out through openings a little higher in the side of the perimeter wall that extended above the roof.

"If their food supply ran low, Noah and his sons could have lowered the big door in the side of the ark and anchored it level with the ocean surface. They could have cast their nets and caught an abundance of fish, not only for the family, but to feed many animals and birds. And speaking of birds, I imagine there were thousands of exhausted birds constantly landing on the roof of the ark. They could not only have killed and eaten these birds but also fed them to the carnivorous animals. They may have also gathered baskets full of floating leaves, roots, and seaweed to dry and feed to the herbivorous animals. With these methods, I believe they could have extended their food and water supply long enough to survive the journey."

Another young lady raised her hand and asked if anyone had actually ever seen Noah's ark on Mount Ararat.

Dr. Lane answered, "Many people claim to have seen it, and many claim they have even taken pictures of it. However, no one has been able to produce the pictures except some taken from very high altitudes using satellites. In my opinion, none of these pictures are very descriptive.

"There are many books that have been written about expeditions to Mount Ararat. If you're interested, check them out. I believe one of the most fascinating and believable stories is about the expedition from Russia in 1916. A pilot and copilot from the Russian Imperial Air Force were flying over Mount Ararat and reported seeing the ark. Other flights confirmed the ark was there. Nicholas II, the czar of Russia, sent two engineering companies up the mountain to find the ark. That was not an easy task. Mount Ararat is difficult to climb. However, they found it, partially protruding out of the ice pack. They photographed it, measured it, and explored the inside, finding rooms with tiers of cages and pens that could have held large animals. The engineers made detailed drawings of the huge vessel. Some of the photographs showed Russian soldiers standing on top of the ark. The mission was a complete success. However, shortly after the expedition returned to Russia, the revolution began. The czar and his family were murdered, and all the information about the exploration was lost. The only information available about their discovery was testimony from some of the Russian soldiers who were on the expedition and the statements from the pilots who originally spotted the ark. Has the makings of a good movie, right?"

The audience agreed.

Another question was asked. "Would all the animals except those that lived in the sea actually have fit in the ark?"

"Yes, I think it was possible. The ark was about four hundred and fifty feet long, seventy-five feet wide, and had three decks. We do not know how many different kinds of animals existed in Noah's time. Many of the species living today could have evolved since then."

There were more hands up, but Matt, looking at his watch, said, "I'm sorry. I have one more lecture today, and I have to leave. Much more information is available to you in the library and on the Internet. I find it fascinating to sit down and read about it. I'm sure you will too." He thanked the audience for their attention, who in turn gave him a standing ovation.

Chapter Nine

Matt, Jim, and two other men were seated at a table close to the fireplace in Luigi's Bistro. It was April in Washington, D.C., but it was still quite cool in the early evening. Matt's lecture had concluded just a few hours earlier, and it was now about 7:00 p.m.

Matt was laughing at something one of the men had said when he became aware of a very attractive young lady entering the restaurant. It seemed rather strange for such a beautiful girl to come in unescorted. Maybe she was meeting someone. She was at the edge of the dining room, her eyes scanning the people at the crowded tables as she waited for the maître d' to seat her. Matt tried not to stare at her, but he was intrigued with her beauty.

Matt had dated a lot of women, but there was something striking about this girl, something different. Several of the men in the room had turned and were sending admiring glances her way.

Long, dark-auburn hair fell loosely past her shoulders. She removed her coat, revealing a brown, knee-length skirt and beige sweater. *Nice shape*, Matthew thought. *This girl could easily be a model.*

James, sitting across from Matt, instinctively turned his head sideways to see who Matt kept glancing at. Smiling, he turned back and teased, "Matthew, I do believe that charmer has caught your eye."

The maître d' had returned to his podium and was engaged in conversation with the young lady. He pointed toward Matt and smiled. To Matt's and Jim's surprise, he then escorted her through the crowded room, stopping at their table. "This is Dr. Lane, madam."

She extended her hand to Matt. "Dr. Lane, please excuse me for interrupting you." Matt stood and took her slender, well-manicured hand. "My name is Ann Tyler. I'm sorry to interrupt your dinner, but I heard you were here, and I need to talk to you. I felt this might be my only chance."

Matt was dumbfounded by the brash approach of this woman but decided to play her game for a few minutes. "That's quite all right," he said. "May I introduce you to my friends? This fellow is James Morgan. James, this is—Miss or Mrs.?—Ann Tyler."

"It's still Miss Tyler," she replied. "I'm pleased to meet you, Mr. Morgan."

James stood up, as did the other two men when Matt introduced Charles Nolan and Clint Brown. He saw their amused faces glance at him.

"Is there something I can do for you, Miss Tyler?" Matt asked. "Would you care to sit down?"

"That's a wonderful invitation, but I'm afraid I haven't the time this evening. I hate to ask this, but, Dr. Lane, could I have just a short conversation with you in private? It's of great importance. I promise I'll have you back with your friends within fifteen minutes."

"Of course, Miss Tyler. Please excuse us, gentlemen. I'll be back in just a few."

"Could we speak on the patio where it is more private?" she invited. Matthew took her arm and guided her through the dining room and out the French doors leading to the outside patio. Several wrought-iron tables and chairs were interspersed with hedges and brick pathways, a charming setting, but no other people had braved the evening chill.

Matt held her coat as she slipped it on. Park-like posts with lanterns illuminated the area and cast a warm glow on Ann. Matt studied her face, noting it was cold enough to see her breath. He guessed her to be in her late twenties or early thirties. She had a beautiful, dark complexion, high cheekbones, and large brown eyes. Her full lips naturally smiled as she spoke. These facial features, combined with a slim, delicately sculptured nose and those lush, pouty lips put her in a class of her own.

They walked together for a few feet, and she paused at a table with two chairs under a lamppost. Looking around to be sure they were alone, she sat down. Following her lead, Matt took the seat across from her.

Ann looked Matt squarely in the eye and said, "I know you only by what I've read about you. I've seen your picture in all kinds of magazines lately. Before that I had heard people talk about you and your father when I was taking classes at the university." She seemed to be searching his soul with those penetrating eyes.

"Just what is it that you know about me? What you hear may not always be true," Matt replied with a sly look on his face.

"Well, I have to admit I was captivated like the rest of the world about what you discovered in Iraq, so I've done some research," she said. "I know your father is an influential United States senator. I know your family has great wealth that originally came from your great-grandfather, who was in the timber and land development business among other things, and that your grandfather and father added to the family wealth by proper management and diversification. I sat in on your lecture this afternoon at the university and realized you're the one person I could trust. At least I hope you are."

Matt was stunned by her knowledge of his background. Composing himself, he inquired, "What do you mean trust, Ann?"

Her brown eyes darted from side to side. Then she leaned forward and spoke in a hushed tone, "I mean I have knowledge of something I think you would be very interested in, and I'd like to tell you about it."

Matt was growing increasingly intrigued with this young woman. "You have me very curious now, Ann. Just what kind of knowledge are you talking about?"

"This is not the time or place to tell you about it. But could we meet soon in a more comfortable setting? A little warmer, perhaps?" she joked. "I could tell you all about it then."

Matt mulled over the idea of meeting again with her. This was a strange encounter, but there was something seductive about this mysterious woman and her closely guarded secret. Maybe there was an adventure behind this cloak of secrecy. Deciding to risk a wasted evening, Matt replied, "Certainly. How about having dinner at my house tomorrow … say, about seven? We'll have dinner, and then you can tell me over a glass of wine."

Seemingly caught off guard by his invitation, she drew back from the table. Fumbling with her purse, Ann stammered, "Please don't get the wrong idea. What I'm going to share with you is very important to me, and it's very serious. It may even be extremely dangerous for both of us by my sharing this secret. I'm not looking for romance, Dr. Lane. I don't think meeting at your house would be a very discreet idea."

"On the contrary, Miss Tyler, I think it makes perfect sense. I didn't mean to imply our evening would be anything but professional. Since I don't usually like to discuss any type of business in public, I'd rather discuss it in private, either at my house or your place … wherever that might be."

"No, my place would not be a good choice," she replied. "I have a roommate who is a dear friend, but I've never shared this information with anyone, not even my own family. Therefore, I'm even concerned about disclosing it to you."

"Okay, it's back to my place then. I'll have Charlotte, my housekeeper, prepare something. My chauffeur can pick you up at five if you will give me your address. After dinner, you can tell me whatever this earth-shattering news is." He smiled at her. "I assure you, Ann, you will be perfectly safe with me."

Ann paused. "Okay, Dr. Lane. Were you serious about having someone pick me up tomorrow night?"

"Absolutely. Johns would enjoy picking you up in the limo. Five, it is."

Ann gave Matt her address and phone number.

Mustering her last ounce of courage, Ann asked one more favor. "You cannot tell anyone about our meeting tomorrow or about our conversation this evening."

"Granted," Matt promised, "but what do you suggest I tell my friends about our now twenty-minute conversation?"

Looking at her watch, Ann stuttered an apology for taking so much of his time. "Can't you say you have a secret admirer who just wanted to meet you, which of course is true, and perhaps she was a little more forward in her approach than most?"

Matt smirked. "I'm sure I can think of something."

As she rose to leave, Matt stood up. "Will you now join us for dinner?"

"No, thank you." Ann was already edging toward the door.

"Then at least let me drive you home." Matt was hoping to gain some insight into this bewitching woman who had suddenly burst into his world. *Is she genuine? What is her secret? There is no doubt this is one liberated, self-sufficient individual. She isn't about to divulge any personal information.* Matt was stymied.

"No, thank you again. I brought my own car and can drive myself home," Ann emphatically replied as she darted out the door.

As he made his way back to his table, Matt was excited about tomorrow night. She was the most beautiful woman he had ever met. What could she possibly want to tell him? It even sounded like there might be some danger involved.

Then he paused for a moment and shook his head to clear his mind. *Maybe I shouldn't be quite so trusting,* he mused.

However, Matt was bewitched by this damsel in distress. *I probably will not sleep very well tonight just wondering what you're going to tell me, lovely lady*

Chapter Ten

Ann crawled into bed. It was late, but she was too excited to sleep. Her mind traveled back over the evening. *I hope I didn't make a mistake in choosing Dr. Lane,* she thought as she lay there in the dark.

She remembered the words her Russian grandmother, Jelena, said to her long ago. "Never tell the story to anyone, Ann — at least not until you're all grown up. And then be very sure you can trust that person. You may be putting his life in danger by telling him. I may even be putting your life in danger by telling you, but, Ann, you're the only one I feel I can tell."

Well, Ann thought to herself, *I'm more than all grown up, Grandma. I'm twenty-eight years old. It's time I told someone. I just hope Dr. Lane is the right person.*

Soon her memories drifted back, and she was reliving that time in her life as she had so many times before.

She was twelve years old, still living in Moscow with her father. Her mother had died several years before, and Ann really missed her.

That summer was special. She spent several weeks with her Grandmother Jelena in a rural farming community north of Moscow. They were having a wonderful summer together. Ann really loved her grandmother. She didn't look or act like most of the older people Ann had met.

Ann last name was Surikova then. Her grandmother was Jelena Malavski Surikova. Ann had changed her name from Ann Surikova to Ann Tyler to make it easier for Americans to pronounce after she and her father moved to the United States when she was fourteen.

As Ann lay in her bed, she began to recall the very detailed story her grandmother told her. She knew the story so well. It was almost like she was there watching it all happen. Finally she drifted off to sleep.

* * * * *

Jelena was standing behind her granddaughter, brushing her long auburn hair. As Ann sat facing the mirror, Jelena could not help but notice that Ann had the same olive skin, high cheekbones, and big brown eyes as she had at her age. It was almost like looking at her own reflection.

Jelena paused from brushing Ann's hair. "Come sit in the living room with me, and let's have some tea."

Ann carried the tray with porcelain cups and teapot into the living room, setting it on the coffee table her grandfather had carved. Jelena poured the tea and put a freshly baked cake on a plate, one of Ann's favorite treats.

The room had a comfortable, homey feel to it. Lace curtains on the large window softened the bleak countryside. The furniture was practical but elegant, reflecting a feminine touch. On a corner shelf were pictures: Mikhail and Ann, Dimitri and Jelena.

As Ann took the plate, she looked at her grandmother seated next to her. "I know you're going to tell me something, aren't you, Grandmother?"

"How would you know that, child?" Jelena asked, smiling.

"I've noticed you seem a little nervous, like you want to tell me something but you're afraid to. Am I right?"

"Yes, you are right, Ann."

"It's nothing bad about my dad, is it? I mean, he's not sick or anything, is he?"

"No, your dad is just fine. But you're right, Ann. There is something I want to tell you. I want to tell you a story. It's a true story, and it's about me. I have worried about telling you this. I wish you were about ten years older, but you're not, and I'm getting very old. So I must tell you. It's about something that happened in my life when I was about your age. Actually, it began when I was about ten and ended when I was fourteen. But before I tell you, Ann, I'm going to ask you to promise me that you won't ever tell anyone else this story until you're grown up and then only to someone you know you can trust."

"Oh yes, I promise I won't tell anyone, Grandmother. Don't worry. I'm really good at keeping a secret. But what about Dad? Does he already know the story?"

"No, he does not, Ann, and you can't tell him."

Ann thought about it for a few seconds. She and her father were very close, but she would respect her grandmother's wishes. "I won't tell anyone. I promise."

Jelena then told Ann the entire story. She included every small detail she could remember. She told her how she had met her best friend, Yuri Pavaloski, when they were both ten years old and how she had noticed the strange lines in the dirt floor of the feed storage room in Yuri's barn, which led to him showing her the secret room beneath the floor.

Then she told Ann about the photographs of Noah's ark that were hidden beneath the floor in the secret room in Yuri's barn, not far from where she was now living.

Ann stirred slightly in her sleep but continued remembering and dreaming of the story her grandmother Jelena conveyed so long ago.

* * * * *

Everyone at school was talking about recent gossip from people fleeing Moscow. Jelena sought out Yuri at recess. "Did you hear that people are being murdered on the streets in Moscow?" she anxiously asked him.

"Yes, it's terrible," he replied. "My father is sure now there will be a revolution, and even more people will be killed."

"Oh, I hope not," she whimpered as tears welled up in her eyes.

"Jelena, I need to tell you something else."

"What?" she asked intently.

"We can't play in the barn together anymore."

"Why not?"

"My mother thinks we're getting too grown-up to be playing games alone in the barn."

She thought about it for a few seconds. "We both know we wouldn't do anything we shouldn't, Yuri."

"Yes, I know we wouldn't, but I don't want our parents telling us we can't be together at all."

"Neither do I," Jelena said. "My mother is already telling me I spend too much time at your house."

"So let's not go in the barn…unless no one is around. Okay?"

"All right." She giggled. couple of weeks later, Jelena walked over to Yuri's house. She was surprised to learn Yuri was home alone. His grandmother was still very ill, and his mother had gone to her farm to help take care of her.

They walked out to the barn just to look at the horses. They had both grown up a lot during the past four years since they first met, and even though Jelena had grown tall quickly and was taller than most of the boys close to her age, Yuri was still taller than she was by three inches.

Jelena was watching Yuri. She was very aware that he had become a handsome young man, tanned and strong from working in the sun on the farm. Other girls at school had also noticed and would flirt incessantly with him. She tried not to show her agitation when she heard him laughing with a crowd of girls around him. After all, she told herself, she wasn't jealous.

Jelena herself looked far different than when they had first met four years ago out on the road in front of Yuri's house. She was now becoming quite shapely, changing rapidly from a young girl to a beautiful young lady. Even the drab, unflattering clothes her grandmother helped her sew couldn't conceal the transformation. The boys at school flirted with her also, but she did not flirt back. She was too attracted to Yuri to pay much attention to any other boys.

They had always just played games together, such as hide-and-seek or playful wrestling, but last week Jelena had grabbed the ball Yuri had been tossing up in the air and wouldn't give it back. Yuri chased her across the yard and caught her, and when he grabbed her from behind and put his arms around her shoulders to get the ball she was hugging, he was surprised and embarrassed when he accidentally touched her breasts. It also embarrassed Jelena. Yuri thought to himself, *I must really be naïve. I never even noticed she had breasts.*

They quickly looked at the front porch, and both were glad to see no one was watching them. Jelena just tossed him the ball and laughed like nothing had happened, but both knew something was different. They were growing up.

While they were still standing in the barn, Jelena sat down on a big pile of clean straw. Then she lay back on the straw and looked up in the rafters of the barn. "Look," she said. "I think there is an owl up there."

"Where?"

"Up there," she said, pointing at the rafters.

Yuri looked up. "I still don't see anything."

"Lie down beside me, and I'll point right to it."

So Yuri lay down next to her on the straw. "Now look right where I point."

Yuri followed exactly where she pointed and finally exclaimed, "I see it — a big barn owl!"

"See, I told you."

They both watched the owl, and the owl watched them with his huge yellow eyes. It was about two in the afternoon, and it had started to sprinkle. Jelena and Yuri lay side by side and listened to the light rain on the roof of the barn. For the first time, they were both very aware of the attraction they were starting to feel for each other. They had always been the very best of friends. They had never fought or argued about anything. They just had fun when they were together, always playing and laughing, but now they both knew the world was changing. They had changed.

Jelena sensed Yuri had turned on his side and was looking at her. Her auburn hair framed her radiant face, and her eyes twinkled with life.

Then she heard Yuri say, "Can I kiss you, Jelena?"

Surprised, she turned her head and looked at him. "Why would you want to do that?"

"I don't know. I just thought of it. I guess it was a bad idea." Yuri blushed.

"No," she said. "Maybe it's not a bad idea. After all, we are best friends. It's just that I've never been kissed by a boy before except for my father when I was a little girl."

"Well, I've never kissed a girl before either, except my mother and grandmother, but I'm sure that's not the same." They both laughed.

Then Yuri rose up on one elbow and looked in Jelena's beautiful brown eyes and a little awkwardly, but tenderly, kissed her. She surprised herself because she didn't just hold still, but she pressed her lips to his and kissed him back. Yuri laid his head back down on the straw. "That was very exciting and very nice, Jelena."

"Yes, it was," she replied.

The owl stood watch as they lay there side by side, holding each other's hand, each lost in their own daydream.

Jolted back to reality, Jelena said, "Yuri, it stopped raining, and if your mother comes home and finds out we have been out in the barn together, we're going to be in trouble."

"You're right." Yuri rose to his feet and pulled her up. "She'll be really upset if she finds out about the kissing part."

"Well, I'm not going to tell," she giggled.

"And neither am I." Yuri laughed as they left the barn.

A few weeks passed. Life was simple and beautiful, free, exciting, and wonderful as only first love can be.

Chapter Eleven

As Jelena quickly put the washed potatoes into the pot on the wood stove, she looked out the small kitchen window for the tenth time to see if Yuri was coming down the road. *Where is he?* she wondered. *Something is wrong.*

Her elderly grandmother sat quietly, drinking tea at the kitchen table. Her mother, sitting in the old rocking chair across the room, was mending her father's socks. The wooden floor creaked as the chair rocked back and forth.

Throwing off her apron, Jelena ached with an urgency to find Yuri. "Mama, I'm through with all my chores, and I brought up and washed the potatoes for supper tonight. Can I walk over to Yuri's? He told me yesterday at school that he would be over here early this morning to help me rake out the chicken coop. It's after one o'clock, and he's not here yet."

"You're only fourteen years old, Jelena," her mother remarked as she looked up from her mending. "You and Yuri act like an old married couple already. You can't seem to stand to be apart. I don't think it's a good idea for you to spend so much time together."

Jelena couldn't think of anything that would be more wonderful and exciting than being married to Yuri Pavaloski. She couldn't let her mother know she felt that way. "We'll probably never get married, Mama. We're just good friends. Is it okay if I go?"

"Well, all right, but don't be gone all afternoon. Papa will be home from the mine this evening, and he will expect you to be here. He'll want a big supper and his family around him."

Jelena's grandmother spoke up. "You go on now, Jelena. Your mother and I will get started making supper. You go have your visit with Yuri. I think he's a very nice young man. But just remember, you know how your papa loves you. You should be here to greet him when he gets home. Between working at the mine and running this farm, your papa works awfully hard."

"Yes, I know he does," Jelena replied as she stood in front of the cracked mirror in the adjoining kitchen brushing her long auburn hair. "I wouldn't miss being here when he gets home. I love Papa!"

Jelena struggled to get into the only coat she had. It was getting too small for her now. She would need to make another coat soon. She knew her mother would help her make it, maybe for Christmas.

Jelena kissed her grandmother and her mother. "I won't be gone long. I just want to know why Yuri didn't come over like he said. He's really worried about his grandmother. Maybe she's gotten worse, or maybe his father came home from Moscow last night."

Jelena went out the door. As she walked across the front yard to the road, she glanced back at the small farmhouse where she had lived all her life. It was only a small farm in a rural community, but Jelena loved living in the country, and they always had food for the table and a warm house to live in. She was thinking maybe someday she and Yuri could have a small house of their own. However, now she was really worried about Yuri. *Why didn't he come over like he said? Could his grandmother have passed away?* She hoped not.

Jelena pulled her coat tighter and buttoned even the top button. It was getting cold, and the sky was cloudy. There were dried weeds in the ditches. Instead of cutting across the fields, she walked down the road to the corner and turned right. She continued down the road to Yuri's house.

As she got closer, she could see a lot of people and horses and buggies in Yuri's front yard. She thought maybe they were having a family get-together. But then she noticed all the women were crying, and as she walked closer, she saw his mother on the front porch sobbing. Her family was trying to console her. She saw Yuri's father sitting on the front steps with his face in his hands. She looked around from the road trying to see Yuri. Jelena was now sure his grandmother had died. She didn't want to bother the family, but she wanted to see Yuri. She thought he could be inside the house, so she walked behind the trees and bushes down the driveway to the back of the house. She could hear the men talking in low tones and the women weeping.

Yuri's grandmother lived with her son on another farm. She had been very ill. Jelena knew Yuri loved her because he often spoke about her. He would need to talk to her about it, as they now told each other just about everything.

Jelena walked past the back porch and around the other side of the house. Her heart was racing, and she noticed her palms were sweating. She was so worried. There was a high pile of cut logs stacked under the living-room window. She stepped up on the wood and, grabbing the bottom of the windowsill, pulled herself up so she could peek inside, hoping to see Yuri and get him to come outside. Peering into the room, she saw a group of neighbors standing around the big, living room table weeping. As the crowd circled the table, she could see someone lying on the table.

Suddenly, she recognized him. She grabbed her chest as her breath went out of her! Yuri lay on the table, not more than five or six feet in front of her. Blue in color, his face looked like stone. His soaking clothes dripped over the table, and water spilled onto the floor. His eyes stared wide open at the ceiling. He didn't move. A cry caught in her throat. She looked at his shirt to see if he was breathing, but his chest didn't move.

She burst into tears and sobbed from the shock of seeing her best friend, the one she shared everything with, the boy she loved, lying dead on that table. She couldn't believe it.

She didn't remember getting down off the woodpile or how she got to the front yard, but the next thing she knew, a young woman, one of Yuri's aunts, held her as she sobbed.

The aunt put both hands to Jelena's cheeks and looked directly into her eyes. With a soft voice, she said, "You're Yuri's friend from down the road. I know who you are." She gave Jelena a handkerchief, dried her tears, and tried to console her. Jelena tried her best to stop crying.

Yuri's mother approached and put her arms around her. She held Jelena close as both their bodies shuddered with grief. The woman held her for a long time. "We have lost our Yuri. Yuri drowned this morning." Tears trickled down her tired face. She choked up and broke down in convulsive sobs.

When she regained her composure, she said, "Yuri's father got leave for the weekend. He and Yuri went hunting early this morning. While crossing the frozen river, Yuri fell through the thin ice. His father tried his best to lie on the ice and pull Yuri back up, but the current pulled Yuri under, and he could not save him. He ran to a nearby farm for help, and they came with axes and ropes, and by chopping another hole in the ice downstream, they were able to pull Yuri out of the river, but it was too late."

His mother then took her by the hand, and they went into the house. As they approached the table, everyone moved back so they could come close. The local doctor arrived and closed Yuri's eyes. Jelena and Yuri's mother held each other tightly, two hearts breaking over the loss of one they loved. Jelena just couldn't believe he was really gone. Yuri looked like he was asleep except his face and hands were a pale blue. Jelena was sure he would wake up at any minute and smile at them.

She reached out to touch his hand. It was icy cold. He really was dead. She had never felt such grief.

* * * * *

Three days later, Jelena attended the service for Yuri at the farmhouse with her mother and father. A crowd of people silently sat or stood around the living room. Some of the women softly sobbed.

Jelena's swollen eyes looked upon Yuri lying in a casket against the far wall. He seemed so far away.

Slowly, numbly, her feet carried her to the heavy, oversized oak casket. *It was made for a grown man,* she thought, *probably the only casket available.*

Yuri's hair was neatly combed. He wore his school uniform. The white linen lining around him had been laid over straw, making it look as though he were lying on a soft cloud. Still, the casket looked too big for a boy only fourteen years old.

Jelena held back her tears. She would never forget this day.

A preacher said some words about Yuri and a prayer. Then most of the people went into the kitchen while others went outside to the porch.

Yuri's father was the only one in the living room. His mother walked away from the casket so grief-stricken she had to be helped to a chair in the kitchen. Jelena sat on the front porch next to the living room window. She looked through the window at Yuri's casket. She watched as Yuri's father said good-bye to his son for the last time. He bent over his son. Jelena could only see his back, but he hugged his Yuri for about a minute. He then slowly rose up, touched his son's cheek with the back of his hand, and, with tears in his eyes, closed the lid.

They all went to the town cemetery, a beautiful wooded area with old tombstones all around. The open grave was not far from a huge oak tree down the hill from the main part of the cemetery. With some difficulty, the grave had been dug the day before. It was winter now, the trees had lost their leaves, and the ground was hard. It was a dismal-looking day with dark, cloudy skies. The wind blew the leaves along the ground into patches of dried grass and onto patches of snow. It was bitterly cold.

Jelena stood with her mother and father. She was thinking how it must have been hard to dig a grave in that frozen ground. Before the casket arrived, she looked in the grave and was surprised to see a concrete box in the bottom of the hole. Then she noticed three wheelbarrows and some shovels over in the bushes. At the end of the grave was a concrete lid lying on several round poles so it could be rolled over the grave after the casket was lowered down. She thought his family must have worked very hard to prepare the grave for Yuri. They would even put his casket in a concrete vault. She was glad for that.

Jelena looked around at the large crowd and thought the entire community must be there, all dressed in black and wearing fur hats and long black overcoats. She saw some of the gravesites had wrought iron fences around them. Yuri's grave would not have that, as to do so was very expensive.

The pallbearers brought Yuri's casket and placed it over the poles above the open grave. They opened the lid for the last time. Everyone came closer to gaze at the young boy's face that now was perfectly still and drained of all life and all color. Jelena looked at Yuri's face one last time and, with a lump in her throat, wept uncontrollably, as did his mother, aunts, and Yuri's grandmother, who had been carried from the wagon to a chair by the grave and was surrounded by her sons.

The preacher said another prayer and dedication of the grave. The casket lid was again closed. Long pieces of linen were then placed under the casket on each end and in the middle, and when it was lifted by the three men on each side, the poles were removed. The casket was lowered to its rest on the wooden blocks in the bottom of the concrete vault. Then the linen pieces used to lower the casket were removed. It was a grim day, losing a lad so full of life. Everyone was devastated.

After the burial was over, everyone drove their buggies back to the Pavaloski's farm to help in any way they could and to try to console the young mother and father. After a light supper of meat, cakes, and tea, everyone left for their own farms.

It was dark when Jelena and her parents returned to their farm. It had been a long, tiring, and very sad day. Jelena tried her best to conceal her grief. But now that she was home, the tears began to fall. She just could not hold them back.

Jelena's father saw how grief-stricken she was. "Why don't you go to bed, Jelena, and I will do your chores."

Jelena was shaking. She hugged her father and kissed his cheek between sobs. "I love you, Papa. Thank you."

Jelena's mother said, "Come; I will help you get ready for bed, and I will stay with you until you fall asleep." Jelena's mother sat on the edge of her bed and stroked her hair until Jelena finally fell asleep.

Sometime after her mother left her room, Jelena woke up again. As she lay in her warm bed, she felt guilty. Yuri, the boy she loved, was not in a nice, warm bed. He was in a box in the cold ground. She still couldn't believe he was really gone.

Suddenly Jelena remembered the secret she and Yuri shared. She had promised she would never tell anyone, not even her mother. Jelena knew what she and Yuri had discovered was something of great importance to almost everyone, but because of reasons she would never understand, the leaders of the Russian army did not want anyone to know about it.

She tried to go back to sleep. The moon was now nearly full. Bright moonlight poured through her bedroom window and bathed the room. Jelena felt so alone. She gazed around her small bedroom and then out the window at the cold and bleak landscape. The trees were dark and bare. Patches of weeds were laced with snow. She had never felt so alone.

"I love you, Yuri, and I miss you more than anyone could ever imagine," she said to herself as tears trickled down her cheeks.

Chapter Twelve

After Yuri's funeral, there was news that the revolution had begun. Unrest and fear fell across the country. Terrifying rumors that the Czar and all of his family had been murdered spread like wildfire.

One morning Jelena was hanging clothes on the line. She heard men's voices and vehicles on the road in front of her house. She dropped what she was doing and hurried to the front yard just in time to see an army car and two army trucks loaded with armed soldiers drive by her house. She watched as the vehicles turned south at the corner. The convoy rumbled along until they entered Yuri's yard. It was about ten o'clock in the morning. The soldiers had their guns drawn.

Jelena crossed the road by her house, traversed the drainage ditch, and crawled through the barbed-wired fence. She darted across the field through the weeds toward Yuri's farm. She had to see what was happening.

She was getting close to the house when she heard the shots. Dropping down into a shallow irrigation ditch, she peeked out through the weeds lining the ditch. The soldiers were going through the house, shouting and ransacking every room. They were searching every building on the farm.

Jelena knew they were looking for those photographs. They must have somehow learned that Yuri's father had printed some additional copies, and they wanted them destroyed.

A cry came to her throat when she heard Yuri's mother screaming as the soldiers dragged her out of the house. One of the officers slapped her several times. Roughly he shoved and kicked her and threw her into the back seat of the car.

Jelena was crying as she watched the soldiers continuing to search the buildings. At one point, a soldier scanned the field where she was hiding. She crouched even lower in the ditch, shaking with fear.

Finally they all got back in their vehicles and departed. Jelena wept as she slowly walked home. In the last weeks, her whole world had been torn completely apart.

Neither Yuri's mother nor father ever came back. There was hearsay that they were murdered by the army. No one could ever imagine why. Jelena knew why. But she had promised Yuri she would never tell, and she knew it would probably be a death sentence to anyone who learned that the photographs existed.

One evening about a week later, Jelena got up enough nerve to go over to the barn. She had not seen anyone at the farm since the soldiers left, not even Yuri's uncle. She was scared and shaking, but she just had to know. She opened the main door and walked into the darkened barn. There were no horses. Yuri's uncle must have taken them before the soldiers came.

Quickly she moved across the barn to the feed storage room. The door had been left ajar. She held her breath and pushed it open. The hinges creaked.

Her eyes strained in the dim light. Breathing a sigh of relief, she saw the sacks of grain still stacked over the access door. They had not found the secret room, or they surely would not have put the sacks of grain back.

She had just started to back out of the room when she heard a noise behind her in the barn. She froze. Her mouth was so dry she couldn't swallow. Trembling, she forced herself to turn around.

A low, raspy voice echoed through the rafters, "Jelena, where are you?"

She almost fainted with relief. It was her father's voice.

"What are you doing in here, Jelena?" he questioned with great concern and a little anger in his voice.

She stammered for a split second as she moved to meet him in the middle of the barn. "Yuri's uncle had some horses in here. I just wanted to make sure they were all right, but I see they are gone. And then I was just looking around."

"Well, let's get out of here, Jelena, and don't you ever come over here again. You have no business here anymore. The Pavaloski family is all gone now, and I don't believe any of them will ever be back."

Jelena never went back to the barn again.

Chapter Thirteen

Russia

She sat in her car and looked at the old barn. She had parked just across the road from Yuri's farm. This was not the first time she had taken this drive. Every few years since she and her husband, Dimitri Surikova, had moved from Moscow back to the small town near here, she would come by herself just to reminisce.

Slowly sliding out the door of her car, she walked across the nearly abandoned gravel road.

It was a beautiful spring day with a warm breeze blowing across the freshly plowed fields. Birds were sitting on the fence, and their warbling brought a smile to her lined and wrinkled face.

Her hair was now mostly gray, wound tightly in a bun at the back of her head. Her long, tailored suit flattered her slight frame. Its purple hue presented an aura of style and grace deserving of respect for the now elderly Jelena.

Not a soul was around. Leaning on the gate recently erected across the driveway to deter visitors, she gazed at the dilapidated house where Yuri once lived. Closing her eyes, she heard the laughter of children resonate from the yard. She saw a handsome lad pushing a girl on a swing under the old elm tree. Her pigtails were flying in the wind as she giggled and demanded, "Higher, Yuri." Precious memories could be so vivid.

Returning to the present, Jelena glanced at the very spot, not three meters away, where she and Yuri had met so long ago. *How quickly life passes,* she thought.

As far as she knew, no one had ever lived here again after the Pavaloski family. Someone farmed the ground because there were always crops in the field, and once a tractor was parked in the yard, but the house had been boarded up years ago.

Tears came to her eyes, and a lump formed in her throat as it always did when she came here and let her memories take her back. Strangely, she had never forgotten the shock of Yuri's death, not long after he had shown her the hidden photographs of Noah's ark.

Jelena studied the barn where she knew the secret room was. No one had made much of an effort to restore the old barn or even try to keep it from falling down, as it was now leaning slightly and was in very bad condition.

She had often wondered if those old photographs were still in that wooden box down in the secret room under the dirt floor of the feed-storage room. Jelena thought that unless the wood floor had rotted and caved in, the secret room had probably never been discovered. Even if it had, no one would know anything was buried beneath the brick floor. The photographs, sketches, and documentation regarding the Russian expedition that found Noah's ark had never been made public. At least she had never heard anything about it.

Yuri showed me the photographs of Noah's ark so very long ago. I've kept my promise all these years. If I die or become senile, the proof that Noah's ark is really buried in the ice on Mount Ararat will never be known. I've kept the secret long enough, she decided.

But whom should I tell? The government has relaxed the restrictions regarding religion, and people can now worship more openly, but the Kremlin will go to great lengths to avoid a scandal or public embarrassment. It would be an embarrassment to find the proof of the ark had been concealed all these years by the communist government. I don't feel I can trust anyone.

Jelena then drove north to her old house. No one was living there, either. Stopping at the edge of the road, she remembered how hard it had been for her family after the communist government took over ownership of their farm. Everything they worked for went to the government. They were given a small allotment to live on, but it was never enough. They never had enough food to eat.

She thought about the terrible explosion at the mine that killed her father. Her grandmother and her mother died four and five years later, about a year apart. They were all buried in the same cemetery where Yuri was.

Tears of joy welled up in her eyes as she recalled the day she married Dimitri Surikova. He was a debonair gentleman, thirty years old, and she was an impressionable, twenty-two-year-old young woman. Dimitri had been a good husband and father.

His family owned a silver mine and small refinery before the communist government took it over. She smiled as she remembered working side-by-side with Dimitri and his family to extract and refine as much silver ore as they could before the government confiscated it. Dimitri hid it in a place he knew they would never find.

She remembered her life with Dimitri after the revolution when they lived in Moscow. Not a day went by that Dimitri didn't tell her how beautiful she was and that he loved her. He declared how proud he was to introduce her as his wife. He was the father of their only child, Mikhail, and they had lived a good life together.

In Moscow, they had to always be careful not to appear affluent. But the money from the silver mine allowed them to give Mikhail an excellent education. Mikhail lived with his daughter, Ann, in Moscow, where he worked as an interpreter for the Russian government.

Dimitri had been dead nine years now.

She never could understand how she would still often remember Yuri. She had always missed not sharing her life with him. She felt a little cheated, even after all these years.

As Jelena drove away, a happy thought crossed her mind. She thought of the upcoming visit of Mikhail and her granddaughter, Ann. Ann was going to stay with her for a few weeks after her father went back to Moscow.

Jelena wondered just how mature her granddaughter might be at twelve years old. *Would she be mature enough to be trusted with a very important secret?*

Chapter Fourteen

Ann was quick to get up early each morning to help her grandmother cook the meals, do the dishes, and keep the house clean. She was really enjoying her time with her grandmother.

The next day Jelena announced, "After we have breakfast, Ann, we're going for a drive."

"Good, Grandmother. Where are we going?"

"I'm going to show you where I grew up.""I can't wait!" Ann replied excitedly. "That's where everything happened in the story you've been telling me. Will we see the barn?"

"Yes, but we can only look at it from the road. We mustn't go in."

Jelena always took the back roads. She knew even though she was a very careful driver, she didn't want to lose her driving privileges. She told Ann, "I might be getting old, but I still love the freedom of driving around the country back roads. And out here, there is usually very little traffic."

She first drove to the cemetery where Yuri and all of Ann's relatives were buried. Ann wanted to visit each and every grave, especially Yuri's.

Farther down the road, Jelena stopped in front of the house she grew up in.

Finally she drove to Yuri's farm and parked on the road. As they looked at the old barn, Ann was very excited and asked her grandmother a lot of questions about it. "There's no one around. Can't we just go over to the barn and peek in?"

"Definitely not, Ann," Jelena scolded. "That old structure is dangerous, and besides, someone might drive by and wonder what we are doing."

"I'm sure you're right, Grandmother, but someday...."

Jelena knew she had made the right decision. She hoped when Ann grew up, she would lead the right person to the lost photographs.

Jelena never told her secret to anyone, just as she had promised Yuri many years ago. Except her granddaughter, Ann Surikova.

* * * * *

Suddenly Ann woke up. It was three in the morning. She had been dreaming again. She turned on her side and pulled the covers a little tighter. Smiling in the dark, she whispered, "We're almost there, Grandmother. The secret you kept all your life will soon be told, and hopefully the lost photographs of Noah's ark will be found for the entire world to see." Still smiling, Ann fell into a restful sleep with no more dreams.

Chapter Fifteen

Ann lived in an upscale D.C. townhouse with an elegant entry and a charming courtyard. All day she had been nervous about tonight's meeting with Dr. Lane. She was concerned and apprehensive about whether she was doing the right thing confiding in a stranger the secret she had kept since she was twelve years old. But she knew in her heart that the world had a right to know her secret, and at last, she felt she had finally found the one person she could trust. Dr. Lane had the means and, she hoped, the desire to act upon the information and bring to light what she felt would be a very important archaeological discovery.

At exactly five that evening, her doorbell rang. Ann opened the door, and Johns tipped his hat and introduced himself as Dr. Lane's driver. Before her stood a distinguished-looking English gentleman in his chauffeur's cap and dark suit. His white beard was neatly trimmed. He was a handsome man about five-feet-eight inches tall of rigid stature.

Johns drove the large car expertly through the traffic, and soon they escaped the city and entered the beautiful countryside. The landscape was dotted with cherry blossoms. Ann brought the window down a little, not enough to blow her hair but enough to breathe in the sweet, fragrant air.

She wore a peach blouse and ivory skirt that hugged her hips and accented her bronze legs, elongated by strap heels. A cream-colored mohair shawl her grandmother had given her was draped softly over her shoulders. Elegant pearls completed her ensemble. Her dark hair fell around her face in curls and extended down her back. Ann hoped she looked professional. Tonight could be the most pivotal time of her life.

As the big car slowed, Ann closed the window and moved to the center of the seat so she could see through the windshield. The sun had set, and there was a pink glow on the horizon. There was still enough light to see that they had entered an area of very large estates, set far back from the road. The heavily wooded, rolling hills hid most of the buildings, but occasionally Ann caught a glimpse of paved, winding roads leading to elegant mansions.

Soon the car turned off the main road and stopped at a large, ornate metal gate. The gate swung open when Johns pushed the button over the visor, and the limo proceeded to a guard shack where, with a smile and a wave, the guard motioned Johns through. A quarter mile farther, the elm-lined drive opened up to reveal a stately manor. The grounds were covered with vegetation, well trimmed, with manicured lawns and gardens. Johns drove the car around the circular drive and stopped in front of a grand two-story mansion with four twenty-foot-tall white columns supporting the massive portico.

As Johns opened her door, the carved walnut door of the mansion swung open, and Matthew came down the granite steps to greet her. Matt shook her hand, smiling. "Well, Ann, did you enjoy your ride?"

"Yes," she replied, still holding his hand. "My first limousine ride. I enjoyed it very much. Thank you, Dr. Lane. What a beautiful home you have!"

"Thank you. Come in, and I'll show you around — and please call me Matt."

She immediately saw that Dr. Lane was sharply dressed in a sport jacket over an open-collared polo shirt, tan slacks, and loafers. Relieved, she realized she had not overdressed.

Matt's smile and warm welcome permitted her to relax. She looked forward to seeing his elegant home.

The imposing entrance led to a high-ceilinged room, not ornate and gold-trimmed like you might see in some of the Newport mansions, but paneled in beautiful walnut with large walnut columns around the perimeter. The floors were marble, as were the stairs at the far end of the room. Twenty-foot-wide steps led twelve feet up to a landing. Stairs went each way, right and left, twelve feet higher to the second floor. Behind the marble steps trimmed in walnut and brass were floor-to-ceiling windows, a full sixty feet wide, exposing the beautiful grounds at the rear of the house. A sparkling pool was on the left side of the rear patio. Brightly colored flagstone extended forty feet out to four steps leading to the garden area abounding with shallow pools and fountains. Roses flourished on trellises and in brick raised areas. What a serene place to relax.

Matt showed her through the dining room with the traditional long table, which could seat twenty-two people, the large modern kitchen off the dining room, the pool room with billiards and regular pool tables, the exercise room, and the theater room with a capacity of twenty-five. He explained that the second floor consisted of several large bedroom suites.

Matthew had designed the entire house and grounds with input from his father. He was his own general contractor, saving money over the two years of construction, but more importantly, he did it because he thoroughly enjoyed the project and wanted to see that it was done exactly as he had imagined it.

Ann could see he was very proud of what he had designed and created. Truly he was an artist/craftsman. He excitedly showed her the garage, which was attached to the house via a short enclosed walkway with windows on both sides. As they entered, the lights came on automatically, and they were on a landing level with the tops of the cars. Due to the sloping grounds, the garage area was built lower than the house. Ann exclaimed, "Wow! This is great! But tell me, Matt, why do you need a limousine? Is it just to impress your girlfriends?"

Matt actually blushed. "Well, we need the limo because Dad does a lot of entertaining and has politicians and dignitaries here from time to time. The local guys usually drive their own cars, but we send our limo for out-of-towners and foreign visitors ... and special guests. Like you."

Quickly changing the subject, Ann asked, "So your father, Senator Clifford Lane, lives here with you?"

"Yes; he has a suite next to mine on the second floor. However, he isn't here very often. He mostly lives in his apartment in D.C., closer to his work, but he comes back when they are not in session. Dad, who is on the Senate Armed Services committee, also travels out of the country quite a bit."

"I know your mother passed away about five years ago."

"Yes, just as I was drawing up the plans for this house. It was devastating to both me and my father to lose her. She and my father were such a great match for each other, and my mother and I were very close. She was only fifty-one when she died." A hint of melancholy crept into Matt's voice. "Dad was fifty-three and is now fifty-eight. He may remarry someday — he is still young enough — but says he probably never will find another woman like my mother. He is doing okay, though. He keeps busy, loves his work in Washington, and feels he is making a difference. I'm proud of him because I know he is completely honest, and that's rare in Washington."

They went down the steps to the floor of the garage and walked down in front of the cars. Next to the limousine was a new pearl-white Mercedes sedan ... then a bright-red Corvette convertible. Beyond the red convertible were several empty spaces, and on the end of the garage was a drive-through car wash. This was a man's garage.

After the tour, they went back inside into the formal dining room. Off to one side was a smaller dining table next to a fireplace, warm and comfortable, beautifully decorated, and with soft lighting.

"I really wasn't expecting all this. You live far differently from what I had expected. I'm overwhelmed with it all, from the chauffeur to the beautiful mansion you live in."

"I wouldn't call it a mansion. It's not like the mansions the Rockefellers and Vanderbilts had in Rhode Island or Hyde Park. It's just a big house."

"Well, it's a very beautiful and well-designed home."

"Thank you. My parents never had great wealth, but we always lived comfortably. When my grandfather passed away about eight years ago, my dad and I inherited his fortune. We both decided to build this house, so we planned it together and built it. I admit it does get a little lonely here with my mother gone and my father away so much," Matt responded with a tinge of sadness.

After a moment, Ann broke the silence, "Perhaps I should tell you a little about myself."

"Before you do that, let's have dinner. Then I'll tell you what I already know about you, and you can fill me in on the details."

Out of nowhere, Johns appeared with ice water and a fresh loaf of bread. Matt poured two glasses of Chablis, and Johns elegantly served them a delicious dinner, starting with escargot.

When placed in front of Ann, she told Matt, "One of my favorite foods."

"I hoped you might like it. I love it, but some people don't care for it — like Jim, for example. I can't get him to even try it," Matt laughed.

The meal continued with green salad, stuffed chicken breast, tiny new potatoes, and buttered asparagus.

After some casual conversation, Ann could not contain her curiosity. "What did you mean you would tell me what you knew about me? We just met last night. You can't know very much about me in that short time."

"Well, let's see. You were born Ann Surikova. You had your name changed to Ann Tyler about twelve years ago. You were born in Russia near Moscow. You were twenty-eight years old last October seventh. Your mother died when you were nine years old and living in Moscow. After she died, you and your father continued to live in Moscow until you were about fourteen. Then you and your father migrated to the United States. Your father was an interpreter in Russia, fluent in five languages — Russian, English, French, German, and Spanish — and easily got a job as an interpreter in Washington. He passed away two years ago. You went to college here in D.C. and have a degree in archaeology. You now work for the Smithsonian. You live with a female roommate in the townhouse that you own, where Johns picked you up this evening."

Ann gaped at him in wide-eyed amazement. "How do you know all of this?"

"I'm sorry," Matt said apologetically, "but in my position and my father's position, I can't be too careful about whom I meet, especially since you were so mysterious about wanting to tell me something. I had a friend do a routine check on you. If it had turned out that you had a long rap sheet for crimes or something else, I would want to know that. Likewise, you apparently checked me out pretty thoroughly before you introduced yourself to me."

"Yes, but only what I could read in the papers and your reputation as a researcher of ancient antiquities. I didn't check your, like you say, rap sheet!" Ann retorted.

Ann was surprised at the strong feelings of resentment and slight embarrassment she was feeling on learning that Matt had pried into her life. She kept telling herself to calm down. *Don't let him know this upsets you. It's very understandable why he had me investigated. After all, I acted pretty mysteriously last night.*

She found herself wondering if he would be the best one to tell her secret to after all.

"Well, I'm very sorry, Ann, but I hope you understand why I did it."

"It just took me by surprise, that's all," she lied. "What else do you know about me?"

"Well, we didn't find any record of you ever being married, which was surprising since — I hope you won't take this wrong — you are a very attractive woman, very beautiful actually. I … we found it unusual. We didn't find any current evidence of you even dating anyone. All your neighbors spoke very highly of you. You're friendly but don't seem to go out much. Your father was well liked where he worked, and that's about all we had time to find out."

"How much I date is none of your business!"

Matt interrupted her, "You're right, and again, I apologize. But *who* you date would have been our concern. Someone could have put you up to meeting me to cause some harm or scandal to me or my father."

"I don't blame you for being cautious. I know I must have sounded very mysterious last night. But you certainly must understand my feelings that my privacy has been violated. I wasn't applying for a top-level security clearance."

The rest of the meal was consumed in an ominous silence.

Deciding to forgive Matt's impropriety and to break the icy chill that had fallen on the room, Ann finally said, "The dinner was delicious. Thank you."

"I'm glad you liked it. If you're finished, we can have brandied coffee in the great room."

"Just coffee for me."

"Ann, I'm sorry to have upset you. Could we call a truce or something?"

"Well, I guess I did get a little emotional, and I do understand why you did the background check," she shyly admitted. "Maybe we can start over."

Charlotte already had a coffee tray on the table in front of the stone fireplace in the great room. It was still cool at night, so the fire was warm and comfortable. The light of the flames danced on the Venetian-plastered walls, giving the area an old-world feel. Dim lighting created a homey atmosphere. Matt guided Ann to the two overstuffed chairs in front of the fireplace.

"So at last you're going to tell me this secret that is of such great importance, right?" Matt asked with a smile.

Ann blurted out, "Before I tell you, you must make me some promises, or I'll just leave now and not tell you. This, I feel, is of great importance to the whole world."

"The whole world?"

"Yes, the whole world!" she adamantly replied.

"Okay, what do I have to promise?"

"First, you can't tell anyone else what I'm going to tell you — unless I agree to it."

"Okay," he agreed.

"Second, you have to take me with you wherever the adventure leads. You can't leave me behind because you think I may be in danger or something."

"Danger? How much danger? Describe danger?"

"I don't know, but there could be some danger involved."

Matt stood up. "Well, I don't know," he kidded her. "I'm only thirty-one years old. I just recently became wealthy. I'm beginning to like this life. I haven't had much time to enjoy this new life of not having to work for my living. Maybe I don't want to be in danger. Jim and I barely escaped with our lives recently in Iraq."

"Well, if you feel that way, maybe I have chosen the wrong person to help me. In which case, I'm glad you were honest with me. I'm sure this will involve some element of danger, and I don't blame you for not wanting to get involved."

"Hold on." Matt had moved, standing directly in front of Ann now, looking down at her. "It's true I don't want to get killed, but you've got me so curious about this darn thing you want to tell me that I guess I'm willing to risk some danger if, as you say, it's of great importance. I love a good adventure. I may regret this later, but okay, I agree."

"Are you sure?" she asked, searching his face for a sign of commitment.

"Yes. Yes, I agree to all the terms and conditions."

"Okay then, please sign this," and she pulled a paper out of her purse.

"Sign what?"

"This agreement. It just says you agree to the terms I just asked."

Matt took the two-page contract from her hands and read the few typed words that simply outlined what she had said. "Okay," he smirked, "I'll sign it, but you should know that it would never hold up in a court of law."

"I know, but it will make me feel better."

"Okay, if it will make you feel better. Here." He signed it.

Ann folded the two pages and slipped them back in her purse.

Chapter Sixteen

They were seated again, in chairs that faced each other in front of the fireplace, in close proximity to allow normal conversation. Ann glanced around the room.

"When I was about twelve years old, my father took me on a train to a small village north of Moscow where he grew up and where his mother still lived, my grandmother. After one week, my father went back to Moscow, and I spent most of that summer with her. I say summer, but it was always cold. I don't think it ever got above sixty degrees all summer long. She was a wonderful woman, and I loved her very much. She was a great cook — just plain food, but she made it all taste very good. During the summer, she said she wanted to tell me something, something very important that she had never told anyone before. She made me promise not to tell anyone until I was grown and then only if I could trust the person."

It dawned on Matt that he must be the one Ann was talking about. *She trusts me.*

"Her name was Jelena Surikova. Her maiden name was Jelena Malavski. Grandmother was born in 1903 in a farmhouse about twenty kilometers from where she lived then. Her father was a coal miner, but he was killed in a mine explosion. She told me, when she was about ten, she used to play with the boy who lived on the farm close to her. He was about her same age. His name was Yuri.

"Yuri's father was a captain in the Russian army in charge of the photography department. He only got to come home to his farm and his wife and son every few weeks. He had a barn built and when the contractors finished, he and Yuri built a room under the floor of one of the rooms in the barn. It was a secret room where his family could hide in case of war."

As Ann continued with her story, she worried she was losing Matt's attention, so she simply blurted out, "The secret room is where Yuri's father hid the photographs of Noah's ark."

Matt quickly set down his glass and leaned closer toward Ann's chair, his body tense and his eyes riveted on her face.

Astonished and not sure he had heard her correctly, Matt asked, "What did you say?" Did I hear you say something about photographs of Noah's ark?"

Ann had Matt's full attention now. "Yes, I said the secret room is where photographs of Noah's ark are hidden. Yuri showed them to my grandmother. He told her he had overheard his father tell his mother that they were photographs of Noah's ark taken on Mount Ararat by the army.

"Yuri's father told his mother he wasn't supposed to have them, but he didn't think they should be destroyed. He told his wife that he was going to hide them in the secret room.

"When Yuri found them, he showed them to my grandmother. She said there were photographs of the outside of a large wooden ship but none of the inside. She told me some of the photographs were taken from quite a distance away, and she could see the ship was high on the side of a mountain and part of it was embedded in ice.

"Yuri made her promise that she would never tell anyone else about the photographs or the secret room. He said his father would be furious if he found out she knew. He said for some reason the Russian army did not want anyone to know about the discovery of the ark and that his father would be in serious trouble if anyone ever found out he had those photographs."

"Unbelievable!" Matt exclaimed as he stood up and ran his fingers through his hair. "No one that I've ever spoken to has mentioned the possibility of other photographs from that expedition, but it makes perfect sense that someone who was involved in developing the photos might have made extra prints. The Russian Revolution started about then, and the photographs, sketches, written testimony, everything about the expedition, was lost — either destroyed or locked up somewhere, maybe in the Kremlin."

Ann was also standing now. Matt looked directly into her eyes, his face close to hers, and taking her hand in his, he said, "Ann, please tell me you know what happened to those photographs."

Shying away and retreating to the safety of the chair and sitting down, Ann stared at Matt as if searching his soul. Hesitating, but with a sigh, she finally said, "I do."

"Tell me the rest of the story," Matt begged.

Ann, with renewed enthusiasm, continued. "After Grandmother and Yuri had looked at the photographs, Yuri wrapped up each picture and carefully put them back in the wooden box. She said there was a waterproof canvas covering the box to keep the moisture out and another piece of canvas underneath it. Then he carefully laid each brick back in place.

"Grandmother said she remembered they left the secret room, covered the access door with dirt, put the feed sacks over the access door, and left the barn. Unfortunately, soon after that Yuri accidentally drowned."

"He drowned?" Matt repeated. "How did that happen?"

"He fell through the ice while crossing a frozen river."

"How sad."

"Yes, it was," she said. "Even though she was young, I think Grandmother really loved that boy. I've never seen her as sad as when she told me about Yuri drowning.

"Anyway, soon after the funeral, soldiers arrived at the farm and searched every building. They dragged Yuri's mother out of the house and shoved her into a car. Grandmother thought they probably killed both his mother and father because they never came back, and everyone in the area assumed they had been killed.

"No one could ever understand why, except my grandmother. She was sure it must've been because of the Noah's ark photographs. She never told anyone, not even her parents."

"Ann, did the soldiers find where the photographs were hidden in that secret room?"

"No. At least she didn't think they found them."

"How would she know?"

"She was hiding in the weeds close to where they were searching. She said she saw them go into the barn and come out again with nothing in their hands. She felt sure they would have shouted to the officer in charge had they found something of interest. Also, a few days later, she said she went into the feed storage room, and the sacks of grain were still stacked on the dirt floor over the access door to the secret room. She didn't think anyone ever found them."

Matt paced back and forth in front of the fireplace.

Ann persisted, "If everyone who knew the secret room existed was dead, no one would ever know it was even there. And even if someone discovered the room, how would they know there was a wooden box buried under the brick floor?" Ann quickly added, "When Grandmother told me the story about sixteen years ago, she didn't know for sure, but she thought the photographs were very likely still buried in that box."

"Is your grandmother still alive?"

"No, she died a few years ago. After she grew up, she married my grandfather, Dimitri Surikova, but he died when I was very young. Anyway, he had this small farm about twenty kilometers from where she grew up. They only had one child, my father, Mikhail.

"My grandfather had been dead several years before I visited her the last time when I was twelve. That's when she told me the story. She had an old car that she drove on the rural roads. The day after she told me the story, she drove me to the area where it all happened.

"First we went to the cemetery. It was fairly large and a short distance from the local village. There were lots of trees, and grass was growing around old tombstones in irregular rows. Grandmother showed me her mother's and father's graves and also the graves of her aunt and a cousin. She said her husband had been buried in a different cemetery closer to where she now lived.

"Then she took me to Yuri's grave. There was just a small stone that had his name and date.

Yuri Pavalovski
Born in 1903. Died in 1917

"We stood for a moment just looking at the headstone, both remembering the tragic story of how Yuri died.

"After driving past the farm where she grew up, she drove me past Yuri's old farm. The barn was still there, but it was in bad shape. There was a metal gate across the entrance, so we didn't go onto the property. We just stopped in front of it and looked at it. I wanted to get out of the car and go into the barn to find the feed room and the hole in the floor under the dirt to see if the pictures were still down there, but Grandmother said no. The old house was still there. It was boarded up and run down. It looked like it had been empty for years.

"Then we left and went back to her house. I stayed a few more days until my father came to take me back to Moscow."

Matt sat down again and looked at her inquisitively. "Ann, is this all for real?"

"Yes, I swear it!"

"But, photographs of Noah's ark? I can't believe it. I mean, I've been fascinated by the story of Noah's ark since I was a little boy. I've read every book I could get my hands on about it. I've always believed it was up there on Mount Ararat just like the Bible says. Jim and I actually climbed Mount Ararat four years ago but found nothing. Are you really sure the pictures she saw were of the ark? I mean, she was only a young girl."

"Well, Yuri's father believed they were photos of Noah's ark, and he told Yuri's mother they were. Grandmother said the pictures Yuri showed her looked like a large wooden ship on a mountain, partly embedded in ice. I think Yuri's father and mother were executed over those pictures. Think about this," Ann said as she stood up and faced Matt. "Mount Ararat is close to the southern border between Russia and Turkey. As you well know, the story of the Russian expedition to find the ark in 1916 is well documented in books that can be found in most libraries and on the internet. There are statements taken many years after the Russian Revolution from the pilot who originally spotted the ship and reported it. There were soldiers who swore they photographed it, measured it, stood on top of it to have their picture taken, and examined the animal cages inside the ark. Yes," Ann replied, "I think the photographs were the real thing!"

Matt reaffirmed what he had stated earlier. "There are recent pictures of the ark on Ararat, but they were all taken from a satellite. It is hard to actually confirm that the pictures are of the ark. They could be a rock formation. Ann, do you realize that out of all the reported sightings of the ark on Mount Ararat by many people over the years, there still are no distinguishable photographs? Many people and expeditions claimed to have photographed the ark, but all of the clear, recognizable photos have somehow disappeared."

Then Matt frowned. "Why have you never told anyone about the old photos before?"

Ann blushed slightly. "Because I've never met anyone I felt I could trust not to just ignore me and go get the photographs for themselves. If they actually lead to the ark, I want to be part of it."

Matt stood up and went to Ann and stared at her. "Ann, do you think the pictures are still there in that underground shelter?"

"I don't know for sure, but I think there is a good chance that they have never been found. If you didn't know the access door was under that layer of dirt, you wouldn't even know it was there."

"But there's a possibility that the wood rotted and the whole thing caved in a long time ago or that water got in the box and the pictures are not even discernible by now."

"Yes, that's very possibly true. However, if the roof of the barn, even though it may have fallen in, still shielded the feed room below so that water and snow have not gotten into the area, it's also just as possible that they are still there, and since they were well wrapped and covered with something waterproof, they may still be very decipherable. Matt, what you think our next step should be?"

"Our next step?"

"Yes, *our* next step. Remember, I made it very clear that I was going to be a part of this adventure from beginning to end, and you even signed a contract to that effect." Her voice was now raised. She stood up and took a step toward Matt.

Reaching out to touch her arm, Matt tried to soothe her. "Now please, Ann, just calm down. Believe me, I intend to include you in every part of this 'adventure,' as you have chosen to call it. That is up to the point where your life may be in danger, and at that point, we'll have another talk about it. But first things first. I have to have time to think about our next step."

"Well, it's very obvious to me that you and I just fly to Russia and try to find the pictures. I speak Russian and —"

"Wait! Just hold on a minute!" Matt interrupted as he waved his hands in front of her. "We need a little better detailed plan than that. First, I will need your permission to share your story with a few select people that I know I can trust."

"Why do we have to tell anyone else? And how do you know you can trust them? If someone else learns where these pictures are, they could get to them before we do, and who knows what might happen. I don't even know how the present Russian government would deal with this, but I doubt that the world would ever see these pictures. In fact, if the wrong people learn what I know and now what you know, our lives could be in a lot of danger. Remember, I warned you the information could be dangerous."

"I know you did, Ann. Of course, you're right. But to see this thing through to the end, we will need a lot of help from a lot of people. I promise I will choose our contacts carefully and will only tell key people about the project and only as we need them to help us. Is that fair enough?"

"Well, I guess it will have to be. But please ... *please* be careful who you tell."

"I promise I will. Tomorrow I will tell just two people. The first person I've known since childhood, and I would not attempt any dangerous project without his help. You already met him last night. He was the first person I introduced you to, James Morgan."

"Oh, you mean tall, dark, and handsome?"

"Pardon me?" Matt was caught off balance.

"The man sitting next to you last night?"

"Yes, he was."

"Well, I just remember he was a very nice-looking man."

"Well, yes, I guess the opposite sex does find him attractive," Matt admitted, envious of the attention Ann had paid to Jim. "Anyway, Jim and I met in junior high school, and we both have always been interested in the same thing — archaeology, ancient artifacts and such. We've been in a lot of countries together and have depended on each other a lot. I know I can trust him to watch my back in tight situations. It was Jim who was with me when we found where the ark was originally constructed."

"Oh, so he's the one?"

"Yes, that was Jim."

"Is he married?"

"Is he married? No." Matt was becoming annoyed that all of her attention was centered on Jim.

"Has he ever been married?"

"No," Matt curtly answered.

"So both of you are in your, what, early thirties, and neither of you are married, but you hang out together a lot. You're both unusually good looking."

"Stop right there!" Matt slammed his cup on the table. "For your information, we are not homosexual or bisexual or anything other than lucky!"

"Lucky?"

"Yeah, lucky!" Matt was assertive.

"What do you mean lucky?"

Pausing for a few seconds to regain his composure, Matt explained, "I mean lucky in several senses of the word. Lucky to still be alive, lucky to have the right jobs and the means to go where we want, when we want, and not be tied down. That's about it. Any other questions about Jim and me?"

This young woman had really gotten to Matt. *Why do I care what she thinks? So what if she is interested in Jim? Just another pretty face. Get control of yourself. I don't need to tell her my life story. Just get on with the plans!*

"If you're concerned, I can assure you that you will be very safe traveling with Jim and me."

"I was never really worried. But I'm glad you told me."

Matt looked at her for a few seconds, wondering, *Is she really that interested in Jim, or is she just trying to see my reaction to her questions?*

Finally, he said, "Anyway, Jim will be the first person I tell. And the next person will be our boss."

"Your boss?"

"Yes, we both work for the university. We lecture, we search, and we bring all our findings to Dr. Ira Jensen who works closely with the curator of the Museum of Natural History. We can also trust him; plus we may well need him and resources from his department before this project or adventure is finished."

"And just what do you mean by the project being finished?"

"I would love to see the ark — if it could really be found — or at least a portion of the ark located and brought down the Turkish side of the mountain and permanently displayed in an environmentally controlled atmosphere and protected from further decay behind large glass walls. But I want anyone and everyone in the world to safely be able to see it, along with any other artifacts that may be found in it."

"Wonderful!" Ann exclaimed as she clapped her hands. "That's exactly what I would love to see happen."

"Then, Ann, let's make it happen. From now on, let's just refer to it as 'the project.'" Matt walked over to a small refrigerator under a granite countertop and took out a bottle of champagne and two glasses. He poured them half full and handed her one and, touched his glass to hers. "A toast to 'the project.' That it starts with the pictures still being in Russia and ends in our dream of the ark being displayed."

They stood in the glow of the firelight, their eyes meeting. They both felt a commitment to find the ark.

Matt drove her home in his Mercedes that night. It was nearly midnight when he walked her up to the door. "I'll be clearing up some business and making some arrangements during the next few days. I'll call you if I need more details about where your grandmother used to live. What's your status at work? Could you leave for a few days or weeks if necessary?"

"Yes, I've already made provisions to take a leave of absence. I made that a requirement when I was hired."

"Great, because I expect you and Jim and I will be on a plane to Moscow before the end of the week."

"I hope so. I've been waiting a long time for this."

"Well, thank you for trusting me with your secret," Matt said. "I promise I'll do everything I can to make it all work. Let's just hope and pray that we can find the pictures and that the images have not faded so much that we can't see anything and that there is enough of the mountain in the background to know where the photographer was standing."

Matt shook Ann's hand, and they said good night.

Ann turned the key in the lock and opened her door. Abruptly, she swiveled around, took a step closer to Matt, and, stretching up on her toes, kissed him on the cheek. "Thank you for sharing my dream!"

Chapter Seventeen

"I can't believe this is really happening," Ann said as she adjusted her seatbelt. The three of them, Matt, Jim, and Ann, were on a plane to Moscow. Less than a week before, Ann had revealed her secret to Matt. Since then, Matt and Jim had researched the family names of Jelena's grandmother and her playmate, Yuri. They had been able to identify the approximate location of their farms.

Professor Ira Jensen from the university had been told, and he found some funding to pay for the airline tickets and their expenses on this fact-finding mission.

"I can't believe it either, Ann. We may actually find real photographs of Noah's ark and from those photographs we could actually locate the ark . . . and it's all because of you and your grandmother," Jim replied, pumped up with excitement.

Ann was worried about the days ahead, hoping things would work out and that they would retrieve the photographs intact and not encounter any problems.

What if someone now lives on that farm? What if the photographs are not there and I brought these two archaeologists all this way for nothing? That would be very embarrassing, to say the least. What if someone has torn the barn, the house, and all the buildings down and filled in the hole? That could mean they now farm the land the buildings used to occupy. I should have trusted someone earlier and revealed my secret years ago when the odds of finding the photographs were more in our favor, Ann thought.

Forcing these negative thoughts out of her mind, Ann began to enjoy the company of the two young men.

Jim was telling her about some of the escapades he and Matt shared as young boys. His infectious laugh punctuated the stories, and his ginger-brown eyes twinkled with mischievous sparkle.

"It's nice to relax," Ann told him as she laughed at another of his jokes.

Jim was full of life and an incessant tease. The light-blue knit shirt he wore was tight and strained, making it obvious he spent hours in the gym.

In a lull in the conversation, Ann turned her attention to Matt, who was lost in thought and staring out the window. She gently touched his arm to get his attention as the flight attendant began serving dinner. He turned, and any hostilities they may have previously had melted from the warmth of his smile. Matt was the natural-born leader of the two men. His work was his first love, and he was always searching for answers.

"Please tell me more of the story about your grandmother and Yuri," Matt asked. "You never went into much detail before, and it's going to be a long flight."

Ann began by saying, "Detail . . . well, that's kind of ironic because my grandmother told me everything in great detail. She told me her story as if she were living it all over again. She even told me Yuri had kissed her once. It was the first time she had ever been kissed by a boy."

This seemed to catch the attention of both Matt and Jim. "Really?" Matt said.

"They were lying on a pile of straw in Yuri's barn one rainy afternoon when he held her hand and kissed her." Ann blushed. "I thought it was very romantic, even if she was only fourteen years old. When she told me about Yuri drowning, she cried. She allowed me to write some of it down in my diary. That's why I remember it so well."

Ann tried to tell every word exactly as her grandmother had told her, including the smallest details. She wanted to please Matt and help in any way she could. She shared Matt's passion for archaeology and research and felt herself being drawn closer to him. At one moment, he could be the epitome of masculinity and, in the next moment, a man of deep compassion. Like the rock of Gibraltar, he was steady and firm in his convictions and actions. She had never before met anyone like this who made her feel so warm and safe.

Ann wondered how Matt felt about her. *Does he find me attractive…intelligent? Will there be any future to our relationship? Or is Matt too absorbed in his work to allow any personal or intimate bond?*

Snap out of this, she told herself. *You have never been very interested in men before, and this is certainly not the time to start. Let's just find the photos and get back home safely.*

"That's a very exciting and moving story, Ann," Matt said. "Thank you for telling us."

"Yes," Jim added. "It certainly had me mesmerized."

"Best try to get some sleep now if you can. We'll be very busy once we arrive in Moscow," Matt advised Ann as he indicated she could rest her pillow on his shoulder.

* * * * *

After they had freshened up, they found that their hotel, located on the airport property, had a restaurant on the third floor.

Per Ann's request, they were seated near a window overlooking the landscape. Crisp white linens, polished silver, and gleaming crystal adorned the round table.

Matt's and Jim's Russian vocabulary was limited, but Ann spoke the language fluently. Relishing being able to take charge, Ann offered, "Let me order. You'll love this."

The waiter brought each of them a bowl of *shchi*. It was a vegetable soup consisting of cabbage, potatoes, onions, garlic, carrots, and roots and was served with sour cream. Accompanying this was some Russian rye bread, very soft and tasty.

Jim especially enjoyed the bread, remarking, "I could make a meal out of just this."

Ann cautioned, "Be sure to save room for the main course."

The main entrée was a mild-tasting fish garnished with a variety of vegetables. Their coffee was served in glasses instead of cups.

While they finished their meal with spice cake, they looked out the window of the restaurant at the city of Moscow. The sun had gone down, and the lights were beginning to come on in the city. As they gazed out the window, they became quiet. Matt was hoping that the results of this trip would be positive, that in a few days they would be leaving Moscow with a treasure map, and the photographs, which consequently could lead them to the ark of Noah.

As he looked at the sights of the city, Matt noticed the reflection of Ann in the window. She was smiling as she gazed at the city where she grew up. Matt felt a surge of excitement in his chest as he watched her out of the corner of his eye. With a tinge of jealousy, he recalled how well she and Jim seemed to hit it off on the plane. He thought, *What a beautiful girl, so fun to travel with, always smiling, and always cheerful. But how will she handle things if the going gets a little tough?*

Even if they were lucky enough to find clear photographs after all these years, actually finding the ark would prove to be the biggest challenge. Many men had already tried over the last few hundred years, and some had died trying.

Finally Matt broke the silence. "I've rented a car to be brought to the hotel at nine in the morning. Let's meet for breakfast at about seven thirty and be off to your grandmother's village as soon as the car arrives." They all agreed.

The next morning, they quickly ate their breakfast. After retrieving their luggage, they checked out and waited out front for the rental car. Matt signed the rental agreement, and they drove the man back to the car rental agency, still on airport property.

Matt had advised them before they left D.C. that they should try to blend in. "The modern-day, local Russian clothing is devoid of bright colors and jewelry, except for a functional wristwatch. Let's try to imitate that as much as possible," he had instructed.

Therefore, that morning Ann wore charcoal-gray, loose-fitting slacks with a black, long-sleeved shirt. She had her hair swept back and tied at the neck with a black silk scarf. Matt approved of her choice of clothing but thought, *Even in drab colors with no makeup or jewelry, this girl still stands out in the crowd. She looks fantastic.*

Matt told Ann, "I'm glad they drive on the same side of the road that we drive on, but you may have to help me with some road signs as well as the instruments. For example, how do you turn the heater on?" They all laughed.

Ann sat up front with Matt and navigated as they drove north. She had been only twelve years old when she visited her grandmother last and had ridden the train most of the way, but she was able to guide Matt along the highway out of the huge city and into the country.

They finally arrived at the village close to where Yuri had lived. They found a small, older hotel, not nearly as modern as the one in Moscow. They walked about two blocks to a small café. Several people sitting in booths gave them inquiring looks. Matt and Jim kept their conversation low and to a minimum as they chose a simple meal and coffee.

Early the next morning, after eating breakfast in the same café, they were on the road again. All the area was farmland with each farm two or three kilometers apart. There were large trees around each farm, which had been planted years earlier for windbreaks. There were modern but small tractors and trucks on most farms now.

Ann showed them where to turn to drive past the farm where her grandmother grew up. Ann had to look closely at each farmhouse to be sure which one it was.

"There!" She spotted it.

She had never been in that house, but her grandmother had driven her past it the day after she had related the story to Ann. Another family occupied the house now, and it looked like it had recently been painted. There was a car in the yard and a bicycle on the front porch. Visions of her frail, wrinkled grandmother so full of spunk and spirit flashed into her mind. Tears clouded Ann's eyes as she wished Grandmother Jelena could be with her now, but she bravely blinked them away as they drove on.

Matt noticed the tears but said nothing, sensing this was a special moment for Ann, not to be shared with anyone.

Down the road about one-fourth of a kilometer, they came to an intersection, and Ann had Matt turn south on the gravel road. Up ahead they could see the trees of another farmstead. Ann said, "I'm sure this is the farm where Grandma said Yuri lived."

As they approached, there was one building that stood out above all the others. The big barn was still standing.

As they drew nearer to the entrance of the driveway that led past the house and back to the barn, they slowed down. Matt made a right turn onto the two-track road and stopped at the gate. It was obvious that the road had not been used for a long time. Weeds had almost covered it up. The house was still standing, but the windows were boarded up.

Jim remarked, "How lucky can we get. Apparently no one is living here. That should make things much easier."

Maybe not even since 1917, Matt thought.

They got out of the car. Jim opened the gate that had no lock and closed it after them. The farmyard was an area of about two acres and was enclosed on all four sides by a barbed-wire fence, probably to keep the animals out.

Matt spoke in a quiet voice. "The farmland is obviously being farmed by someone who keeps his machinery somewhere else."

They stopped and looked around. Among the trees was an old outhouse, a granary, and another smaller building, which was probably used as a tool shed. They saw one old, rusted plow and other antiquated pieces of farming tools in the dry weeds along with miscellaneous pieces of old wooden planks and a stack of round wooden poles.

Matt said, "These poles have been here maybe two to three years, probably the start of a corral or pole barn."

Looming above these buildings was the huge, dilapidated barn, quite old and leaning a bit, but still standing. Wooden shingles were missing from the roof, and some areas had been patched with metal many years ago. Faint signs of paint streaked the weathered, gray wood.

With Matt in the lead, they continued walking up the old two-track path from beside the house to the barn. Ann warned him to watch for snakes, as there were some in the area that she was pretty sure might be poisonous.

Matt was nervous and kept glancing back up the road. *Maybe we should come back tonight in the dark*, he thought. *If someone stops, how will we explain what we are doing here?* North across the field and on the other side of the road, he could see the trees around the farm where Ann's grandmother used to live, but there was no activity anywhere.

Matt stopped and, handing Jim the car keys, said, "Jim, go move the car inside the gate and pull up behind these bushes. That should lessen the chance of someone knowing that we're in here. It's only a matter of time until someone drives by."

Jim moved the car and closed the gate.

As they approached the barn, the entrance door on the south side was open, sagging on its hinges and creaking as it was gently moved by the breeze. It was about ten in the morning and a sunny April spring day. Birds were singing in the trees, and the air in the country was crisp and cool.

They stopped at the barn door and looked in. Even though there were lots of holes in the roof and walls, it seemed dark inside, at least until their eyes became accustomed to the dim light. Matt stepped through the door, and Ann and Jim followed. The dirt floor had patches of weeds growing here and there, and a musty smell of rotting old wood and animal droppings permeated the air. Pigeons had roosted in the barn, and straw and loose hay were strewn about.

Ann's eyes immediately swept across the barn past the horse stalls to a door in the corner of the barn. "That must be the feed storage room," she blurted as she hastily moved toward the door.

Suddenly, she stopped in her tracks. A huge, dark-colored snake lay coiled in her path. Ann had startled him. She froze. The snake readied itself for a strike at her legs.

Instinctively, Matt put his arm around Ann's waist and pulled her to safety. He could feel her tremble as he held her for just a second and then slowly released her.

"Thank you. I should have heeded my own warning. I was just so excited to find the photos."

They gave the snake a wide berth, with Ann grasping Matt's arm. Jim tossed some rocks at the snake, and it finally uncoiled and slithered away from the path they had taken.

As they approached the door to the feed storage room, which was half open, they had to squint to see in the room. There were quite a few cobwebs inside but no feed, just an empty room with a dirt floor.

Matt stepped back outside the room, cautiously picked up a two-foot-long piece of wood, and started scraping away at the dirt and old spilled grain in the far corner of the room. Jim grabbed a board of similar size and started helping him.

Matt had retrieved his flashlight from his back pocket and gave it to Ann. "Can you give us some light over here please?"

From the shape of the room, Matt was guessing which corner the access door would be in. Their eyes were becoming accustomed to the dim light, but they could see even better with the flashlight. After they had moved about four inches of dirt and created a lot of dust in the air, Matt's board struck wood. He and Jim worked faster now and cleared away an area about three feet by three feet in the corner, exposing a four-sided crack in the floor approximately two feet by two feet. The access door showed signs of old roofing tar paper still attached.

"The story Grandma told me was true," Ann said excitedly.

Matt bent down to get a closer look. "Yes, let's just hope the photos are still down there and readable."

Jim was dubious. "I've got my doubts that we're going to be that lucky after all this time has passed. Surely someone found them during the past hundred years. I mean, they were put here when? . . . 1916 or 1917? That's a long time ago. In fact, I'm surprised the floor we're standing on, with the weight of all three of us, has not caved in, but it seems solid. Let's get this access door open. I'm getting really anxious to see if those photos exist."

The old heavy-plank access door seemed solid, as did the rest of the floor around it under the dry dirt. They had to look around the barn for something to help them pry it up. Matt found an old hammer head with broken handle and an old wooden-handled screwdriver with the handle split and half gone. Between the two tools, they finally managed to lift out the heavy door. Shining Matt's flashlight down in the hole, they could see it was full of cobwebs, and it smelled dank and musty.

Matt said, "Just a minute. Jim, go take a look in the car. I remember a book of matches in the glove compartment, and while you're there, see if anyone is around. It would be a little hard to explain to the owner of this farm or his neighbors what we are doing here, especially if we're under the floor of this old barn."

"Right," Jim said and started for the car.

"Ann, let's look around and try to find something to make a torch to burn away enough cobwebs to get through. We could run into another snake down there."

Ann shivered. "I hope not. I'm still shaking from the last one."

Matt and Ann found a stick, some old canvas, and what they thought to be some motor oil and fashioned a makeshift torch. Jim came back with matches. "I didn't see anyone, but I moved the car farther into the bushes. Someone would actually have to drive in here to see it."

"Good. Now let's just hope we don't accidentally burn this old barn down with our torch," Matt said with a tone of uncertainty. They all nervously chuckled but realized that could easily happen, especially since they had no water to put the fire out. Matt carefully lit the oil-soaked canvas and, leaning down, waved the torch in the hole. A few minutes later, he was in the hole with the torch, and most of the cobwebs were gone.

"Come on down," he beckoned to Ann and Jim, "and bring the screwdriver and flashlight."

The torch lit up the room of red brick walls and red brick floor covered with a heavy dust. As Matt moved the torch around the room, he observed an old lantern sitting on the floor in one corner. It was so rusted he was sure the kerosene would have evaporated by now. The rest of the room was bare. The old ladder they had come down on was still fairly solid. The area looked like very little moisture had ever gotten in, but there was a definite musty, stale odor. It looked like no one had been here since Ann's grandmother and Yuri were here.

"Okay, Ann," Matt said. "Which bricks do we remove in the floor to locate the box with the pictures in it?"

"I'm not sure. I don't remember Grandma saying exactly where the hole was, just that it was in the floor."

Jim had been moving around the room searching for a clue. "Matt, bring the torch over here in the corner. These bricks look like they are not as level as the rest. They appear to be sunken in a little deeper than the rest of the floor. Where is that screwdriver?"

In a few minutes, the key brick was out, and under it was wood. Matt and Jim quickly lifted the rest of the bricks out, exposing an old wooden box. The box was about sixteen inches by sixteen inches and appeared to be about four inches thick. As they lifted the old box out, they could see it was sitting on an old piece of rubberized cloth, possibly a rain cover.

Probably something from the army, Matt thought.

"Just like my Grandmother said — the old rain cover under and around it to protect it from the moisture." As Ann spoke, the torch withered and died out, plunging them into darkness. She gasped, and this time it was Jim who put a reassuring arm around her shoulders. Ann turned the flashlight on.

"Come on," Matt said as he led them to the ladder. "Let's take it outside to open it. The light will be better." Matt went up first and leaned down to help Ann out.

They came up out of the room, carefully handling the old box, afraid it might fall apart in their hands. They carried the box to an old worktable built along one wall of the barn and put the box down.

Matt turned to Ann, "This is your adventure, Ann, your project. Go ahead and see if you can get the lid off."

Ann slid the box out of the beam of bright light coming through a hole in the roof in case the bright light might damage the photographic images on the old paper. She started prying the top part of the wooden box off the bottom. The lid was not mounted with hinges but was made to overlap the bottom, and it was stuck tight. Jim helped her pry it off with the old screwdriver. Finally the lid popped off. The box was empty.

They all stared at it.

"No ... No! I can't believe it. I was so sure the photos would be here. Where are they? The soldiers must have found them after all." Tears were flowing down her cheeks.

Matt had been preoccupied in thought. "I don't think so. I don't think the soldiers found them. If they had or if anyone else had, for that matter, they probably would not have bothered to bury the empty box again."

"That's right," Jim concurred, trying to dispel Ann's bitter disappointment. "At the point when the revolution became real and the new Communist government either hid or destroyed all documented proof of the existence of Noah's ark, Yuri's father probably became concerned that someone at the lab knew he had made the extra copies. So he must have decided to get rid of the photos. He would be the only one who would take the time to put the box back in the hole and put the bricks back. If the soldiers searched and found the obvious hiding place, they would have been convinced he had the pictures, and he and his wife would have been tortured to tell where they were."

"What do you think he did with them?" Ann whimpered as she wiped tears from her eyes with her sleeve.

"He probably burned them. That's what I would have done," Jim indicated. "Don't feel bad, Ann. Matt and I have learned that you win some, you lose some in this business."

They closed up the box, and Matt took it back down the ladder. He put the box in the hole, and put the bricks back in the floor. When he came up, he and Jim replaced the access door, covered it with dirt, and tried to make it look like they had never been there.

They drove back to the hotel in silence, each deep in his own thoughts.

Chapter Eighteen

The atmosphere in Matt's room that night was filled with disappointment and frustration. They had eaten dinner together quietly. Ann had barely touched her food. Her dream from all those years was gone. She had built up the hopes of Matt and Jim, and now their dreams of seeing the photos and finding the ark were shattered.

Looking dejected and with her eyes cast down at the bare wood floor, Ann apologized, "I'm so sorry, guys. This is such a letdown, and I feel so bad about getting all our hopes up." She shifted her torso trying to get comfortable on the rickety, old chrome kitchen chair.

Jim consoled, "Don't feel bad, Ann. This isn't the first time Matt and I have followed a hot trail on an ancient artifact hunt only to hit a dead end. Right, Matt?"

"Oh, absolutely. This is only one of many disappointments for us in our many years of chasing clues. We could tell you some real stories." As Matt spoke, the springs of the sagging bed squeaked when he stood up and started pacing back and forth.

"Thanks, fellows, but believe me, I'm really sorry."

"Forget it," Matt said. "Besides, we may not be completely out of clues. I've been thinking about some of the things you told Jim and me on the airplane yesterday."

"What things?" Ann asked.

"If you recall, I asked you to tell us every detail of the story your grandmother told you, which you did. In fact, I was amazed you could remember the story so well — the secret room, seeing the photos of the ark, Yuri lying on the table, and the funeral. Also, you said your grandmother and Yuri put the box back in the hole, and Yuri put a piece of waterproof material on top of the box before he put the bricks back."

"Yes, I'm positive that's what she said. I tried to remember every detail she told me."

"Well, there was nothing on top of the box today except the bricks."

"You're right. There wasn't any waterproof cover on top of the box, only under it. I hadn't noticed that this afternoon."

Matt continued, "If the waterproof cover had been on top, perhaps folded a few times making it a half inch thick, the bricks wouldn't have been a half inch lower in the dirt. Remember, the bricks over the box were lower than the floor. That's how we knew where the box was located."

Jim asked, "So if Yuri's father took the pictures out to burn them, then why did he also take the top rubberized rain cover?"

"It could be nothing, but it could mean something, like he still needed the rain cover to protect the pictures in a new hiding place. Also, Ann, didn't you think it sounded just a little odd the way Yuri's father kind of laid his body over Yuri's body as he told him his final good-bye before closing the coffin? You told us yesterday your grandmother observed him bending at the waist and kind of laying his upper body over his son for a few seconds, right? Didn't she say that? She must've thought it a bit unusual, or she would never have mentioned it. I mean, who would even remember such a thing unless it was quite unusual, much less think it was important enough to tell you so many years later?"

"It sounded a little unusual the way she said it. But she said Yuri's father was really grief-stricken."

Jim leaned forward. "Matt, you don't think he somehow slipped those pictures in his son's casket, do you?"

Matt shrugged his shoulders. "I'll admit it's a long shot, but Ann said his father also built a concrete vault for the coffin. How often would you do that in 1917 unless you were royalty or you wanted that wooden box protected?"

"But why would he do that?" Ann asked. "Put the photos in his son's coffin?"

"I don't know. He probably didn't do that at all. I said it was a long shot. But if he did do it, my guess would be that he didn't believe the pictures should be destroyed, that they should be saved for the sake of mankind. He didn't know he and his wife were soon to be killed, and they probably were killed. In future years, when it was no longer dangerous to have the pictures, and if all the other copies had been destroyed, he would know where the evidence was. Maybe he had hoped, just like we do, that if all the people in the world could learn that Noah's ark is really on Mount Ararat, what is written in the Bible would have a lot more credibility. It would be the only actual artifact ever found that is described in the Bible. I think finding it would be the greatest discovery of all time. If more people believed in the Bible and followed the commandments like 'Thou shall not kill', maybe we would live in a more peaceful world."

"Matt, you don't need to preach to Ann and me," Jim said, winking at Ann. "I think we already believe it. At least I know I do. You should've been a preacher. That was a great sermon."

"You know that wasn't preaching, Jim. You know I don't preach, but some things do make common sense."

Chuckling, Jim moved across the room and slapped Matt on the back. "You know I'm just kidding you, Matt. I'm hoping it would make life better for everyone too."

Ann was amazed. "You guys really are as determined as I am to bring Noah's ark to the world."

"Yes, we are," Matt said. "I hope my little outburst didn't offend you, Ann. Sometimes I get a little angry when I think about all the needless killings that never seem to stop."

"Heavens, no. I hope you are right, that proving the ark exists could make a difference."

Jim piped up and said, "Even if it only saves one person from being murdered in this world, our efforts will have been worth it … because that saved life could be mine." They all laughed. "However, bro, do you think we'll be forgiven if we have to disturb the dead and open a grave? I'm assuming that's what you have in mind?"

"I'm afraid you're right, Jim. That is exactly what I have in mind. I think it's time someone found the ark, and yes, I think we will be forgiven. There may be nothing in that casket but the bones of a fourteen-year-old boy who died in 1917, but we've come this far, and we can't give up now, not as long as there is one more chance."

Matt knew he had to find out if the photos were in the coffin. "We can't try to go through the proper channels to have the body exhumed. I'm sure we would never get permission, at least not for several years. But if we're caught in the act, we could all end up in a Russian prison for many years. You two think about it tonight, and if you decide you don't want to risk it, let me know in the morning. Believe me, I'll understand."

"I'm scared, but I'm in," Ann said. "I don't need to wait until morning to decide, but please let's come up with a good plan, and let's be very careful."

Jim concurred. "You know I'm in, buddy. But like Ann said, we have got to get this done and not get caught. Prison would not agree with me."

Matt smiled at the eagerness of his companions. "If we are all together on this, I've already got a plan in mind. Let's get some sleep, and I'll see you in the lobby at seven in the morning."

Chapter Nineteen

By eight thirty the next morning, they were on their way to the local hardware store. It had rained a little during the night, but the sun was now brightly shining. Driving through a residential area to avoid Main Street as much as possible, Matt remarked, "Other than all the advertising written in Russian and the absence of American automobiles on the streets, the town looks a lot like a small town in the Midwest."

There was a park with quite a few trees in the center of town, not far from a school. A few people were out walking and visiting with their neighbors on the street. An elderly man resting on a park bench raised his index finger and slowly waved at them as they passed by. They parked around the corner while they waited for the store to open.

Matt told them his plan. "At nine, Ann, you go in and buy two more flashlights and batteries. Here are enough rubles for the purchase."

Shaking her head, Ann protested, "I have rubles of my own."

Matt turned to her in the passenger's seat. "We are working on the university's expense account. Use this money, but save the receipt. I'll need to turn in all of our expenses." Matt reached over and put the money in Ann's hand.

Matt knew he wouldn't turn in the small receipts to the university, only the cost of the plane tickets. Ira was always after him to turn in all his receipts for reimbursement, but he just shrugged it off. He'd laugh and tell Ira, "I don't want to break your budget. I enjoy working for you too much."

Looking in the rearview mirror, he told Jim, "Go into the store after Ann, but don't let on you know each other. Buy a block and tackle that will lift at least five hundred pounds and fifty feet of half-inch nylon rope. I don't think any one will notice the three of us all getting in the same car at different times. I'll leave the car door unlocked. I'll follow later and buy a fold-up ladder, some heavy wire, wire pliers with a cutter, and a tarp. Each of us buying part of what we need won't create as much suspicion as it would if one of us went in and bought it all. Let's just hope the man who sells us this stuff in the hardware store hasn't noticed us in town. We probably stick out like a sore thumb, so be careful what you say."

"Good luck, Ann," Matt and Jim both said as she exited the car.

"Just don't leave me here. I'll be right back."

* * * * *

Soon they were back in the car heading down the road with everything they needed except the block and tackle. All Jim could get was a come-along with a steel cable. He and Matt agreed it should work anyway.

As they drove east out of town, the road took them through a narrow farming belt, a valley where the terrain was a little irregular. On the right side toward the south, the land was farmed for several kilometers out, but on their left side, the flat land only extended a short distance. Beyond that was a small range of hills covered with scrub oak and pine trees.

About four kilometers east of the town, they crossed a bridge over a creek and headed up a small hill. On the left side at the top of the hill was the gated entrance to the old cemetery.

There were a great number of trees, mostly pine, but also a smidgen of large oak trees. The road going into the cemetery was gravel and continued straight back into the dense trees before making a loop that led back out to the main road.

Jim opened the unlocked gate, and they drove in. Matt stopped the car at the far end of the loop. They all got out and started looking around. Parked that far from the road in the trees, Matt reasoned the car would not be easily seen from the road.

It was deadly quiet. Even the birds weren't singing. There were old tombstones everywhere, just placed at random. The cemetery was not well maintained. Tall grass and brush hid some of the smaller grave markers. A few of the family grave plots had wrought-iron fences around them, but most of these hadn't seen any fresh paint for years and appeared abandoned by their families.

Ann and Jim trudged west down the hill in the direction of the town where they had stayed last night. Below they could see the stream they had just crossed. They were looking for the oak tree where Ann remembered Yuri was buried.

Matt went to the edge of the trees and looked east, the direction they were headed before they entered the cemetery. There was a field but no farmstead as far as he could see. He turned and walked back. From the car, he then walked north through the trees until he came to a drop off. He was facing the low mountains in the distance. Down the hill from the cemetery, on the other side of the creek that curved around the base of the cemetery hill, was a farm. Not what he wanted to see.

Matt stood at the edge of the trees and watched the farm below. He couldn't see any people around the house or the old barn. There were no animals in the corral attached to the barn. The buildings looked like they hadn't seen any paint for forty years, and there were a lot of weeds around the place. He couldn't see any farm machinery or cars, but there were car tracks, and nothing had been boarded up. Matt thought, *Someone could be living there; maybe they are just in town. We do have the cover of all the trees and brush, and the house is probably a quarter mile away tucked in behind the cemetery. But we will just have to be really quiet in case someone does live there.*

Ann remembered approximately where Yuri's grave was but not exactly, and many more people had been buried here in the years since she was here with her grandmother. Ann didn't know where her grandmother's grave was since she wasn't able to come back for the funeral but had been told she was also buried here.

Jim called softly to Ann and beckoned her to join him by a big oak tree. "Is this Yuri's grave?"

Kneeling down, they cleared the grass away from the broken stone.

"Yes, it is," Ann said as she removed more debris from the stone.

Jim signaled Matt, who was searching on the other side of the cemetery.

When Matt arrived, he whispered that there was a farm close by so they needed to be quiet and cautious. Then gently taking Ann's hand, he pulled her to her feet. "I think I found your grandmother's grave. Come with me, and I'll show you."

Matt and Jim let her have some time alone at Jelena's grave while they looked at Yuri's tombstone and tried to imagine how tonight's work would go. They knew Ann wanted to drive past the house her grandmother was living in when she visited her years ago, and they would have to stop at Yuri's farm to pick up three poles for a tripod, a pick, and some shovels, all of which they had seen around the barn at the farm. They had their night's work cut out for them.

Matt and Jim both knew they were crossing the line here. If they were caught, they would be in such serious trouble that even Ira couldn't help them.

When they left the cemetery, they drove to the neighboring town where Ann's grandmother lived when Ann visited her. After that, they went back to the small town where they were staying, had lunch, and went to their rooms to rest since they intended to work all night.

About five in the afternoon, they had an early dinner and arrived back at Yuri's farm before dark. They had passed a few cars, trucks, and tractors on the road, but there was not much activity. Most of the farmers gave a casual wave as they passed.

Soon the poles were all tied under the car with one end tied to the bottom of the front bumper, and the other end tied under the rear bumper. They would have to be careful not to drive too fast or straddle any ruts so the poles would not drag or tear loose.

The two men went over to the building they thought was the tool room and found another shovel and a hacksaw, which they borrowed. Then they just sat in the car and talked until about eight.

At one point, Ann said, "It's really none of my business, but can I ask you guys something?"

"Sure," they both agreed.

"You have indicated you practice karate, often carry guns, have been all over the world, and been in some perilous situations."

"Yes, that's all pretty much true, although you make it sound a little melodramatic," Jim acknowledged.

"Have either of you ever had to kill someone? I'm not talking about Iraq. I know what happened there."

Neither man replied, so she pressed on, "Should I repeat the question?"

Jim looked at Matt, hoping he would answer.

Matt was pensive but finally said, "Yes, it's true we have had to fight our way out of some threatening predicaments, but luckily neither of us has ever yet had to shoot or kill another person, at least not until Iraq. We don't know if we hit anyone there or not. It all happened so quickly. I don't remember actually hitting anyone. What about you, Jim?"

"I shot toward the rocks they were hiding behind mainly to prevent them from shooting at us. I don't remember actually hitting anyone either. If we did, it wasn't intentional. We were just trying to get away."

When it was fully dark, they went back to the cemetery. Matt immediately went to the edge of the trees and looked for lights or a car at the farm. He didn't see any lights, but if someone lived there, they could already be in bed and their car could be in the barn.

By midnight, the three poles were standing over the grave like a tripod with the tops lashed tightly together at the top with the heavy wire and the come-along suspended from a rope sling above the grave. The ground was not too hard, and they had only dug down about three feet, each taking turns, when they hit the top of the concrete vault.

The moon was shining brightly now, so they hadn't needed the flashlights much. The car was parked back in the cemetery far from the road. The steel gate had been closed when they arrived but not padlocked, so they didn't need the hacksaw. Earlier, a couple of cars had gone by on the road but didn't even slow down.

Matt and Jim were in the trench they had dug alongside the vault. They had just rigged a rope under the lip of the old concrete lid when they heard cars coming.

Ann was alone on top beside the trench. She whispered from above, "There are two cars."

They all froze and listened.

When he heard them slow down and stop at the gate, Matt's heart started beating fast. He heard the gate creak as it swung open, and both cars drove through into the cemetery. Helplessly, he watched as Ann crouched behind the oak tree. Matt couldn't see anyone, but he could hear the cars just a few yards from them up on the cemetery road, stopping about even with them. Then some doors opened, and two men started talking in low tones.

Matt didn't dare move a muscle for fear a shovel would fall over and clang down on the concrete lid or a branch would snap under the weight of a foot. Neither Jim nor he had brought a gun because of the airport security. Never had they been so vulnerable. Matt chastised himself for getting Ann involved. They would just have to talk or fight their way out of this one.

In a few minutes, one of the cars started up. Matt heard two girls yell good-bye in Russian as one couple got in their car and backed out onto the road and left. Then a car door slammed shut. They didn't dare move. They listened intently for any sound. Matt was now quite sure they were just young lovers and hoped they would soon leave. A half hour went by, and finally the car started. If they were lucky, the car would just back up and leave.

Instead, the car drove in to turn around, and when the couple saw their parked car, they must've thought it was another couple of lovers, just like they were. They honked their horn three times. *Beep, beep, beep*! Matt cringed when he heard the horn blast. A girl and a boy laughed as they drove back out the gate and down the road toward town.

Matt and Jim scrambled out of the grave and rushed to Ann.

"Wow, I thought we were had when they first pulled in," Jim said.

"Me too," Ann spoke softly. "I don't think I've ever been so scared."

"Let's hurry," Matt urged as he finished securing the rope. "I just hope if anyone is at the farm, they didn't hear that horn blaring."

"But," Jim mumbled, "they didn't close the gate. I'll go up and close it so no one else stops." Jim left and came back in a few minutes.

Matt and Jim hoisted the heavy concrete lid up about four feet. Then they stepped back into the trench they had dug alongside the concrete vault. The trench was long enough for all three to stand alongside the vault with their knees about level with the top. The lid of the vault hanging above blocked off most of the moonlight. With Matt in the middle and Ann to his right and Jim to his left, Matt turned on his bright flashlight, and they all looked in the vault. The old, rough, oak wood of the coffin was dried and warped, but it was not caved in, which surprised Matt. He handed the flashlight to Jim while he pushed on the old, rusty latch to open the lid. It wouldn't budge. Reaching into his back pocket for the broken screwdriver they had used to remove the bricks and open the wooden box, he began prying up on the lid. The catch ultimately pulled out of the dried wood.

"Jim, it's going to take both of us to lift this monstrosity."

The lid was all one piece. Tugging and pushing, they eventually raised the lid of the casket, the corroded hinges protesting and squeaking all the way.

Jim turned the flashlight inside the coffin. There in the bright light, they all stared at the face of Yuri Pavaloski. Seeing his actual face and features right there in front of them was unreal. Matt was expecting to see bones and a skull. None of them had expected this. It gave them a jolt, followed by an eerie feeling.

A cold breeze blew past and ruffled some of Yuri's old, tattered clothes. To their surprise, he still looked like a fourteen-year-old boy asleep in front of them. They could see he had been a handsome young man. His combed hair was still in place. They noticed his skin was just a little tight. His body was mummified.

When Matt had recovered from the shock, he studied the corpse more closely. "That was some embalming job. Maybe one of his father's officer friends in the Army Medical Corps did it. He looks like he hasn't been dead very long. Certainly not for over a hundred years."

As each turned their flashlights on his body, they could see the boy had, indeed, been buried in a man's casket because there were about two feet at the right end between his feet and the end of the casket. It was an almost indescribable scene as the three of them stared at the boy Ann's grandmother had loved so long ago.

But there were no photographs!

Stumped, they again shined their flashlights all around in the coffin. Then Jim began to unbutton Yuri's coat. The button came off, and the coat easily pulled apart, exposing the white shirt Yuri had been buried in. It was stuck to his skin and was badly discolored from body fluids, but the photographs were not there under his burial clothes.

Finally Matt and Jim stopped, paused, and then looked at each other. Jim said, "Ann, can you please hold my flashlight?"

As Ann held both lights, Matt looked at Jim. "I'll lift; you search."

Ann knew they were going to look under Yuri's body for the package. Matt put his hands under Yuri's shoulders and slowly began to lift his body up. Yuri's body was stiff and did not bend at the waist. Ann quickly shined the light under him.

"There," Ann said. "There's something under him. That's got to be it."

They could see a square piece of flat board lying on the linen cloth under the body. Jim quickly slid it over, revealing an oilcloth package. He reached in and removed the package so Matt could lay the body back down. Anxious to see if it actually contained what they hoped it would, Matt laid the package on top of Yuri. Ann pressed closer, straining to see. She shook with excitement as she directed the light beam on the package. Matt carefully unfolded the oilcloth exposing several old photographs lying upside down, slightly bent and kind of yellow, but not stuck together because of white linen sheets between each picture. They all stared in astonishment.

Matt's breathing was rapid and irregular. "Okay, keep your fingers crossed. Here we go." His hands trembled as he turned over the first photo.

Ann gasped as Jim blurted out, "Look at that!"

"It's perfect," Matt said, "a wooden ship protruding out of the ice."

Ann bent closer with the light. "Oh my God! I can't believe it. We are actually looking at the ark."

For a moment they forgot where they were. Quickly taking control, Matt whispered, "Shh — We've got to be quiet, but let's look at the other pictures."

The photos were now spread out over Yuri's body. "Look, each photo was taken at a completely different angle — some close, some far away, but each one is very clear. Hold your light on this picture, Ann," Matt pointed.

As Ann shined the light beam on the photo Matt had selected, Jim hoarsely muttered, "Rocks!"

Matt turned to Jim with a big grin. "Yes, rocks. This photograph is the only one that shows a rock outcropping in the background. We can match these rocks in the background and find where the ark is under the ice."

"You're right, Matt. This is unbelievable."

Matt whispered, "We'd better hurry and get the grave closed and get out of this cemetery."

Carefully he gathered and repackaged the precious photos. They straightened Yuri's jacket and with Ann shining the light on Yuri's face one last time, they closed the lid. Then they lowered the top of the concrete vault back down.

"I'll take the package to the car and hide it in the spare tire compartment. You two start filling in the grave," Matt said.

They had just finished shoveling the last of the dirt over Yuri's grave, and Matt and Jim were wrestling the headstone back where it had originally stood when someone shouted in Russian, "Put your hands in the air *now!*"

Chapter Twenty

They wheeled around toward the loud voice, two bright lights shining directly in their eyes. Matt, Ann, and Jim were stunned but slowly put their hands in the air. Blood rushed to Matt's head as his heart pulsed with fear. They'd gotten careless, and now they were in danger.

The same voice yelled, "Alex, I think we've caught ourselves some grave robbers." Stepping forward from the trees was a burly man holding a rifle. Another stocky man approached from the other clump of trees, pointing his rifle directly at Matt.

The first one with the booming voice was a giant of a man about forty years old, well over six feet tall, and weighing, Matt guessed, around 230 pounds. The other man was probably in his late thirties and about five feet ten inches. When they lowered the flashlights out of Matt's eyes, he saw they were powerfully built guys wearing flannel shirts and caps pulled down over deep-set eyes. Scraggly beards hid the rest of their faces. These men were more than likely the farmers from the nearby farm.

Not wanting the men to guess that Matt and Jim were not Russian, Ann spoke up quickly. She knew as soon as the farmers heard Matt and Jim speak, they would know they were foreigners. "Who are you, and what do you want?"

The older man barked, "What do we want? We want to know what you're doing digging up graves in the middle of the night?"

"Yeah," the other man said. "Karl and I live on the farm right over there behind the cemetery." Ann's eyes followed as the man pointed toward the trees. "We've been standing there in the trees for the last several minutes watching you in the moonlight filling the grave back in."

The giant man declared, "Robbing graves is a very serious crime in these parts. We are really good at killing things with these guns, so don't try anything."

The farmers shined their flashlights, illuminating the tools the men had been using. "What did you take out of the grave?" the other man demanded.

Ann replied, "We are not grave robbers. My grandmother's buried here in this grave."

"Your grandmother?"

"Yes, my grandmother."

The threatening bully concentrated his light on the tombstone Matt and Jim had just put back in place and sneered. "I don't think your grandmother's name would have been Yuri, who was born in 1903 and died in 1917."

"Don't you see," Ann squirmed as she carried on her argument in Russian, "someone has switched tombstones." She didn't know what to say that would even start to explain what they were doing, but she was terrified. She knew Matt had been right when he said they would spend years in prison if they were caught.

"According to my family records, my grandmother should be buried here. But the tombstone said a young boy is buried here. I was sure my grandmother, Jelena Surikova, was buried here just three years ago. I was at her funeral, and I know she was buried right by this big oak tree. We arrived here this afternoon to pay our respects and found someone else's tombstone where hers used to be. I know you may not believe me, but it's true," she pleaded. "I would not let my cousins, Matthew and James, leave here until we dug up the grave to prove my grandmother was buried here, and I was right. We found her in her own coffin, and her rightful place, and now I can relax. I don't know why anyone would have exchanged her tombstone for this young boy's tombstone, but you can bet tomorrow I'm going to find out. It was probably just kids playing a prank."

When she finished her story, the two Russians were looking at her with a bewildered look on their faces. Karl snarled, "Did you ever hear such a story, Alex?"

"Nope." Alex shook his head, spitting on the ground.

"Do you believe that story?"

"Nope," replied Alex, spitting again.

"Please believe me," Ann begged. "We didn't steal anything. Do you see any treasure lying around?"

"No, but you probably took a ring or gold from her teeth. And we'll find it in your car. I take it that your car must be parked up above us in the trees somewhere. Anyway, that's our local policeman's problem, not ours, so just march ahead, all three of you."

"Wait," Ann pleaded. "You know that a young boy who died in 1917 would not have had an expensive ring or any other kind of jewelry, and he wouldn't have gold in his teeth, so why would we dig him up?"

"I don't know, lady. I think you're all three crazy, but like I said, our policeman can get to the bottom of this. When he opens his office at seven, it's going to be his problem.

"Your two cousins haven't said a word. Why is that, lady? Don't they speak?"

Matt was flabbergasted that Ann had stalled the farmers this long. Maybe this gal had more grit than he thought. Neither he nor Jim had spoken yet, knowing they didn't speak the language well enough to pass as Russians. They especially didn't want these two guys to know they were from the United States. Somehow, they would have to overpower these men before they could phone the police. If they were somehow able to get away, they didn't want to later be caught boarding a jet bound for the United States at Moscow airport.

Not backing down from their captors, Ann again went on the offense. "No, they don't speak Russian. They were born in Russia, but they were taken to Australia when they were very little and never learned to speak Russian. If you speak English, just ask them why we opened up my grandmother's grave. They don't understand Russian, so they couldn't understand what I said to you. Ask them yourselves in English," she demanded.

"We don't speak English," Karl said. "Besides that, they probably speak Russian and know exactly what you told us. Enough time wasted," he growled. "Now, if you don't get going, I'm going to shoot you; so march. Don't any of you try anything. Just walk where Alex here points with his flashlight. We're all going to our farm, and at seven, we're calling the police. So move."

Both men had their guns cocked and ready. There was no choice. No more stalling; they'd have to cooperate for now. Reluctantly they marched toward the adjacent farm, Alex leading the way and Karl coercing them to move faster. When they crossed the creek on the exposed rocks, Ann slipped and fell into the frigid water. Jim grabbed her and half carried her to the other side, wrapping her in his jacket. She did not know if she was shivering from the cold water or from fear. She flashed a slight smile at Jim letting him know she was okay.

When they came to a barbed-wire fence separating the farm from the other property, Karl roughly shoved Matt down, indicating he should crawl under as Alex held up the wire. Matt felt the wire catch his shirt and tear, but he crouched lower and got under. Jim and Ann quickly followed Matt, and soon they arrived at the farm.

Stopping in front of the barn, Alex went to a tall pole and switched on the yard light. Disappearing into the barn, he came out a few minutes later with some cotton rope.

The farmers then marched them all into the living room of the farmhouse. There were two doors on the far wall that opened to other rooms. Peering into one of the small rooms, Matt saw an unmade bed and an old chest of drawers. The living room was small, meagerly furnished with an old couch, faded and badly worn; an old wooden rocker; and a dingy-looking, overstuffed chair that matched the couch. There were a few black-and-white photos of elderly people mounted on the walls.

Matt mulled over their situation. *These men are probably brothers who never married and farm together. Maybe they even grew up in this house.*

Alex pushed them through the living room and through another door. He pulled a string hanging from the ceiling, and a single light bulb came on above them. The prisoners found themselves in the kitchen.

It was evident there was no woman's touch in this old house. Dirty dishes were stacked in the sink. An old stove, refrigerator, and a cupboard were the only furnishings other than a large wooden table with four mismatched, wooden chairs. The pungent odor of onions wafted through the room.

Alex moved three chairs away from the table over to a bare wall and motioned for the three of them to sit down. After tying Jim's and Ann's hands and feet to the round vertical rungs of the chairs, he didn't have enough rope to tie Matt's feet, only his hands. He didn't tell Karl or he would have to go back to the barn to get more rope.

After they were tied to their chairs, Karl made a pot of coffee and told Alex, "We've got to stay awake and call the police at seven sharp in the morning."

Alex brought the rocking chair into the kitchen from the living room. The minutes slowly ticked by as Karl and Alex played a card game and slurped their coffee.

Right after his hands were tied to the rungs of his chair, Matt discovered one of the round rungs in his chair was cracked. He had been rubbing the cotton rope up and down over that sharp edge for almost two hours now. He had to move his hands slowly so he wouldn't get caught. The rope still showed no sign of weakening. He hoped Jim could somehow get loose.

Matt was really worried now. He or Jim had to stop these men from calling the police. He wasn't sure the Russians were telling the truth about not speaking English, so he didn't dare tell Jim and Ann he was working to free himself.

Matt and Jim had quietly spoken to each other using the best Australian accent they could muster just in case. They tried to bolster Ann's feeble story by saying they couldn't understand who would have moved the headstones. "It must've been teenagers just playing pranks," Jim said.

Matt struggled to break the rope binding his hands, to no avail. At seven, Karl dialed the local police office. Matt sensed their fate was being sealed. With at least one rifle trained on them at all times and no way to get their hands loose, nothing could be done to prevent the inevitable. The phone rang several times but was not answered, so Karl hung up.

In desperation, Matt continued rubbing the rope over the sharp edge faster in short strokes, hoping Karl and Alex wouldn't notice. He had been surprised when Alex ran out of rope and couldn't bind his feet. Now if his luck would hold out, he just might get his hands loose.

Karl dialed again about five minutes after seven, and Matt's heart sunk when he heard Karl speak to the police. He asked the policeman how soon he could get to their farm. "Me and my brother, Alex, are holding three people, two men and a woman, at our farm. We caught them when they were just finishing filling in the grave of a boy who died in 1917."

The policeman must have asked Karl to repeat the story Ann had told about the grave belonging to her grandmother. Karl chuckled as he relished telling the story once again.

Karl hung up and said, "He's coming out right away, Alex. Go get the pitchforks!"

Startled, Matt was terrified when he heard Karl tell Alex to get pitchforks. Glancing at Ann, he saw her eyes wide open, her lips trembling. Jim also appeared to sense something sinister was about to transpire. *Why on earth did Karl tell Alex to get pitchforks?* Matt did not speak Russian well, but understood enough Russian to know just about what had been said in every conversation all night. But now he was doubly concerned for his friends, especially for Ann.

In a few minutes, Alex came in from the barn with two pitchforks. Matt noted the tines on each one looked sharp and menacing, and Alex was taking full advantage of the fear he saw in Ann's eyes as he waved the sharp prongs in front of her face. The crazed look in his eyes as he brandished his pitchfork slowly back and forth in front of all three of them with the tines of the pitchfork just inches from their faces was a show of power of a sibling who had probably been dominated by his brother all his life. Karl continued to hold his rifle on the three.

They remained like that for almost twenty minutes, no one saying a word. Soon they heard a car coming up the road. Karl peeked out the window. "He's here." Then he spoke to Ann. "Alex and I would just as soon the police don't know we have these here guns, so if you know what's good for you, you won't mention them. He won't pay attention to your saying we had guns anyhow, but tell your cousins not to say anything about them. If you do, we'll sneak down to that jail he'll be taking you to and shoot you through the cell windows. You'll probably be there a couple of nights before they take you to Moscow. Shooting you through the windows in the jail will be just like shooting fish in a barrel, and no one will ever know who did it. They'll just think people in the town didn't take much to grave robbers. So repeat what I just said to your cousins and hurry."

Even though Ann knew Matt and Jim had understood most of the conversation, she repeated it to them in English for the benefit of Karl and Alex. She tried to use an Australian accent but was sure it didn't sound very much like she came from the "land down under."

Karl quickly took both guns into one of the bedrooms and hid them. Then he returned to the kitchen and joined Alex, holding their pitchforks with the sharp tines, ready to stab them if any sudden moves were made.

A knock on the back door pierced the silence. Karl shouted, "Come in!"

As soon as the policeman entered and saw the three strangers sitting on kitchen chairs with their hands and feet tied, he drew his pistol and told Karl and Alex to lower their pitchforks.

Matt assessed the new arrival, a fairly tall, slim man about thirty-five years old. He had on a uniform that reminded him of a US forest ranger, complete with shined boots, hat, and a badge pinned on his shirt. The scowl he cast toward Ann indicated he did not believe her story.

Matt realized the three of them were in the worst possible situation. He had hoped somehow to escape from the two farmers before the law had gotten involved. Now they would be arrested and charged with a serious crime. If they made any attempt to escape and were unsuccessful, even more serious charges would be added.

The policeman began, "Okay, what are your names, and where do you live?"

Ann spoke first. "Sir, I speak Russian, but my two cousins here do not. I was born and raised in Moscow but moved to Australia when I was about fourteen years old. My name is Annabelle Gorsk, and I live at 1424 North Wallaby Lane in Melbourne, Australia."

Ann kept her first name since she was sure each of the three had probably spoken to each other during the night, and the two farmers might have noted the name each gave didn't match. She made up the address and hoped he wouldn't ask how to spell Wallaby. She wasn't sure she knew how to spell it herself.

"And my two cousins are brothers." Ann thought Jim and Matt looked enough alike that they could possibly pass for brothers. Ann was desperately searching her mind to come up with a last name for Matt and Jim that would satisfy the policeman, who had handed his pistol to Karl and was taking notes in a notebook.

She didn't have to come up with a last name because the policeman then put his notebook away and grabbed the pistol from Karl's hand. "I'll get the rest of the information after I lock you up. But first tell me what you are doing here and why you were digging up the dead."

Ann said, "My cousins and I are very close. We were seeing where our families lived, and we were visiting our grandmother's grave." She then told the same story she had invented for Karl and Alex and tried to make it sound as believable as she possibly could.

As Ann retold the story, Matt finally felt the rope he had been trying to cut through for the past few hours break free. Each wrist was still tightly bound and his arms ached, but his arms were now free from the chair. He realized he had to act quickly and overpower all three men. The policeman had the gun in his hand, but it was lowered a little, and the two pitchforks were standing across the room in a corner, tines pointed to the floor. This would be the only chance they had, and he knew he had to make his move work the first time. There would be no second chance.

The policeman and both farmers were standing in front of Matt, Jim, and Ann sitting and tied to their chairs. Matt had been careful not to move his feet at all, hoping the policeman would not notice his feet had never been bound. Matt sat in the middle with Jim on his right hand and Ann on his left. The policeman was standing in front of Matt but looking at Ann as she told the story. Karl and Alex were standing to the left of the policeman, in front of Jim. They were also intently listening to Ann's unbelievable story.

Matt moved his leg lightning fast and kicked the policeman right between his legs so hard and so fast that he dropped his gun and doubled over on the floor in a fetal position, groaning. Alex dived for the gun that had landed on the floor in front of Ann's feet, but Matt stepped on his hand just before he could reach the gun and kicked him in the face, stunning Alex.

By this time Karl swung a hard right fist at Matt's face, catching him with a glancing blow just to the left side of Matt's eye. Matt then doubled Karl over with a hard left to his stomach, followed with a hard right to the side of Karl's face, driving him down to the floor.

The policeman, still in excruciating pain, recovered enough to reach for the gun in front of Ann's chair. Matt grabbed for the gun at the same time gripping the policeman's hands. The policeman held his finger on the trigger. Matt fought to wrestle the gun away from him as they grappled around on the floor.

The gun discharged close to Ann's feet. She jolted, still bound to the chair.

Matt repeatedly hit the policeman in the face with his elbow until he released the weapon. Grabbing the weapon with both hands, Matt stood up, totally exhausted, sweat mixed with blood on his face.

From the corner of his eye, Matt saw Jim standing partway up. Forcing his weight down on the chair several times, Jim finally broke the sturdy chair and released his bound hands and feet.

Alex and Karl were still lying on the floor, bleeding and moaning with pain. The policeman started to get up, but Matt threatened him and motioned him to stay on the floor.

Matt helped Jim get his hands free. Then Jim untied his feet and released Ann. "Crikey, good on ya, mate!" Jim declared, trying to fake the Australian accent. "I was getting a little worried there."

Ann nervously stuttered as she asked, "We've got the upper hand now, but what do we do with these fellas? Do we dare tie them up and leave them here?"

"We'll tie them up and fast before someone comes looking for the police or stops at the farm to buy some hay," Matt replied. "Ann, give Jim a hand while I keep the gun on them."

Jim was already using the ropes to tie their hands behind their backs. The three Russian men were all a bloody mess and were angry, especially the policeman, who proceeded to tell them in Russian what a big mistake they had just made and that they would now face many years in a Russian prison. Jim put the policeman's hand cuffs on him. Ann found some long underwear in one bedroom, which Jim cut up and used to gag the three Russians.

"What are we going to do now, Matt?" Ann asked quietly.

Matt took Ann aside. "Jim and I are going to take these three for a ride. We'll be back in about an hour and a half. You climb up to the cemetery after we leave in the police car. No one has seen our car yet, so let's keep it that way. Pretend to be looking at graves until we return."

Ann touched Matt on the arm. "You're not going to hurt them, are you, Matt?"

"Not unless they try to escape," Matt replied.

Within minutes, Jim was in the driver's seat of the police car, the three Russians were in the backseat with their hands still tied, and Matt was sitting with his knees in the passenger's seat facing the three men in the backseat. Matt kept the gun trained on them but held it low in case they met another car on the road. Each time Matt or Jim spoke, they tried to sound Australian, not yet knowing if the Russians could understand them. Most of the speaking to the Russians was done by gesturing with the police revolver pointed threateningly at each of them.

Jim drove toward the mountains on the dirt back roads. They saw farmers in the fields but met no one on the road. After almost thirty kilometers on a rough, single-lane road, they finally came to a heavily wooded area. Jim pulled the car off the road in a secluded spot and stopped. They got the three men out of the car and marched them into the woods. After a short distance, when they were sure they were not visible from the road, Matt called a halt. The Russians were wide-eyed and shivering from fear. Speaking to them in Russian as best he could, Matt said, "If you cooperate, no harm will come to you. But if not, we will shoot you. You understand?" He hoped they could comprehend what he was trying to convey.

They appeared puzzled, so Matt repeated what he had said, using a few more hand gestures. Finally they acted like they understood. Jim held the gun, and one at a time Matt untied their hands and had them remove their shoes, socks, shirts, and pants. The two farmers were wearing a kind of long-john type underwear, and the policeman had on only boxer shorts and undershirt. Matt had the policeman remove his hat also.

Matt considered having them remove their underwear. This may have bought them a little more time to get back to Moscow before the three Russians could get someone to help them, but he decided to let them keep their dignity and keep their underwear on. *Besides*, he thought, *even though it is almost nine, it is still extremely cold in these trees.* Matt didn't want any permanent harm to come to these men.

The three were standing in their skivvies with bare feet in heavy woods with rocks, grass, shrubs, and trees all around them. Matt had retied the farmers' hands behind their backs and put the policeman's cuffs back on him. Matt and Jim gathered up the Russians' clothes. Then Matt turned the three men around so they had their backs to him and Jim.

All three were sure they were going to be shot. Even though they were still gagged, it was easy to understand they were crying and begging for their lives.

"Run," Matt commanded in Russian. The threesome scurried away, ignoring the sharp rocks cutting their bare feet.

When they were out of sight, Matt and Jim sprinted to the car, threw the clothes in the backseat, and raced back to the cemetery. They met two cars on the road as they got closer to the cemetery, but they just put their sun visors down and kept their heads low, not waving or even slowing down.

They left the police car in the cemetery where their rental car had been parked and tossed the keys and now unloaded gun into the woods. Ann was so relieved to see them she ran and hugged them both. They could only hope it would be many hours before the three Russians could find someone to help them and get back to town.

Stopping briefly at the hotel to grab their suitcases, passports, and check out, they were on the road back to Moscow within minutes. They were all exhausted from lack of sleep and stress.

When they arrived in Moscow, Matt dropped Jim and Ann off at the airport. He returned the rental car himself just in case the policeman had gotten to a telephone and alerted the authorities in Moscow that two men and a woman would probably be returning a rental car. He gave Ann and Jim money to buy tickets. He had Ann buy two one-way tickets to Washington, D.C., and Jim buy one ticket for himself.

Soon Matt joined Ann at the airport with Jim hovering close by but not joining them. Just as they started boarding their aircraft, several security officers and Russian policemen hurried by their gate and stopped at the Qantas airline gate, just a little way down from where they were boarding. They all turned toward the crowd waiting to board and soon were taxiing down the runway.

After they were in the air, fatigue set in, and they slipped into a restless sleep.

* * * * *

Washington, D.C.
The next day

Ira Jensen was on pins and needles. Last night Matt had called from Moscow. The university was closed, but he had left a simple message on the answering machine, "We have the key!"

When Ira heard the recording, he was elated. He knew Matt couldn't give any details. The Cold War KGB was one of the best spy agencies in the world, and no one knew how many phone calls to the USA were monitored even now.

As Matt, Ann, and Jim entered Ira's office, they greeted each other with great jubilation. Excited and grinning from ear to ear, Matt closed the door behind him as he entered and snapped the lock in case someone should just walk in. Ira followed Matt to the large desk.

Removing the package from his briefcase, Matt said, "Wait until you see what we have, Ira." Then he placed each photograph side by side on Ira's desk.

As Ira stared in disbelief at each image, he could barely speak. Jim pulled a chair over, and Ira collapsed into it. His eyes were moist; his hands were shaking. "Actual pictures of Noah's ark! I just can't believe it. I can't believe it."

They all had tears in their eyes as the reality of what they were looking at began to sink in.

Matt explained to Ira as he continued to stare at each photograph, "Last night we repackaged each photo in these preservative envelopes to prevent more deterioration. We will make copies this morning in the photo lab. Then we will turn them over to you. Have you mentioned our project to anyone yet?"

"Huh?" Ira mumbled. Regaining his composure, he replied, "No, no one, Matt. President Jacobson asked where you two were, and I just said I had you on another hunt, to which he replied, 'Okay. Just keep me informed as to how they are spending our money.' He always says that. I told him I would certainly do that as always."

"Ira, we're going to have to ask you to keep the photos in your safe after we've copied them until we get the ball rolling to get permission to hunt for the ark. That will take some time. I'm hoping the fact that we have the photos will make the difference, but we can't let the press or anyone know about them yet. If the tabloids get wind of this story, they may say the photographs are fake, not true, anything. That could hurt our chances of getting permission to search on Ararat."

"I know, Matthew. I'll not show them or talk about them until you let me know."

Ira turned to Ann, offering her a seat. "Please tell me about your trip. Were the photos right where your grandmother said they would be?"

"How about ordering some coffee and caramel rolls, Ira?" Matt interrupted. "Have we got a story to tell you!"

Chapter Twenty-One

Armed with the actual photographs of the ark and a modified story of how the photographs were recovered, Ira Jensen began the diplomatic process to obtain permission from Turkey to search on Mount Ararat for the ark. After many back-room meetings and a series of negotiations and concessions, surprisingly, permission was granted. The American ambassador to Turkey received a letter granting permission for a small team to search for the ark. The diplomatic process had taken many weeks.

Ira received the news in the form of a letter from the ambassador delivered by courier. After he read it, he excitedly called Matt on his cell phone with the news. Matt was elated that they were being allowed to search. "There are stipulations, Matt," Ira said. "Basically, most are simple. First and foremost, you were specifically named to lead the search team. You're to be the project manager, and you will correlate your efforts with a representative from the Turkish government. The search is to be kept secret, and all information regarding the search will be highly classified. Let's see . . ." Ira paused as he reviewed the contents of the lengthy stipulations. "Oh, yes, there will be no blasting of the ice, no defiling of the sacred mountain, several things you will need to read and become familiar with. However, I hate to tell you this, Matt, but there is some bad news in the stipulations. It involves Ann."

"What is that?"

"No women will be allowed in the area where the search for the ark is conducted — a lengthy thing about women not being allowed above the twelve-thousand-foot elevation, some religious rules about the defiling of the sacred mountain. Ann already knows about the Turkish ruling. She was here in my office when the official permission to search for the ark was delivered, and she read it all with me. She was elated about getting permission to search and very happy for you and Jim, but she had a hard time accepting that she could not be a part of it. It's very unfair. If it hadn't been for Ann, the photos showing the ark would probably never have been found. She was very depressed when she left my office. I think she was holding back tears."

Matt told Ira, "Let's not give up yet. I want Ann to be in on the discovery of the ark if it's at all possible. I've got an idea that might work, but don't say anything to her. I don't want her to get her hopes up and then be disappointed again if my idea doesn't work."

After Matt hung up, he thought about the problem and then dialed his father's office.

Within a few days, a directive was issued through all the proper channels. It stated the Turkish government had reconsidered its initial ruling regarding women being allowed on expeditions to Mount Ararat above the twelve-thousand-foot elevation. Women would be allowed to go there if accompanied by a man. Ann was elated when Ira called to tell her. Ann asked if Ira knew what had changed their minds. He replied, "I don't know, Ann, but I know Matt had something to do with the change being issued."

The next day, the three "ark hunters," as they were now jokingly referred to, were in Ira's office along with University President Wayne Jacobsen and two other senior members of the university. All had seen the incredible photographs and were aware of the need for secrecy. The meeting had been called to review the plans and budget for the ark expedition. After the detailed plan that had been worked out was unanimously approved, President Jacobson asked, "By the way, Matthew, what changed the minds of the Turks that allowed Ms. Tyler to go on the expedition?"

All eyes were on Matt, who shifted uneasily in his chair. He was somewhat flushed as he answered, "The thanks go to my father and the American ambassador to Turkey. I knew my father was acquainted with Ambassador McLain, so I called my father and told him the story of how Ann led us to the photos. I then asked him and the ambassador to get together and, without insulting the Turkish government, simply point out to them that Allah apparently had no problem at all with women being on Noah's sacred mountain. Allah had watched over and protected the four women who lived on the ark, Noah's wife and the wives of Shem, Ham, and Japheth. Apparently the Turkish government agreed."

Everyone applauded. President Jacobson said he would personally thank them both. Ann added, "And I, of course, will write and let them know of my personal appreciation, but I'll never be able to thank you for making this all possible, Matt."

"Actually," Matt said, "if you like, you can all thank them in person. Each of you is invited to our home this coming Friday evening for a reception. Both my father and the ambassador will be there as well as several other important Turkish diplomats."

* * * * *

Ann was ecstatic about being at last invited to meet Matt's father. But then she had a scary thought. *What if he doesn't like me?* She spent the next two days thinking of little else, selecting her dress, and every other detail.

Jim offered to pick her up and drive her to the party.

As Ann was putting on her dress, she found herself wondering again what Matt's father, Senator Lane, looked like. *Is he tall? Does he have blue-green eyes like his son?* She wished she had seen his picture at his house when she first told Matt about the photographs. Above all, she hoped he would not be disappointed in her.

She wore a beautiful light-pink cocktail dress with matching pumps, complementing the stunning pink topaz pendant with matching earrings set in gold, which had been a present from her grandmother. Her hair hung down her back in ringlets. Ann sighed as she appraised her reflection in the mirror. *Grandmother would be so pleased.*

Jim rang Ann's doorbell promptly at six p.m.

Taking a deep breath, Ann opened the door.

Jim rocked back on his heels. "H — Hello," he stuttered. "Wow, I guess I'm not used to seeing you all dressed up. You look like a million bucks. Are you ready? I mean . . . obviously you are ready."

Ann returned his obvious adoration with a warm smile as she took his arm and they walked to his car.

161

Matt met them at the door when she and Jim arrived. He was mesmerized with her beauty. Putting his hand on his chin, he looked at her and said, "Hmm … I can't put my finger on it, but somehow you look different than you did when we were in Russia." They chuckled.

"And you both look much more handsome and distinguished in your tuxedos rather than the clothes you were wearing in Russia."

"Touché," Matt replied.

Matt and Jim together took Ann around and introduced her to the dignitaries. Finally, Matt introduced Ann to his father.

Senator Clifford Lane was a distinguished-looking man, the Sean Connery type, and equally as charming. Ann noted he did resemble Matt, tall and handsome.

He was quite impressed with Ann, not only because she was stunningly beautiful but also intelligent and captivating. There had been a change in Matt these last few weeks; he was more thoughtful, more reflective. Senator Lane sensed Ms. Tyler could be responsible and invited Ann to have lunch with him in the near future.

Later, Ann thanked both Matt's father and Ambassador McLain for their help in allowing her to go. The ambassador said, "Ms. Tyler, we were glad to help, but we're not sure we did you any favors. Are you sure you want to go? Mount Ararat has claimed many lives, mostly people trying to find the ark."

"I know the dangers, and I know I could easily be hurt or even killed, but I've lived with the thought of someday finding Noah's ark since my grandmother told me about the photos of the ark when I was twelve. There's no question in my mind. I must be part of it if I possibly can."

Chapter Twenty-Two

Mount Ararat

The wind was buffeting the Bell Ranger helicopter so hard Matt was having a difficult time controlling it. As they worked their way higher and higher in the thin air, a heavy gust came over the ridge in front of them, and the chopper was blown sideways. Ann, in the backseat next to the Turkish military officer, grabbed her seat and pulled her seat belt even tighter. The Turkish officer sitting alongside her spoke only broken English but muttered a few words in his own language under his breath. Ann made out the word *Allah* several times. They were trying to go over the ridge to get above the Ahora Gorge but were making little forward progress.

Finally Matt shouted at Jim over the roar of the big engine, "We're not going to make it this way! We're at about thirteen thousand four hundred feet, and I can't get any higher. I'm going to have to get behind the peak and try to set her down out of the wind! We'll just have to hike the rest of the way! We can walk around the side of the peak and then work our way up. That will put us at about the right elevation above the Ahora Gorge. From there we can confirm the landmarks that match the photographs."

Matt finally found a place behind the rock outcrop where the wind was only blowing about twenty to thirty miles per hour, and he was able to set down on the ice below the rocks. He shut the engine down. It was now quiet except for the whistling of the wind, which was rocking the big chopper.

He looked back at Ann. "Remember when I said if the time ever came when I was really worried about your safety, we would have to talk about it? You wanted to be a part of the entire adventure. Well,

I've been worried about you before, but now I think the danger is even more real. Jim and I should go alone on this one."

Jim added, "No doubt about it, Ann. This part is extremely dangerous."

Matt continued, "As you well know, Ann, many people have lost their lives doing what we are going to do — walk across this glacier. It is melting underneath even though there are high winds and blowing snow on top. We can't fly close enough to see the landmarks in a conventional aircraft, and we obviously can't get close enough in a chopper due to high winds every day. We're running out of time. Winter will be coming soon. We have to get this project started before the Turkish government changes its mind about allowing this operation. We've come too far to stop now."

Ann rebutted, "Wait a minute. You two are not going to stop me from going with you. I know it's dangerous. I've probably read every book about the ark and Ararat that both of you have. I assume you two are familiar with the video Fernand Navarro and his son, Raphael, took of each other on July 5, 1955. About this same time of the year, I might add. It showed the father pulling a piece of wood out of the ice, five feet long, very old and very heavy. It was hand hewn. Do you remember he had to cut it into two pieces to get it down off the mountain?"

"Of course, Jim and I are familiar with the story, Ann. I have a DVD copy at home, but what's that got to do with whether you go today or not?"

"What's that got to do with it?" she exclaimed. "They found that wooden beam at the 13,500 foot level. That's just one hundred feet higher than where we are right now. As soon as we walk around the mountain and locate the rocks in the background from the photos, we can climb up one hundred feet and be right where they found the wooden beam in 1955. Who knows, we might even be able to see the outline of the ark down under the ice. I'm going, and you can't stop me."

"Come on, Ann, be realistic. The chance of our finding the ark today in this wind and with this blowing snow is pretty remote. After we have established the exact location and have people and equipment up here, I promise you will be a big part of the search."

"Enough talk." Ann opened the door. "We're wasting valuable time. I'm going. If I fall in a crevasse and you can't get me out and I die, at least I will die pursuing my dream. I absolve you of any responsibility. So let's get our gear and get moving."

Matt and Jim glanced at each other, resigned to the hopelessness of changing Ann's mind. They could only shrug their shoulders. As he opened the cockpit door, Matt was worried, very worried. *Ann has no idea just how dangerous this could be.*

The Turkish escort declined to go with them. So Matt showed him how to operate the radio in the helicopter in case they had an emergency and didn't come back. They got their heavy gear on — insulated jackets and pants, climbing shoes — gathered the ice axes and climbing ropes, and headed across the glacier into the wind. They went single file about fifteen feet apart, all tied to each other with a climbing rope. The wind was not as strong on the glacier as it had been higher up in the helicopter, but it was still blowing fiercely. It was cold, but not freezing yet. The ice was still melting under the ice cap, making it extremely treacherous to walk on. Matt was in the lead with Ann in the middle as they trudged through the snow, working their way around the east side of the mountain.

They had been trekking almost three hours, stopping often to rest and drink water. Matt raised his hand and pulled out his copies of the photos. Jim and Ann gathered around him as they all looked at the photos and at the side of the mountain and at the edge of the gorge far below them. "We're getting close, but the ice cap is getting steeper!" Matt shouted, wrapping his hands around his mouth in an effort to be heard.

There was a huge sloping area between them and the edge of the gorge. The thought of falling and sliding down the ice cap over the edge to sure death made Matt shudder. This canyon was even deeper than the Grand Canyon.

The sky was becoming more foreboding and dark, and the wind was increasingly ferocious. It was like walking in a blizzard. The snowpack on top of the ice was deep, and Matt was breaking the trail. He was breathing hard now, his heart was pounding in his chest. It was difficult to pick out the best trail, but he had to avoid the blue crevasses that were now all around them.

He worried about the two behind him, especially Ann. *If anything happens to either Ann or Jim because I led them into danger, I could never forgive myself.*

Matt peered into the oblivion behind him but could not see his companions. Only the rope connected them to each other. With the wind howling in their ears and the low visibility, it was impossible to communicate with them, but he hated to keep stopping. They had to be back down the mountain before dark.

Finally Matt stopped to get his bearings, trying to see the outcropping of rocks high above on the ice pack. Ann and Jim had maneuvered to the same spot. Both were cold and their breathing labored, but neither complained.

Matt dug out his waterproof copy of the best photograph, and Jim helped hold it so the wind couldn't tear it out of his hands. The weather conditions were deteriorating as Matt spoke loudly to be heard above the wind. "We're real close now, but we have to go higher. Let's take a break, eat an energy bar, drink some water, and retie ourselves farther apart. We're going to need a little more distance between each of us to climb over that." He folded the photograph and put it away.

Ann and Jim focused where Matt was pointing above them. There were several ice ledges, each with vertical walls five to six feet high with shades of blue pockets all around them.

As they rested, Matt reflected on the past few weeks. He would have liked to wait for a better day to do this search. They had been staying in hotel rooms at Dogubayazit at the foot of this mountain for almost two weeks waiting for the weather to clear. This was the best day they had yet; at least it seemed so this morning when they left. He knew the weather on this mountain could change quickly, but he was still surprised that the good weather this morning could have gotten this bad already.

After the quick break, they started again. This time they were tied twenty feet apart. The terrain got really rough, and Matt was using his ax to climb up sometimes six or seven feet before he would reach a level area. At a snail-like pace, they continued working their way higher up the mountain as they also moved farther west.

Still in the very jagged ice but closer to the smoother area of the ice above the gorge, they stopped again. Matt was comparing the photograph with the terrain. Suddenly he realized the rock outcropping way above them looked exactly like the one in the photograph.

Excitedly Matt shouted, "This is it! The correct angle! The ark is just above where we are now."

"Fantastic," Jim shouted.

"I knew it! I knew we were just below!" Ann said.

Jim and Ann huddled around Matt with the wind whipping the snow around them and looked at the photos. The bow of the ark sticking out of the ice and the unmistakable outcropping of rocks in the background confirmed what Matt was saying. They had the correct angle; only the ark was still higher up. They turned and started again on a steeper climb.

It happened so suddenly that no one had any warning. A large area of the ice that both Matt and Ann had just crossed collapsed into a deep chasm behind Ann and right in front of Jim. Ann fell backward as Jim fell forward into the abyss so quickly that neither of them could stop his fall. Matt was yanked hard by the rope as the two fell.

Dropping immediately to the ice, Matt grabbed his ax and quickly stuck it in the ice and held on. Lying flat on his stomach, with the rope tugging hard at his waist and holding on with both hands to the handle of the ax, Matt dug the cleats on his boots as deep into the ice as he could from that position. His feet were only five feet from the edge of the crevasse. That meant Ann was down about fifteen feet and Jim was hanging twenty feet below her.

Matt was afraid to move. If he tried to turn over on his back, he knew he would quickly be pulled into the hole with Ann and Jim. He tried yelling to them but could not hear anything except the howl of the wind. He had never been so scared in his life. *Jim and Ann may be unconscious from the fall or could even be dead from a broken back or head injury. I can't hold on forever.*

Matt was tense and shaking. Soon his hands would be numb from the strain and cold, and he would lose his grip. His toes ached from the strain they were in. Matt didn't know what to do, so he just held on with every ounce of strength he had.

Minutes ticked by. He didn't dare move. He was afraid they all three would fall to their deaths. He had been in this strained position now a long time, and even though he kept shouting Jim and Ann's names into the snow, there was no reply. *I have to try something.*

Matt tried raising his right leg to see if he could pull the rope up a couple of inches. He dug his right toe into the ice a couple of inches higher and then pushed down on his right leg as hard as he could at the same time he pulled on the handle of the ax. He actually did pull it up about two inches. He rested a minute and did the same with his left foot and gained another two inches. *Could I be pulling the weight of both Ann and Jim with the rope on the edge at that angle?*

His mind was wrestling with his dilemma. Then the cold realization hit him. He wasn't raising Jim and Ann. The rope was just stretching and cutting into the edge of the ice. This would soon cut the rope.

Matt was really getting tired now. He had been in this position too long and knew he would soon start to lose his grip on the ax. Every muscle in his body had been aching so long he was beginning to go numb. He had to work harder and harder to force his fingers to keep gripping the ax.

This is it! This is how all three of us will die because there's no way I'll ever cut the rope to save myself and send Jim and Ann to sure death.

Terrified, he felt his fingers began to slip down the ax handle when he heard a weak voice from the hole. It was Ann! During a lull in the wind and straining, he heard, "Hold on, Matt. Don't let us go."

A surge of adrenaline enabled Matt to tighten his grip on the ax. He yelled, "Hurry, Ann!" but he knew she couldn't hear him because he was yelling right into the wind.

It seemed like an eternity, but suddenly Matt felt a release from the tension on the rope. *Please don't let this mean they fell.* Quickly he drove two pitons into the ice, tied off the rope, and inched his way closer to the crevasse afraid to get too close for fear the edge would break off.

"Ann? Jim? Are you all right?"

"No," Ann weakly replied. "I'm terrified. I can't even see the bottom. I think my leg is broken."

"Stay calm. Don't try to move yet. What about Jim?"

"I'm okay for now, Matt," Jim shouted from below Ann. "I'm on a ledge with a foot hold."

"Ann, can you use your ax and your good leg to work your way up if I keep pulling on the rope?" Matt asked.

"I think so."

"Good girl. Take it slow. Jim, you'll have to work your way up at the same time. Can you do that, buddy?"

"We're on our way. Just keep pulling on that rope."

It took almost thirty minutes with all three of them struggling to finally get Ann out and then another fifteen minutes to haul Jim up to the top. When they were all on top, they lay on the ice, gasping for air. Their muscles ached from the hard strain and exertion.

As soon as Matt and Jim caught their breath, they immediately went to Ann and examined her leg. "Her leg is definitely broken," Jim said.

It was then Matt noticed the gash in Jim's jacket. Blood was spurting out. Immediately, Matt sprang to his side, pulling Jim's jacket and wind shirt off. Putting a layer of gauze and tape over the jagged cut on his shoulder to slow the flow of blood was the only first aid feasible now. Within seconds, he was helping Jim get his wind shirt and jacket back on to stop exposure to the elements.

Hurriedly, he turned his attention to Ann who was writhing with pain. Assessing the injury, Matt quickly formed a splint with a couple of stakes from his backpack and immobilized her leg.

Ann feebly tugged on his jacket sleeve. "The day was not a total loss anyway. We found the right spot to dig." She then reached into her pocket and pulled out a dark chunk of wood. "I found it in the ice as I was climbing out."

Ann drifted into unconsciousness again.

"Lead the way, Jim. It took us several hours to get here, and it's going to take us a lot longer to get back." Matt prayed for strength to get them all back safely before hypothermia set in.

Matt scooped Ann up in his arms, and they started back to the helicopter. Jim was getting weaker and stumbled several times and had to rest often, but sheer guts and determination kept him moving forward. Matt called out words of encouragement often even though he himself was struggling with the weight of Ann in his arms. Occasionally, Ann would moan if he slipped or bumped her leg. He pressed her head into his shoulder trying to protect her from the wind. *She is so soft and vulnerable. How could I have been so insane to have allowed her to come on this trek? I should have been tougher when I tried to talk her out of coming today.*

They were really struggling now. Jim had lost so much blood that there was no way he would be able to make it back to the helicopter. Matt knew he might have to leave him and come back after he got Ann to safety.

Suddenly Matt spotted a shadow moving toward them. *Was it a mirage?* No, it was the Turkish military officer coming toward them across the glacier. It was getting very late, and he had gotten worried about them. Quickly assessing the situation, the officer slipped an arm around Jim and half dragged him back to the helicopter. Again adrenaline coursed through Matt's body as he pushed forward and thanked God for the miracle.

* * * * *

It was dark when they finally lifted off the mountain. Matt flew directly to the clinic at Dogubayazit.

The doctor looked at the deep gash on the back of Jim's shoulder. He had lost a lot of blood, and the cut was almost to the bone. Ann's leg was broken. The doctor set Ann's leg and put a cast on it. Then he cleaned and stitched Jim's jagged wound and kept all of them overnight in the clinic. Matt had already collapsed from sheer exhaustion and faded into a fitful sleep.

Very early the next morning, Matt was up checking on his companions. Jim was sitting up in bed enjoying the attentions of a charming nurse. He gave Matt a thumbs-up and grinned.

The doctor was just leaving Ann's room and informed them both that she was resting comfortably and was mildly sedated. Matt quietly slipped into her room and moved close to her bed. She looked so beautiful, her long brown hair flowing over the pillow. As she lay there sleeping, Matt bent down and softly kissed her. He still felt guilty for putting her in so much danger over the past month — not once, but twice.

Ann's eyelids fluttered as she slowly awoke. Tears started running down her cheeks when she saw Matt. Quickly he moved to hold her and try to assure her everything was all right. "Jim? Where is Jim?" she sobbed.

"He's just fine. I just spoke to him a moment ago in the next room."

She started to regain her composure, and Matt was now forced to release her from his arms. "Oh Matt, how long have I been asleep? I must look terrible." She started to sit up, but then the pain reminded her of her broken leg. "Ow!" Gingerly she tried to move her injured leg to a more comfortable position.

"Are you okay?" Matt asked, moving closer to help. "Maybe you had better just rest." He moved the pillow under her head and helped her lie back down.

"I guess I'll have to."

"I feel terrible about this, Ann."

"Don't you dare feel bad about this, Matt. We both know I knew the risk, and there is no way I would've let you talk me out of going. So I broke my leg. It will heal. But I put you and Jim in jeopardy because of my stubbornness. I'm so sorry Jim got hurt and I put you through such an ordeal. How can I ever thank you for saving our lives? I understand you carried me all the way back to the helicopter. How did you do that?" Ann began talking fast and excitedly.

"You better calm down. You've been through a lot of trauma. I think you'd better take it easy."

"He's right," Jim said as he walked in, one arm in the sleeve of his robe and the other in a sling under the robe.

"Hi, Jim." Ann greeted him with a big smile.

"How's the leg?"

"It hurts. How about your shoulder?"

"It hurts," he replied.

"Oh, I am so sorry."

"No need to be. Matt and I apparently will be indebted to you forever for saving our lives yesterday."

"What?"

"Maybe you'd better explain that," Matt said as Jim came closer and stood beside Ann's bed next to Matt. "I'm remembering yesterday a little differently than that. My arms still ache from Ann saving me," he said.

They all chuckled.

"Well," Jim began, "two doctors stopped by my room last night while making rounds. I knew one was the emergency room doctor who took care of us when we came in. I had never seen the other doctor before, but we talked for quite a while. I told them exactly what happened. They both said it was a good thing there were three of us roped together. Apparently, these guys hike on the mountain sometimes and were familiar with accidents that occur there. They said if Matt would have been where Ann was and taken the same exact path, the way the ice caved in, we would have both fallen into the crevasse and probably never would have been seen again. But since there were three of us, when Ann and I fell in but Matt didn't, he was able to stop our fall and hold on until we regained consciousness. So thanks for insisting on going with us."

"You mean I don't have to go through my life with all this guilt because of my stubbornness?"

"I guess I'll have to thank you too, Ann," Matt said.

"Don't you dare thank me. We all know that's pure speculation, but it does make me feel a little less guilty."

They all agreed that Jim would take Ann back to D.C. as soon as she could travel. When Jim recuperated, he could then stay in D.C. to help with the paperwork end of the project, at least for a few weeks.

Yesterday had been a really hard day for all of them, but they were still elated. They now knew where to start the search. They were also very aware that the search for the ark on this mountain was not going to be easy.

Chapter Twenty-Three

Matt was still at the base of the mountain in the Turkish village of Dogubayazit. Cupping his hand around the phone at his ear, he strained to hear what Ira was asking.

Matt replied, "Four Turkish government officials and a team of six engineers arrived the day Jim and Ann left. We've had long meetings every day, some lasting far into the night. We've covered a lot of ground and now agree what will be needed for the project to succeed.

"The engineers are really sharp, especially one named Muhammad Baig. After the enclosures are complete, he and the electrical engineer, a young fellow named Adem Emir, will remain at the site with me. Mohammad is probably close to sixty and is soft spoken and intelligent. He speaks excellent English. He's been a good interpreter for me. I really like both men. We work well together, especially Muhammad and I. He will be the liaison officer when we get settled on the site. Muhammad will also set up and operate the communications room. The Turks are very concerned about the communications. They don't want anyone eavesdropping."

"Has the weather cleared enough to fly up to the site?" Ira inquired.

"Yes, I've taken everyone up, three at a time. The engineers have determined where the target should now be. They have done many calculations to allow for the movement of the glacier since the photographs were taken. We've ordered a lot of heavy equipment, and it will arrive any day now."

"Sounds like the wheels are starting to turn."

"Yes, they are," Matt replied. "I'll try to keep you informed unless they ask me to not use a telephone to communicate with you."

"I understand."

After learning Jim and Ann had arrived safely, Matt said good-bye and hung up. Reflecting about the conversation, Matt knew by referring to the ark as the target, Ira understood. But if anyone was listening in on the conversation, they probably also understood. This could cause problems. He would have to limit the calls.

* * * * *

A few days later, ten Mercedes semi-tractors pulled up to the base of the mountain with the first of the equipment Matt and the engineers had requested. Soon, a steady stream of heavy-lift helicopters were carrying men and equipment directly to the target site. Twenty-nine days later, the site was complete. The construction crews, having been warned about the secrecy of the project, were now gone.

On Monday morning at ten, three helicopters landed on the site. Matt, Muhammad, and Adem met the government officials at the heliport. Matt had been expecting them. They had requested a tour of the site when it was complete but before the search began. Matt and his crew were proud of what had been accomplished and were happy to show them. The sun was brightly shining on the ice cap, and the wind was barely blowing.

Standing on the ice outside the structure, the men all exchanged greetings. Most of these men had been in the initial meetings at Dogubayazit. They were all astonished at what had been built on the glacier and were anxious to see inside.

Everyone understood and spoke some English. They asked Matt to conduct the tour, and Muhammad and Adem would clarify in Turkish, if necessary.

Matt began, "As you are well aware, gentlemen, this beautiful morning with the sun shining is unusual. In a few hours, it will probably be cloudy, very windy, and very cold. Often it gets too windy up here on this ice cap to land or take off in a helicopter. Therefore, we keep our helicopter and two snowmobiles some distance from here in another dome building, a little more protected from the high winds. We keep two snowmobiles here for an emergency run to the helicopter if anyone should get hurt or if it's too gusty or windy to land at this location. As we all agreed in Dogubayazit, we had to create a safe, workable environment in which to conduct the search. We built it as quickly and as efficiently as possible.

"We began by lifting one small bobcat tractor up here with which we smoothed off the surface of the ice as much as possible where the three structures were to be erected. To safely accomplish this, we removed the cab from the tractor and secured the operator with a safety line. We didn't want to lose the operator if the bobcat fell into a crevasse. Luckily, it did not."

The men all agreed that had been a dangerous but necessary task.

"Because of the slope of the ice cap toward the Ahora Gorge below us, we could not level the long main search building, but the cafeteria, sleeping dome, and showers/bathroom area are fairly level. The terrain dictated where the structures had to be erected.

"There are three separate temporary structures here. They are all made of the same material, a heavy fabric covering structural aluminum framework. Each building is securely anchored deep in the ice. The manufacturer guarantees each structure will withstand a 110-mile-per-hour wind.

"This first building next to the heliport is a forty-foot diameter dome." Matt opened the door, and they all entered a six-foot-wide corridor with a door on each side of the walls. "The rooms on each side are showers and portable toilets. This building is fairly level, has an insulated floor, and is heated to about sixty-five degrees. The hot water for showering is limited, and it gets cold pretty fast when you're getting dressed." Everyone chuckled.

A narrow, six-foot-long, half-round tunnel and one set of doors led to the next enclosure. Matt told the group, "This dome is eighty feet in diameter and also has an insulated floor. We are in the lounge area now. This area is for everyone to use when they are off duty. As you can see, it contains couches, easy chairs, a small library of books and magazines, tables for card playing, vending machines, and a coffee station.

"All around the perimeter are sleeping quarters, and this room is our communications room."

They all crowded in. Muhammad showed them the short-wave radio, the only form of communication allowed on the mountain. His desk sat behind a large bank of file cabinets. He explained that daily records were being kept on everything from food and diesel fuel orders to weather reports and daily work schedules.

Continuing the tour, Matt proceeded through another short tunnel with a set of doors that led to the wall of the large main structure. They stepped off the insulated floor onto a galvanized steel grating. The size of the structure in front of them was impressive.

Matt explained, "The building you've just entered is our largest structure. It is three hundred feet long. You're standing in the middle of the longest wall. It is one hundred fifty feet uphill to your right and one hundred fifty feet downhill toward the Ahora Gorge to your left. If you look straight ahead, you will see the far wall one hundred fifty feet away. In other words, this structure is three hundred feet long and one hundred fifty feet wide. We believe we have it centered over the ark. And we believe the roof of the ark is thirty to thirty-five feet below the surface of this ice."

Everyone stood in awe at the huge structure. It was overwhelming to realize they were standing in this building on the glacier on Mount Ararat. And beyond that, Dr. Lane believed it was erected over Noah's ark in the ice thirty-five feet below. Even though some had helped plan all this, they were speechless. Matt waited while they took it all in before continuing.

"If you look up above at the center, you will see the lights and a track with a cable crane attached."

The entourage was excited as they looked up at the roof of the huge structure. The room was very well lit with lights hanging down from the roof seventy-five feet above the floor.

"When we start melting the ice, the heating machine will be suspended from that track that runs down the center. The heater can be rolled most of the length of the building if necessary. We will start in the center of the building. We will melt a fourteen-foot-diameter hole straight down, hopefully to the top of the ark. We will be using a high-intensity, electric heater mounted on a rotating seven-foot arm. The electrical power will come from two large Caterpillar diesel generators mounted in protective buildings outside the structure. Each generator has its own five-hundred-gallon diesel fuel tank. The workers will, of course, wear rubber boots and warm protective clothing. The water from the melting ice will be continuously pumped outside. Men will be lowered in and out of the borehole in a metal cage suspended from the track above."

Matt could tell by the reaction of the officials that they were impressed. He allowed time for questions, which he and Muhammad or Adem answered. Matt then resumed the tour.

"You will notice it is cold in this big structure and the floor under the grating is ice. I'm glad to see all of you received the message advising you to wear warm clothing today."

They all smiled.

"We have to keep the temperature just below freezing in here, or the ice will melt and our enclosure will start to sink. The only heat in this building will be down in the melting hole.

"Now if you look to your right again, back up the slope to the high end of this building, you will see we have petitioned off that end. We had to level off the floor about fifty feet out into this structure. That is our cafeteria, which also has a little heat. Let's proceed to that area and we'll try to answer any questions you might have."

The dignitaries did have a lot of questions. They were very impressed with the facility, but also very concerned about the project. A lot of money was being spent. They needed to be reassured that the ark would be found, and soon. Two hours later, the government officials left.

Matt quickly gathered his crew around him. "Gentlemen, let's melt some ice."

Chapter Twenty-Four

Matt hadn't realized how much he had missed Ann. He had been so busy the past few weeks. They had encountered some minor problems but overcame them, and the borehole was getting deeper. But now, Matt was lonely for the companionship of Jim and Ann.

Some days the wind was too bad for the helicopters to come up. On the days when weather permitted flights only partway to the project site, they had established some fairly safe routes over the ice flow and used the snowmobiles and tracked bobcat to ferry supplies from the area where the helicopters could land. They had erected a forty-foot-diameter dome to keep the snowmobiles and bobcat in, close to where Matt had originally been forced to land the Bell Ranger.

Communications were fair but not great. He hadn't spoken with Ann at all since she left weeks ago. He seldom talked to Jim, and when he asked Jim how she was, he would just say she was doing okay.

One evening Matt was in the communications room talking to Ira Jensen on the short-wave radio when Ira said, "It sounds like Jim finally found himself a lady friend. You should do that yourself, Matt, when you get home—unless, of course, you already have a Turkish girlfriend with you up on that mountain. You're not getting any younger, you know."

What Ira said struck Matt to the core. It couldn't be. Jim would've told him. Trying to act casually interested but inwardly praying Ira would not say Ann's name, Matt inquired, "Don't remind me of how old I'm getting, but I hope I never get as old as I feel after all the around-the-clock work up here. By the way, who is this lady Jim has latched on to?"

"It's Ann Tyler. I understand they have been seeing quite a lot of each other lately."

Matt was stunned. All he could see was an image of Ann in the clinic the day she left the mountain—beautiful, fragile Ann, her eyes sparkling with excitement, her brown hair cascading down in soft curls, her lips slightly parted in a mesmerizing smile as she thanked him for saving her life. Never would he forget the soft, warm feel of her hand in his as they said good-bye.

Matt was jolted back to reality as the static on the line cleared, and Ira continued, "Well, Paula and I ran into them the other night at the movies, and I've overheard some of the girls working here talking about seeing Ann and Jim together a few times. They think it's so romantic. But of course, these girls get excited if someone they know goes out with the same person more than once. To hear it from these girls, you'd think Jim and Ann were practically engaged. Maybe Jim's going to settle down finally. Ann is really a special girl, don't you think, Matt?"

"Yes, she is."

Even though Matt had a huge lump in his throat, he managed to say good-bye to Ira without showing how heartbroken he was. After he hung up the phone, he sat in the dark of the communications room. He had never felt so low and alone in his life. The news had been such a shock to him. It had almost made him physically ill. He sat there for more than an hour. Matt hadn't realized he had such deep feelings for Ann. After all, she was just a good friend.

He had never even gone out with her alone, just the two of them. Life had been such a whirlwind since they first met. There just hadn't been any time, any opportunity. During the weeks while waiting for permission to search on Mount Ararat, Ann had been busy at the Smithsonian. The three of them had gone to dinner together twice, and they had all three met for drinks with Ira and Paula. Even though he knew he was really attracted to Ann and always tried to get seated next to her at dinner, there just hadn't been any time to date. *How could I have been so stupid? I have just been so all-consumed by the possibility of finding the ark that I couldn't think of anything else. Why has this simple news hit me so hard? It is just so unexpected. I may never now have a chance to really know her, to be a part of her life and have her as a part of my life.*

He finally regained his composure and left the communications room. He walked past the workers and noisy machinery down in the pit and went outside. With only the stars to light the sky, he could see faint lights of a village way off in the distance.

He should have known Ann and Jim would get together. They were always joking and laughing. Jim was not as serious-minded as he was. Jim was a great catch for any girl. Both men seemed to attract lots of pretty girls, but their independence had always been very important to them, so neither wanted to be obligated to anyone. Matt remembered that on his thirtieth birthday, they had partied alone and drank a toast to the fact that they had both escaped Cupid's arrow. That was last year. That was before they met Ann. Now it seemed they had both fallen for the same girl.

Then, again Matt brightened. *Maybe I'm feeling bad for nothing. Just because Jim and Ann have gone out together several times doesn't mean they have fallen passionately in love with each other. It's ridiculous for me to let what Ira said upset me so. But then . . . why didn't Jim tell me he had been dating Ann?*

Matt tried to convince himself it was just a rumor, but he knew in his heart that Ann and Jim were much more than just good friends. Well, so be it. He vowed that when they returned to the mountain, he would act as always, and when they told him about their feelings for each other, he would act surprised and wish them well, and he would mean it. But for now, it was just too painful. He hoped they wouldn't come too soon. He would need some time to get over this.

* * * * *

Matt spent most of his days down in the hole where they were melting the ice. Matt and Muhammad had been confident that they would be able to see the ark at thirty feet, but they were at thirty-four feet now and still nothing. The heaters were working twenty-four hours a day. It was a continuous effort to keep enough diesel fuel in each of the five-hundred-gallon tanks beside the huge diesel generators.

They had already spent several million dollars on the project, most of the money coming from the Turkish government and a portion coming from the university, with a deal that Jim had helped negotiate. Matt knew exactly how much money they spent each day. Muhammad logged everything by hand, item by item, from large expenses like helicopter rent and structure fabrication to lock boxes to hide keys on the snowmobiles and Bobcat. It seemed people were always putting the keys in their pockets instead of on the key rack. Matt had to review and sign every report.

The government and the university expected to get their money back after the ark museum was opened at the bottom of the mountain. With a modest price of admission, everyone could see as much of the ark as could safely be brought down, plus all the artifacts found. Visitors would be able to sit in comfort in the auditorium and see videos of the entire recovery operation. Everything had been extensively filmed thus far, from nothing on the ice to where they were at this point. They had a permanent Turkish film crew who stayed at the site, filming every helicopter lift and the construction of all the buildings.

Matt looked over at the lights around the borehole, reflecting on how much had been accomplished since they arrived on this glacier. It seemed unreal that the Turkish government had been so cooperative and helpful, and through modern technology, heavy-lift helicopters, excellent engineering, and a great effort from these very people working with him now, all this had been accomplished. If someone had told him just a few months before that he would be in this shelter on the glacier of Mount Ararat melting the ice to find Noah's ark, he would never have believed it.

* * * * *

Matt was in the pit when Jim and Ann arrived back on the mountain. Ira had said they could come as soon as Jim completed writing a grant request and Ann had recuperated from her broken leg, but that was the only notice Matt had received. He was kneeling,

182

preoccupied with the work. He didn't even see them come down in the cage lowered from the overhead crane to the bottom of the pit.

Jim tapped Matt on the shoulder. When Matt turned and saw Jim, he sprang up and gave him a bear hug. They patted each other on the back like the old friends they were, excited to share all the news with each other.

As Matt stepped back, he saw Ann standing to the side, beaming as she smiled warmly at him. Caught up in the moment, he grabbed her and swung her around, perhaps holding her a little too tight, a little too long. She giggled as he put her down. He vowed his desire would remain a secret. Never would he do anything to hurt his two best friends. He turned and shut down the pump that had been making all the noise so they could hear each other.

"How's the leg, Ann?"

"I just got out of the heavy cast last week. I can now put weight on it. I didn't want to come back here until I could walk and be of some help."

Ann was wearing a fur-lined parka with the hood up. The fur outlined her radiant face and auburn hair. Her flawless cheeks were slightly rosy from the freezing temperature in the room. She was clapping her gloved hands in admiration of the project.

She is even more beautiful and exciting than I remember. After all the women I have known, how could this one girl attract me so? Is it just knowing I probably can never have her, never share my life with her? This has to stop. This is just immature thinking. I had never even thought about sharing my life with her until I learned that I probably never could. That has to be it. These ridiculous, immature feelings will probably be gone in a couple of days.

Matt quickly recovered from his conversation with himself and replied, "Good idea. And, Jim, how's the shoulder?"

Jim was also dressed in warm clothing, as they had been advised to do earlier since the large dig area had to be kept at freezing temperatures. Matt could see Jim's breath in the cold, "It's been healed a couple of weeks, but I've been busy trying to explain to everyone why you're spending so much money up here." They all laughed.

Jim added, "I'm really impressed with the facility — so much built in such a short time. Coming over here on a snowmobile from where the chopper had to land sure beats the way we got here the first time." They chuckled.

Matt questioned, "If they didn't bring you all the way over in the chopper, we must have high winds outside again. I've been so busy in here, I haven't even looked at the weather today."

"It's very cold and windy," Ann told him. "I think winter is setting in."

"How is the project really going, Matt?" Jim asked seriously.

"I hesitate saying this, but I'm getting really concerned. Just look at this pit we're standing in. We're down almost thirty-nine feet, and still nothing. I've got a high-powered light, and every day I polish the floor and shine the light straight down, but still no dark shadow appears in the ice. We've rechecked our position with the rocks and the angle several times where the photographer had to have stood. We've allowed for movement of the glacier. The dome is dead center over where the ark should be, but it's just not here."

"Could it be even deeper in the ice?" Jim inquired.

"I don't think it could be much deeper. I hope it isn't. I'm already getting worried about the safety of being down thirty-nine feet in this pit without more shoring. A pit this diameter is almost impossible to properly shore without interfering with the ice-melting equipment. When I study the photos of the ark, it appears that the ice had melted down enough that the bow toward the gorge is resting on solid ground. I don't think it can be over seventy-five to eighty feet thick here. Allowing the ark to be forty-five feet high — we're down thirty-nine feet — we should at least see it through the ice below."

"Not if the roof caved in," Jim said. "What about a radar or sonar machine?"

"The Turkish government won't allow either brought up here. The engineers say those machines won't work in these conditions anyway."

"I understand." Jim shrugged his shoulders.

"I've got another idea," Matt said. "I ran it past Muhammad, the chief engineer, and he agrees it's worth a try. We are going to try it in the morning, provided the crew and equipment we ordered arrives.

Let's grab some dinner, and let me show you around some more. I'll show you where you can sleep in a warmer facility than this iceberg."

"Good," Ann interjected. "It's, like, freezing in here."

"It *is* freezing in here. We have to keep it below thirty-two degrees so our big enclosure won't sink."

They rode in the cage up to the top. Matt introduced them to Muhammad, Adem, and the crew who were going down into the pit for their shift. They stopped in the dining hall and went through the food line set up cafeteria style. Then they sat down at a table and talked for more than an hour.

The food was basic but good. It was provided by a Turkish catering company, and since Matt, Ann, and Jim were the only American workers at the site, the dishes prepared were all Turkish. They had lots of rice dishes, mostly served with chunks of lamb or shrimp, and all kinds of vegetable dishes and eggplant specialties. They also had cabbage leaves filled with meat wrapped in delicious little bundles. The desserts were all extremely tasty, especially baklava. The thin layers of flaky pastry between layers of walnuts and olive oil were delicious. The cafeteria sometimes had sutlac, a Turkish rice pudding. Matt's favorite was "Turkish delight," consisting of simple ingredients such as honey and flour. And, of course, Turkey's famous rich black coffee was always available.

As they were finishing dinner and having coffee, Ann said, "Matt, the dinner was really delicious. Didn't you think so, Jim?"

"Yes," Jim replied with reservation. "It was good, but since I don't speak Turkish and I believe you do, maybe you could talk the cook into ordering what is needed to make some good old burgers and fries on the next food order up the mountain." Chuckling, Matt and Ann shook their heads. Leave it to Jim to lighten the mood.

Ann had inherited an uncanny ability to easily learn foreign languages from her father. She had been studying the language spoken in this area since they first knew they were going to eastern Turkey. She could carry on an everyday conversation and understood it better than Jim and even Matt. She had already impressed the engineers and workers she'd been introduced to today.

Matt continued talking about his work. "I feel I have a good working relationship with the Turkish engineers. Muhammad is my right-hand man. We couldn't have accomplished all of this so quickly without him. He speaks excellent English and also handles our communications room. The crew consists of hard-working men, and they treat each other with respect. The Turks are extremely excited and optimistic about locating the ark. They love to look at copies of the Russian photographs. That really keeps them fired up. They know we must be close to finding it, but it is becoming very frustrating because were running out of time. This late in October, the weather conditions are deteriorating each day. Winter is already upon us, and we will have to quickly close the site down at the first forecast of a bad storm and leave until spring. It is just too dangerous to be here in the winter."

Jim nodded, a bit disheartened. Changing the subject, he announced, "Nothing major happening back home. Ann and I can't believe the newspapers haven't yet been alerted to this project. It's still being kept secret from the world."

"Good," Matt said with relief. "The Turkish government doesn't want to be embarrassed if we can't find the ark."

They talked for a long time. Finally, Matt took them to the sleeping quarters and showed Jim where his small private room was. Jim opened the door and flipped on the light switch, illuminating an area about ten feet long and six feet wide. Opposite the door was a small closet, and beyond the closet was a small sleeping cot. Matt said, "The living quarters here are not the greatest, but we're all lucky. We have private quarters. Only a few of us have separate rooms. The rest of the crew have bunk beds in one large room. The portable toilets and shower stalls are down this hall in the small dome attached to this one."

"This will do nicely. I'm just glad to have a warm bed. I'll see you guys in the morning," and Jim closed the door.

Matt then escorted Ann to her room. It was the same as Jim's except Matt had installed a deadbolt lock on her door, and her room was next to his. After all, she was the only woman on the mountain, and there were about thirty men. Before she went in, Matt said, "I think you are safe around all of these men. The Muslims have very strict laws and extreme types of punishment for those who don't obey the laws, but just be careful, especially in the shower area. You have your own private shower room with a lock inside, but still be careful."

"I promise I will exercise the utmost caution, Matt. By the way, it's good to see you again after all this time."

"It's good to see you too."

Ann opened her door and stepped inside. "I'll see you in the morning. What time did you say? Six?"

"Yes, in the dining hall. Good night, Ann."

"Good night, Matt."

Matt lay awake a long time. It had been bittersweet seeing her again. He couldn't believe how attractive she was. He had noticed every Turk who had spoken to her today had also taken note of her extreme beauty. And the way she smelled … even after her long flight and helicopter ride up the mountain with her heavy cold-winter clothing. She smelled alluring, just a hint of some perfume she always wore, or Matt mused, *Was that just her?*

Matt was afraid tomorrow Jim was going to tell him that he and Ann were in love. Matt told himself that would be great. Ann couldn't have found a better guy. Jim would always be a good husband, and Matt would still be a free man, no one to hold him down, still free to travel the world and explore caves looking for artifacts from ancient civilizations. He loved doing that; it was always an exciting adventure. It was his life.

So why did the thought of losing Ann make him feel so bad? He knew that even continuing to do all the things he loved to do would somehow never be the same now that he had come to know Ann, had fallen in love with her, and then lost her to his best friend.

* * * * *

The next morning they all met for breakfast, as they had planned the night before. Jim and Ann arrived about ten to six, and Matt was already drinking coffee. Ann was wearing heavy khaki-colored pants and her brown parka with the hood up. Matt watched her coming in with Jim, and they were both laughing. Matt thought again how remarkable she looked with the hood framing her face and that beautiful hair. He started to feel the pangs of jealousy but forced those feelings out of his mind and greeted them with a big smile.

Jim asked if the equipment had arrived.

"Not yet, but I expect three big choppers to land at any minute."

Matt had explained his plan the night before. He and Muhammad had been thinking that the ark might have slid downhill a little more than anyone had initially calculated. They had polished the walls of the ice and shined bright lights all around the walls especially the down-slope side, but there was no dark shadow. So they had hired a crew of four experienced, hard-rock miners to start tunneling sideways.

The familiar thumping whirl alerted Matt that the helicopters were approaching. Soon after they landed, he was helping unload four miners and all their equipment. They had brought air chisels, a huge air compressor, and heavy steel jacks to shore up the roof of the tunnel.

By two in the afternoon, the miners had chiseled about ten feet sideways into the ice. Matt and Jim had agreed the night before that the roof had possibly caved in in some parts of the ark but probably not where the vertical walls inside were. They hoped that each time the ark had been exposed to the outside air the ice inside had not melted. They reasoned that ice inside should support the ice pressing down from the outside.

After 6:00 p.m., the miners quit for the day. Matt, Jim, Ann, and the Turkish engineers went into the pit. It was hard to walk with all the tools and equipment the workers had left lying on the floor. The tunnel was now about four feet wide, seven feet high, and twenty-two feet long from the edge of the fourteen-foot-diameter pit. The shoring left a hole about three feet wide and six feet high. Matt grabbed the high-powered light and started into the entrance to the tunnel. Ann grabbed the coil of power cord and went in behind him. Matt had a towel in his hand to polish the ice at the end of the tunnel. The sides were very rough, like chipped ice. Matt could barely see into it. They came to the end of the tunnel, and Matt started wiping the ice, trying to smooth it while Ann held the light. Jim was behind Ann, and the Turks were behind Jim, all hoping to see some sign of a dark shadow in front of them, but after five minutes, they all agreed there was nothing.

Sullenly, they turned to walk out. After a few feet, Ann stopped abruptly. "Look. What's that?"

"Where?" Matt asked.

"At the side of the tunnel where I'm standing," Ann pointed. Matt shined the light toward the side wall, but the ice was so jagged, he couldn't see anything. "I caught a glimpse of something dark, but I can't see it now. Move the light back where you were."

Matt went back to the end of the tunnel and tried to shine the light where he had just been.

"There." Ann indicated the spot where the light beam was shining. "Keep the light there, Matt. Look, Jim. Is that a shadow or what? It seems to be about three or four feet out from this wall."

Muhammad sprang into action and grabbed an air hammer that had been lying on the floor of the borehole. The air compressor was still on, and he hastily began chipping ninety degrees to the right side of the tunnel wall directly toward the dark shadow. Matt, and then Jim, took their turns manning the heavy hammer, and after about thirty minutes, they had chipped out a hole thirty inches in diameter and forty-eight inches deep. Exposed about eye level was the end of a huge, heavy beam. The wood was very old, and the end was badly cracked.

Matt crawled back into the round hole and touched the end of the wood. It was still quite solid. Excitedly, he reached into his pocket and took out a tape measure and measured the end at twenty inches wide and twelve inches high. He was elated just to touch the end of this large piece of wood that would not normally be in this ice at this elevation on this barren mountain. He knew it had to be a piece of the ark.

As soon as he crawled out of the hole, Ann said, "Boost me up, Matt. I want to see it."

Matt bent over and linked his fingers, forming a step for Ann. She put her foot in Matt's hands and he raised her up to the hole, and she crawled back far enough to reach out and put her hands on the edge of the large piece of wood. Tears filled her eyes.

After the two engineers and Jim had each had their turn at lying on their stomachs and reaching in to touch the end of the beam, Matt sent for the film crew. They filmed what had been discovered. Everyone was highly emotional. After all this time and effort, to finally find something just seemed to be what they needed. They could tell from seeing the end of the beam that it had substance, and they could see it did extend away from them back into the ice, but they couldn't tell how far. Maybe it was only three or four feet long, but Matt hoped it was much longer.

Matt then pointed out, "We can't keep crawling on our stomachs back into the hole to chip alongside the beam. We must extract the beam the proper and safe way. Tomorrow morning we will have the miners enlarge the tunnel wall enough to stand up in and shore it up as they go. Remember there is over thirty feet of ice bearing down on the top of this. The miners will have to extract the beam tomorrow. They've already worked a long, hard day."

As they all walked back out of the tunnel and onto the floor of the borehole, there stood the four miners, all geared up and waiting to go into the tunnel. Matt knew he couldn't communicate with them, so he turned to Muhammad, who shrugged and said, "When word spread through the complex that we had found some wood in the ice, I had to keep everyone back up on top or the entire crew would have been down here with us, including the cooks and dishwashers. When the miners heard about it, they offered to extract the beam. They told me not to worry about any overtime pay. They are as excited as everyone else and want to see the beam. They also want to make sure the tunnel is properly shored up and safe."

So the miners went in, and four hours later they brought out the very heavy, hand-hewn beam, sixteen feet and ten inches long. It was somewhat warped and twisted but not rotten. The beam was covered with a heavy coating on all four sides except for a strip on the twenty inch side where it had been attached to another piece. Matt said to Jim, "It's covered in pitch. It not only kept the water out but preserved the wood."

As they all marveled at this large piece of the ark, Matt said, "I've always wondered why Noah was told to build the ark and cover it inside and outside with pitch. Covering it outside would seal it so it wouldn't leak, but why would they take on the enormous task of also covering the entire inside of the ark with pitch? Now we know. It was to preserve the wood, the perfect plan. The ark was covered in pitch inside as well as outside and then buried in the ice. This had to be to preserve it."

The hand-hewn beam had four round holes on one end with dowels still in the holes. The other end was splintered and had been broken off. It was longer than the diameter of the borehole, and part of it still lay in the tunnel. A lot of ice had been chipped out to allow the beam to turn ninety degrees and come out the original tunnel into the borehole. There was a safety fence anchored in the ice at the top around the borehole to keep anyone from accidentally falling in. Behind that barrier were all the rest of the workers, anxious to see the beam.

Using the overhead electric wench, they hauled the heavy beam to the surface where everyone had a chance to touch it and marvel at the hand-hewn surface. They all knew it had to be a piece of Noah's ark. What else could it be?

As Ann held the light so everyone could see the wood clearly, they all jumped up and down and shouted, "I knew we'd find something!" Everyone, including the Turkish engineers, hugged each other repeatedly. It was such a great reward to have finally found a large piece of the ark of Noah.

The next morning as Matt, Ann, Jim, Muhammad, and Adem were eating breakfast, Matt told them some of his thoughts. "It seems like the ark has been purposely hidden and preserved until now, when there seems to be such brutality and violence in the world."

Ann answered, "I agree, Matt. It sure appears that the ark was purposely preserved."

Jim said, "Just read the paper each day or listen to CNN. There's no doubt that the murders, rapes, and killing of innocent people are at an all-time high."

"But on the other hand," Muhammad commented, "the majority of human beings throughout the world are basically good and oftentimes wonderful, helpful, giving, and loving people."

"I don't know the answers to the mystery," Jim exclaimed, "but I sure hope finding the large piece of wood means we're getting close to finding the ark."

Adem said, "It has to be a piece of the top perimeter wall, don't you think, Dr. Lane?"

"Yes," Matt replied.

Suddenly, they felt a slight tremor. It only lasted a couple of seconds. All conversation stopped. The entire cafeteria became quiet. Everyone waited. Many of the workers showed signs of fear and panic. Several seconds passed before the workers began to relax, and conversation slowly resumed.

Muhammad spoke. "I guess that was just a little reminder of what can happen on this mountain."

"You mean an earthquake?" Jim asked.

"Yes," Muhammad replied. "This is very unnerving for the workers. Hopefully that won't affect us getting our crew back next spring."

Muhammad whispered, "Are you all familiar with the big earthquake that occurred on this mountain?"

"Yes, we have read about it," Ann confirmed, "but tell us the story anyway."

"Well, it happened in 1840. A very large earthquake occurred right here on Mount Ararat. The quake was so devastating it completely destroyed a large monastery and an entire village. Many people died in that quake. It was centered at the Ahora Gorge. The complex we're in right now is just the few thousand yards up the ice above the Ahora Gorge."

As Muhammad spoke, a small crowd had gathered to listen. Matt could see the fear in the eyes of the Turkish men. He knew they were thinking that maybe being up here on the slick ice that sloped down to the Ahora Gorge in an earthquake was not such a good idea. Maybe Allah didn't want them to find the ark after all. Everyone knew a strong earthquake in their present location could easily destroy the project and kill them all.

Muhammad, recognizing the concern of the workers, added, "But the mountain has slight tremors like the one we just felt quite often. I'm surprised we haven't felt them before. We probably won't have another big one for a hundred years. Meanwhile, the pay is very good, and it will be wonderful when we discover the ark."

Slowly, the men began to relax and disperse.

The next day they received a warning that a major winter storm was coming, and they were ordered by the Turkish government to quickly secure the site and be off the mountain within twenty-four hours.

The entire project had been enclosed with a twelve-foot tall, chain-link fence with security wire on top. It was anchored in the ice and had signs in several languages every ten yards, stating, "Keep out! Property of the Turkish Government."

Before the twenty-four hours were up, the site was secured and abandoned until spring. The helicopters could still fly but not from the main landing site. They used snowmobiles to track across the glacier to the secondary landing site. There the snowmobiles were left in the auxiliary dome, which was securely anchored in the ice.

The large wooden beam was carefully packaged and shipped to a laboratory in Ankara. There they would protect the wood and carbon-date it.

Before they left the mountain, Matt gathered his key personnel — Jim, Ann, Muhammad, and Adem — for one last meeting. "Finding that wooden beam was really timely. If we had not found anything at all, Muhammad and I were both aware there was a good chance the project would not continue in the spring. It's hard to imagine how a hand-hewn, old wooden beam that size could have been on this mountain, this high up, if it didn't come from the ark, but anything is possible. It could even be some other old artifact that had to be jettisoned from an aircraft maybe fifty years ago as it was trying to gain enough altitude to get over the mountain. Let's all hope the carbon dating doesn't reveal it is only a few hundred years old. If it's not found to be around five thousand years old, we may have a real problem."

Soon everyone was back in Dogubayazit. The entire crew had dinner together. The next morning they said their good-byes and departed just before the first real winter storm hit the mountain.

Chapter Twenty-Five

Matt, Ann, and Jim left Mount Ararat on a Thursday, and by Saturday all three were back home in Washington, D.C.

One afternoon, they were all in Ira's office recapping their adventure on the mountain when Ira's secretary brought in a large envelope and put it on his desk. "Maybe this is the report you have so anxiously been waiting for," she said as she exited the room, closing the door behind her.

All conversation stopped in anticipation. Ira sat down behind his desk, facing them and started to open the envelope. "This does look like what we have been waiting for. It was mailed from Turkey. Hopefully it is the results of the carbon-dating tests on the two pieces of wood you brought down from the mountain — the huge beam and the small piece Ann found when she and Jim fell into the crevasse."

"Don't remind me of that day," Ann said.

They all held their breath as Ira opened the inner envelope.

"Come on, Ira. What does it say?" Matt said.

Ira continued to read for a few seconds. Then his expression turned into a big grin. "Both pieces are the same type of wood and both are well over five thousand years old. Looks like you might have an ark on your hands!"

Tears welled up in Ann's eyes as she reached out with both arms and gave Matt a big hug. "Congratulations, Matt."

"Congratulations to you, Ann. We never would have found it without your photos," Matt pulled Ann from the chair and started waltzing around the room.

They were all so excited they couldn't stop talking about the good news. "To Noah's ark," Matt said as he raised his cup in a toast. "May we find the ark in the spring."

"We will find it this spring!" Jim replied as they cheered.

When Jim and Ann had arrived back on the mountain, there had been no hint of them having a romantic relationship. Of course, they had been extremely busy, and Jim and Ann's visit to the site had been cut short because of the storm. They had all three been the same as they were in Russia, serious but still laughing. Matt assumed they had probably agreed not to disclose their relationship until they were back in D.C. He was bracing himself for the news so he could appear to be happy for them.

Ann had said she would have to go back to her job right away and would probably be pretty busy for a while. Matt knew Ira was planning to ask her if she would be interested in working for him. But Ira had not yet approached her, knowing she was way behind at her job by now, and she was concerned. He knew if she left the Smithsonian, she would want to leave on good terms.

It was a Wednesday evening. At seven, Jim called Matt at home and asked if he was going to be home all evening. Matt confirmed that he was. Jim said he wanted to talk to him and would be over in about thirty minutes.

When Jim arrived, Matt offered him a drink or some coffee. "No, I'm good. I just want to run something by you."

"Okay," Matt said. "What is it?"

"I was in Ira's office this afternoon, and he wants me to fly to Borneo tomorrow. Seems some new ruins have been discovered back in the rain forest, and he wants me to scout around and see if it would be worthwhile to send you and me backpacking. I guess the ruins are a long way from the nearest major city with only paths, no roads. When I get there, I'm supposed to gather as much information as I can about the ruins — where they are, when they were built, and if any other archaeologist has already been there. If I need to, I'll rent a small plane and fly out over the area and get some idea about how hard it would be to pack in there. I should be back in a couple of weeks. Ira said you couldn't go because he wants your written reports on the ark project."

"Borneo! Wow! We've never been there."

"I know. I wish you were coming."

"Well, I would much rather be going with you than getting all the reports turned in, but you know how Ira is about his paperwork."

"How well I know. But don't worry, buddy. If this turns out to be something worth investigating we'll be backpacking again on another treasure hunt. I just wanted to let you know where I'll be for the next couple of weeks. Get that paperwork done so we can leave if this pans out. This could last a few weeks and help occupy our time till spring. If we go, maybe Ann could go with us."

"Yeah, maybe," Matt muttered.

"By the way, Ann and I had dinner together a few times and caught some movies while we were back healing our wounds. I didn't think you would mind. It's okay with you, isn't it, Matt? She really is quite a lady."

Even though Matt had prepared himself to hear even more than they had just dated, he found himself saying, "No, why would I mind? I mean, yes, she is a great gal."

"Well, when you didn't date her after we got back from Russia, I just assumed you only wanted to remain good friends with her. Even though we were in pain when we had to leave Turkey the first time, we both enjoyed being together on the long flight back. We had a lot of laughs. At least, I enjoyed the trip, and I think she did, too. Anyway, I asked her if she'd like to go to a movie when we got home, and she said yes, and that's how it started. Are you sure it's okay? You don't mind? 'Cause if it's a problem, let me know. I mean, we've been friends a long time."

It's no problem," Matt said, but with a big lump in his throat.

"Okay, then. See you in a couple of weeks."

Matt watched the tail lights of Jim's Jaguar disappear down the drive and out the gate. As he walked back into the house, he couldn't believe how he felt. He had hurt so badly for the last several weeks, but deep inside he had hoped he was wrong. Now he knew he had been right. Matt slumped on the couch in front of the fire, his hands shaking.

Charlotte came in. "Are you all right, Matthew?"

"Yes, Charlotte, I'm fine," he said, hoping in the dim light she hadn't seen the tears in his eyes.

Get a hold of yourself, Matt. You're a grown man, thirty-one years old. You don't cry. You never cry. You have hardly shed a tear since your mother died.

* * * * *

Ann had been working long hours trying to catch up at the Smithsonian. She took her shower and slipped into bed. It was ten on a Friday night, but she couldn't sleep. She couldn't understand why he hadn't called her. Had she said something or done something to offend him? Maybe she just wasn't his type.

On the flight back from Turkey, the three of them were seated just like the flight to Russia — she in the middle, Jim on the aisle, and Matt by the window. They were so happy about their discovery. They were so close to finding the ark now. Surely within a short time next spring, they would find it.

Johns picked them up at the airport, and they dropped her off first. It was late. Jim walked her to her door. Matt stayed in the car and was fidgeting with his briefcase. He looked up at her and smiled. "See you later, Ann."

She felt sure, now that they were home, he would call her. The least he could do was phone her as a friend would. Tears welled up in her eyes. Didn't he know how she felt about him? She really couldn't show much affection on the mountain. She knew that would be inappropriate, but now they were home. She just couldn't stop thinking about him. She longed for him to just hold her hand, hold her close while they were dancing, anything, but he hadn't even called. Ann drifted off to sleep.

* * * * *

Matt picked her up for their date; then they were dancing. The orchestra was playing "The Way You Look Tonight." Just being in his arms was thrilling, like a dream come true!

Suddenly she was wide awake. Then she realized it was only a dream. As she lay there, tears wet her cheeks. She knew she had to get over him. If Matt cared at all, he surely would have called her by now. He could've called to see how she was doing, if her leg still hurt, or to talk about next spring.

I guess if Jim wants to date me again when he gets back, I'll go. What the heck! He's a great guy!

* * * * *

A week later, Ira notified Matt that he had heard from Jim. The Borneo project would have to be put on hold for now, and Jim would be back in a few days. Matt couldn't concentrate. He kept telling himself he was acting like a schoolboy with a crush, but he knew his feelings were a whole lot deeper than that. Everything seemed so wrong, so out of control. He had always been in charge of every thought, every emotion. Now his life was in turmoil. Ann consumed his every thought. He had to tell her how he felt no matter what the outcome might be.

It was dark when Matt stopped the Mercedes in front of her townhouse. His headlights turned off automatically, but he just sat there listening to the rain on the roof.

The street was quiet. No one else was around. Matt had not realized it was so late, but through the falling rain he could see a light in her window. He grabbed the umbrella off the passenger's seat and started up the walk toward her front door. Suddenly it started to pour; a lightning bolt lit up the entire area followed by a loud clap of thunder.

He stood in the dark under the cover of the entry way. *What should I say? Should I have called her first?*

He wanted so much to believe that Ann felt the same way about him as he felt about her. Maybe he had only imagined it, but at times Ann seemed to make excuses to be close to him. Then again, what if she was really in love with Jim?

How does this look — me knocking on her door, trying to steal her away from Jim while he is out of town? I can't betray my best friend. Jim trusts me.

It was still raining hard as Matt got back in his car and drove away.

Chapter Twenty-Six

Somewhere in Turkey

Abdul was dreaming when the ringing of the phone by his bed woke him up. He sat up in the small, sparsely furnished room. He turned the lamp on as he listened to the voice on the other end.

"Listen carefully. A problem may develop in the near future, and it's imperative that you be prepared to handle it if the need should arise."

"What kind of a problem?" The forty-three-year-old Abdul asked. He was six-foot-two, with a husky build. His face was clean-shaven except for a heavy mustache. A scar from a knife wound ran vertically in front of his left ear. His eyes, hair, and complexion were dark.

Abdul listened intently as he sat on the edge of his military-style bed. His small bedroom was the only sleeping quarter in this wood-framed building. The larger room was his office. Through the open blinds, he could see the yard light illuminating the single-story dormitory where twelve men slept. A dog was barking in the background.

There were three more buildings in the small complex, all within sight of his office. One was a tent-type mess hall, and another tent contained latrines and showers.

The third building next to his office was a large metal building. It held the secret as to why they were there in this remote area. Here were stored the weapons of war that they delivered to wherever they were instructed. It also housed his helicopter.

The complex was well-hidden in a heavily wooded area up a canyon. The only road into the dead-end canyon passed through a sheep farm. The organization Abdul worked for owned the property. No one who didn't belong here got through the gates.

Abdul knew his camp was just one of many places the organization he worked for had established throughout the Middle East. This operation was in eastern Turkey, not far from Mount Ararat.

The voice on the line continued. "I'll just state the facts as I have been instructed to do. Three American archaeologists backed by the Turkish government have erected a large complex on Mount Ararat. They're trying to keep their covert actions secret by stating they are studying the ice movement. This is a lie! We have an informant within the government. This is another search for Noah's ark."

"Why is anyone concerned? There is no ark on Ararat. If there ever was, it was ground to sawdust by the glacier a thousand years ago."

"Don't interrupt. Just listen. The site has been abandoned until spring. Our informant says he has seen photographs that were taken of the ark in 1916 by the Russian army. They have already found a large beam from the ark. When they continue the search in the spring, we will have an informant among the workers. If the ark should actually be discovered, the informant's job will be to immediately call you and then disable the radio before they can inform anyone of the discovery. Your job will be to destroy anything they found and anyone who saw it."

"You mean if Noah's ark is actually found, they want me to destroy it? Why?"

"Why should this surprise you? Think about it. You and I are paid very well. The organization we work for is very powerful. They have people planted in governments all over the world. They keep things stirred up. You see what I mean, Abdul? They help cause unrest. Then they sell arms to small factions throughout the world. Our employer doesn't want peace on earth. They want war on earth. If the world learns Noah's ark has actually been discovered on Mount Ararat, that may lead to people reading and believing in the Quran and the Bible. People may actually begin to believe it is wrong to kill another human. It's too late for us, Abdul. That's how we make our living, or have you forgotten? You may not know this, but our employers are atheists. They don't believe in the Quran or the Bible, and they don't want any one else believing in them. They don't want anyone finding proof that the story of Noah and the ark are true. News of that magnitude could be the very thing that would bring an era of peace. Our employers don't want peace. To quote them, 'Peace is bad for business!' The ark cannot be discovered. Do you understand? It's your job to see that it isn't. You understand me, Abdul?"

"Yes, sir." He shivered as he replied.

"It will be an easy mission for you. There are a few unarmed civilians up there, plus three security guards who are armed only with pistols. They guard the main gate and are not expecting any problems. There is but one form of communication, a short-wave radio. It will already be disabled when you arrive. I will call you and keep you informed as I learn more details. Just be sure you're ready to move and move quickly if the need arises."

When he hung up the phone, Abdul was both angry and excited. He began pacing the floor. Jumbled thoughts went through his mind.

He knew the people he worked for lived their lavish lifestyle because there was always a war or conflict somewhere in the world. He didn't have to be told all of this and treated like an imbecile. Abdul didn't know who the people were who owned the corporation he worked for. His instructions and his lucrative paychecks were always delivered by courier. He did know, however, that they made a lot of money selling arms.

His job had always been to procure and deliver the weapons where and when he was directed. He and those who worked for him delivered everything from assault rifles to rocket launchers, often to opposing sides of the conflict.

He doubted that finding Noah's ark was going to change that for any extended length of time. However, he reasoned, *I don't need anything holding up my paychecks. I have too many expensive habits. I have to start preparing for this mission, and we must be ready.*

Exactly how many people were on the mountain? Did they really not have any weapons? What about satellite phones? Did they really have only one radio for communication from the mountain?

Abdul was deep in thought as he lay back down. Staring at the ceiling, he would sleep no more tonight.

Chapter Twenty-Seven

Spring on Mount Ararat

The weather was warming a little. The morning sun was shimmering brightly on the snow.

Matt helped the workers remove a few rocks that had fallen from the rocky peaks above during the long cold winter. They had bounced across the ice and hit the structure, but no major damage had occurred. When that task was finished, Matt went inside. Muhammad, Jim, and the electrical engineer, Adem, had just returned from checking the generators.

Matt directed, "Inform the crew we are going to relocate the main search structure. Have them start disassembling the heaters. The company that installed the structures will arrive at ten in the morning to begin the move. We'll be really busy for the next two weeks. Then we can start the search again. The enclosed walkway between the main structure and the sleeping dome will have to be extended also."

As Matt worked with the men, he was having some doubts. It had been bothering him for some time. First, he felt privileged that the Turkish government had invited the three of them back to continue the ark search. After all, Matt thought, the Turkish engineers now have the photos and could have just continued the search themselves.

Matt was still worried that during these past years, some summers were quite warm. The ark could have completely thawed out, fell apart, and now be just a heap of wood at the very bottom of the glacier, in which case they would probably never find it.

He stopped what he was doing. Matt wondered if that might also be why they were invited to be in charge — someone to blame if they were never able to find it, a scapegoat. If the Turks took over the search totally without the Americans and were unable to find the ark, rumor would be that the Americans could have found it.

But Matt didn't have time for politics. He was sure the ark was there. He was still in charge, and together, God willing of course, they were going to find it.

After two weeks, they had moved the main enclosure plus the generators and fuel tanks sixty-four feet (approximately twenty meters) east in the direction where they had found the beam last fall, and they had extended the covered walkway to the sleeping dome. Then in the center of the large structure, they started another fourteen-foot-diameter borehole.

Matt was determined to speed up the search. After confirming with the electrical engineer that they wouldn't need another generator, he ordered two more of the specially designed electric ice-melting machines, two more pumps, and more fire hoses to pump the ice water out of the boreholes. He hired more workers and started two more boreholes, each one hundred feet in opposite directions, directly below the overhead track that ran the length of the building. Within thirty days, all three boreholes were approximately thirty feet deep. Every twenty-four hours, they could melt about one foot of the ice in each hole.

It gave all the workers a foreboding feeling to be down in those fourteen-foot-diameter holes more than twice as deep as they were in width. The ice was slick and polished like glass.

Each evening after dinner, most everyone except the crews operating the heaters in the three boreholes and those sleeping who would soon relieve them, would gather around the table where Matt, Jim, Ann, Muhammad, and Adem were sitting and listen to the stories each would tell. Even the dishwashers would rush to get the kitchen cleaned up so they could be there. The round-the-clock pit crews rotated their shifts, so they only had to miss the get-togethers every third evening. Many of the Turkish crew had studied English the past winter so they could understand more of what was said, but Adem and Muhammad translated when necessary.

Everyone enjoyed this special time. They drank coffee, ate dessert, and listened to whomever wanted to tell a story.

They had copies of the ark photographs, and they would pass them around, each man studying the details of the ark. They especially enjoyed the stories Matt and Jim told about the trip to Iraq and the cave. They laughed about the story of the lion. They were in awe when Ann told about her grandmother, the secret room, the hidden photographs, and Yuri accidentally drowning. Hands would raise, and they would very politely ask questions.

After a while, Mohammed would say, "We'll talk some more after dinner tomorrow night." The young Turks didn't want to see the evenings end, but they did have the next night to look forward to.

One night in the group meeting after dinner, Ann said, "I just think it is so strange that out of the many photographs people claim to have taken of the ark over the last fifty or sixty years, none can be found, except these that we have."

The young Turks were listening intently.

"For example," Ann continued, "I have read that during World War II, the ark was spotted from the air, protruding from the ice. Many pilots from several different countries apparently flew over it and took pictures. Even photographers for the U.S. military newspaper, *Stars and Stripes*, took photographs from the air and printed them in the newspaper. Thousands of young soldiers, sailors, marines, and air force personnel saw the pictures and read the story, but apparently no one saved even one copy of the article. And get this, the publisher of the newspaper can't even find that issue in its archives."

The crowd of men around Ann shook their heads. Shrugging his shoulders one of the workers said, "It seems impossible they can't find even one copy."

"Another of these stories that has always fascinated me," Matt chimed in, "was about an American oil executive. He was riding in a company helicopter over Mount Ararat when they saw the ark. The oil man took a whole roll of film and showed the pictures to a lot of people who remembered seeing them. Some said they could even make out the planking on the side of the vessel. But, mysteriously, the man was murdered, and the pictures were stolen and have never been seen again."

Jim said, "It's like Allah wasn't ready for the ark to be shown to the world yet."

One of the young Turkish cooks stood up and said loudly in broken English, "But he is ready now because we have the pictures."

"Yes," Matt shouted to everyone, "and we're going to find the ark!"

Everyone cheered.

After the storytelling ended, Matt saw Jim head out to the borehole area and take the cage down to the bottom of one of the boreholes with Muhammad. Jim had taken over a lot of the work Matt had been burdened with, and Jim and Muhammad had become good friends.

Oftentimes, Ann would be right down in the borehole with the crew, laughing, joking, keeping up morale, and working. She was willing to do anything to speed up the search, from helping the crew run the ice-melting heaters to shoveling snow that had blown onto the heliport. She was also a great help to Muhammad with keeping the records up to date and properly filed.

Every man up there seemed to respect her, and they loved it when she would engage in conversation with them in their native language.

Matt put on his parka and went outside. He often went out by himself after the storytelling just to look at the sky so full of stars and to see the twinkle of lights way off in the distance at the base of the mountain. It was quiet, peaceful, and he could clear his head.

All winter he had deliberately avoided being alone with Ann. They had been together at the group get-togethers back in Washington, Christmas parties, and birthdays. But when he visited Jim, he took Ira or Charlotte and Johns with him, just in case Ann was there. He didn't want to be alone with her. He hoped his feelings for her would finally fade away. He didn't want to care about her, to think about her or how she looked, how she smiled. He felt so foolish. Ann had never really shown that she had any feelings for him, so why couldn't he just accept that?

He knew lots of other girls. Why couldn't he transfer these feelings to one of them? He knew he couldn't. He didn't understand why, but he just couldn't. Anyway, he was a good actor. No one knew how he felt about Ann, and no one ever would.

Matt was so deep in thought he didn't hear the door open and close.

Suddenly someone was standing beside him. Startled, he turned and looked at Ann, her face bathed in the moonlight and outlined by her dark hair and her parka. She didn't smile. She just looked at him.

"Hi, Ann. I didn't hear you come out."

"Can I talk to you, Matt?"

"Of course, anytime."

"This is hard for me." Ann lowered her eyes and turned her face away. *Was that a tear in her eye?* "What is it, Ann?"

"How do you get someone you really care about to care for you?"

"I don't understand. Is it Jim? I know Jim cares for you. Did you two have some kind of a disagreement?"

"I'm not talking about Jim," Ann said as she turned toward Matt. "I'm talking about you."

Matt was shocked. His heart was racing. "But what about Jim?" he said, cursing himself for such a stupid remark. What if she meant she loved Jim, but was concerned about his friendship?

"It's never been Jim. It's always been you. I can't help it. I love you, Matt. I can't hide it any longer."

Totally surprised, Matt turned to look at her. Then he stammered, "I can't believe you're telling me this."

Ann held her breath, not knowing how Matt felt.

Then he turned his face away and said, "If you only knew, Ann. If you only knew."

"What, Matt? If I only knew what?"

He turned to face her again as he said, "I love you too, Ann."

"You do? Are you sure?"

"Yes, I'm sure. I've never been more sure of anything." With a lump in his throat, he took her in his arms in the moonlight on top of Mount Ararat. Then Matt kissed her, and they held each other for a long time.

When Matt talked to Jim in private that night, Jim said, "I'm genuinely happy for you, Matt. By the way, there was one little thing I forgot to tell you when I confessed Ann and I had gone out a few times. I should have told you that all she ever wanted to talk about was you. I was convinced that I could win her over, so I planned to continue dating her since you didn't seem interested. A couple of months ago, I realized that she was never going to be more than a good friend. I suggested that I tell you how she felt about you, but she wouldn't let me. I'm really glad for you, Matt. Ann is a prize any man would love to win."

Chapter Twenty-Eight

It was about 7:30 p.m. It had just gotten dark outside. Matt, Ann, Jim, Muhammad, and Adem, plus several key personnel, had just finished dinner and were all gathered around a large table in the dining hall. They were discussing the day's progress. Everyone was getting concerned. They still had not encountered even another piece of wood. Matt never mentioned his fear that the ark had finally just collapsed, but he was afraid they were all beginning to think of that same possibility.

As they were talking, Matt happened to notice the coffee in his cup vibrate a little. He thought at first it was just because people were bumping the table. The conversation continued, but Matt was watching and listening. He couldn't put his finger on it, but something wasn't right. He couldn't hear anything wrong, only the steady hum of the generators. It sounded like the big Caterpillar engines were running smoothly, nothing out of balance with them that would cause vibration.

Then he noticed it again. Some ripples in the coffee in his cup. Matt held up his hand, and the conversation stopped. All eyes were on Matthew.

"What's wrong?" someone questioned.

"Everyone be really still for a second and look at any coffee in a cup or water in your glass. Don't touch the table." All eyes went to any liquid in a glass or cup on the table.

Muhammad spoke. "I don't see anything. It doesn't feel like a tremor."

"Well, something is wrong, Muhammad. Let's get everyone out of the boreholes."

Neither Jim nor Muhammad had noticed anything wrong, but obviously Matt had. They jumped up with three others who had been standing around the tables, rushed out through the cafeteria doors and out on to the ice, racing for the boreholes. Within ten minutes, everyone was out of the boreholes and in the cafeteria. A few workers were still in the other two buildings sleeping or showering, getting ready for their shift. They were not aware of what was happening.

The men gathering around Matt were apprehensive, becoming frightened. One of the Turkish workers inquired, "What's going on Mr. Matt? Is there going to be an earthquake?"

The coffee and water were now still. "I don't know, but a few minutes ago my coffee was dancing by itself in my cup. It only lasted a few seconds. I think it was a light tremor."

"You mean like in an earthquake, Mr. Matt?" someone else quizzed.

"Yes, but it's gone now. No, there — there it is again!"

Everyone standing leaned in over those sitting to observe the now obvious movement of the liquid. They couldn't feel anything under their feet or from the tables.

Quickly Matt commanded, "Let's get everyone out of the kitchen and dining room. It's probably just another slight tremor, but I'd rather not take any chances."

Matt got up and quickly moved to the kitchen to help everyone evacuate and to make sure the cooking equipment was off. Then the floor started to shake.

Matt yelled, "Don't panic! Just grab your coats and calmly leave the cafeteria!"

Everyone headed for the only door at once. Panic was setting in.

"Slow down," Matt directed. "Let's not trample anyone. Calmly go down to the sleeping quarters."

Without delay, everyone left the cafeteria and the storage area. Jim and Muhammad checked to make sure everyone was out. Within minutes, they were all outside the cafeteria on the walkway that led down to the entrance to the sleeping quarters. They could feel the ice vibrating slightly under their feet and were starting to panic again. Abruptly the vibration stopped.

There were twenty some men gathered around Matt, Jim, Ann, and the two Turkish engineers all asking, "What was that? Another earthquake maybe?"

Someone questioned, "Is it over?"

Muhammad answered, "Yes, I believe it was a small earthquake. It's probably over, but let's do as Matt said and calmly walk to the sleeping quarters."

Matt took Ann by the hand. "Stay close to me."

She grabbed his arm with her other hand. "I'm not about to let you go."

Matt and Jim took a quick head count and started to walk down the grating.

The workers were excitedly talking as they scurried down the twelve-foot-wide grating close to the wall of the main structure toward the double doors that would lead them to the next dome. The lights of the main building were shining brightly, reflecting across the slick ice surface between the three boreholes and the grating they were on. The lights still on in the boreholes were reflecting up, causing a spotlight to show three large round circles on the fabric above. Next to each hole was a steel cage sitting on the ice that had just been used to bring the crews up to the surface. Each cage was attached to a cable at the top that led to the overhead track.

Matt was in the lead. *We really don't need an earthquake. A bad quake could split the ice and swallow the entire complex and everyone in it.* He tried to walk faster to push the group along.

Suddenly, before they were halfway to the entrance, the door from the sleeping quarters burst open. Out poured ten men. They were putting on their coats and in a panicked state all speaking Turkish. They rushed up the grating to meet Matt. When they reached the main group, they abruptly stopped.

They were pleading with Muhammad. "Wouldn't we be safer in this room with the heavy steel frame work?" Muhammad had to interpret their concerns to Matt.

Matt answered, "Tell them no. We will be safer in the sleeping quarters if there is a strong earthquake."

Matt couldn't move at all with this crowd pressing up against him. He didn't want to panic these men anymore than they already were, but he wanted to get everyone away from the boreholes just in case they really did have a big quake. Matt thought even though the tremors had stopped, something just didn't feel right.

They were moving too slowly as they walked. Finally, Matt told Muhammad to tell them that the three boreholes had weakened the ice in this room. If there was a strong earthquake, the ice could crack open a fissure line right through those boreholes. This building and the overhead crane could collapse.

Just as Muhammad finished translating, the grating started to gyrate again. The crowd panicked, started running wild-eyed, screaming and yelling, down the grating.

Matt, Jim, and Muhammad yelled, "Don't panic!" but the workers were shaking with fear. Some slipped and fell while others toppled over them.

Now that he could move, Matt started walking quickly down the grating with Ann. He tried to spot Jim but couldn't see him in the melee. The ice under the grating was shaking hard now. The vertical aluminum beams that met at the top of the structure, supporting all the weight, were moving back and forth violently, bending the braces that spaced them. The fabric covering began to be stretched tight and then released and then stretched again, causing a loud, popping sound. The hanging lights swung wildly. Then with one violent action, everyone was thrown down to the grating. Matt tried to stand up again, but it was impossible. There was grinding of metal on metal. Ann was on her knees, huddled in a ball. Matt threw himself over her, trying to protect her, holding her tight as she shook in fear, squeezing his arm. Then, almost in unison, the three steel cages fell into the boreholes, adding even more weight to the structure above them. The cages, now suspended, were swinging back and forth, banging on the sides of the boreholes.

A loud roar started building. It seemed to be coming from under the ice. The sound got louder and louder, like a giant wild beast.

Everyone was still down on the grating. They could not stand up. No one had gotten to the sleeping quarters.

Matt was afraid for everyone, especially Ann and Jim. He raised his head and searched around the crowd for Jim, Muhammad, and Adem. He could not locate them in this sea of men, all together on their knees or lying on their sides in a tight ball. He looked back down at Ann. Movement under the grating caught his eye. Fear gripped his whole being. The ice was parting right under the grating they were on.

In only a few seconds, it went from a couple of inches to a foot wide and was still growing wider. It was a jagged fissure running right down the center of the walkway. Everyone could hear it cracking under them. Ann saw it under her. She squeezed Matt's arm harder and screamed, "Look, Matt!"

"I see it!" Matt shouted back.

It was now three feet wide and growing wider. It looked like it was going to keep widening until the twelve-foot wide grating and everyone on it fell to their deaths.

Matt couldn't move one way or another with everyone crowding them so tightly, and all the while the deafening roar got louder, and the structure shook so hard Matt was sure it would collapse in on them.

He raised his head and tried to stand but still could not. The grating under him was shaking too violently. He yelled as loud as he could. "Everyone crawl to the outside of the grating! Crawl to the outside of the grating!"

No one moved. They either didn't understand his English, or they were too afraid to move.

Then he heard Muhammad yell at everyone in their native tongue. He also heard Jim shouting, "Crawl to the outside of the grating!"

Still no one moved. Many of the men were praying.

The fast-widening fissure was now six feet wide and growing wider. Matt's heart was in his throat. He felt responsible for all these people. He felt helpless, but he was not going to give up. *Ann and I are not going to go down with this grating, even if I have to carry her over all these men. We are not going to die like this!*

The loud roar continued, ascending to a deafening scream, and ended with the loudest crack of thunder Matt had ever heard. The sound was so loud it hurt his ears. It was more like an explosion. It came from the ice by the boreholes. Everyone felt the concussion as if a bomb had gone off. Then the shaking stopped, and the crevasse forming under them ceased to widen.

Matt and everyone else rose up and looked toward the boreholes. In the beam from the lights, there was a heavy mist of chipped ice particles drifting down like heavy snow. They stood up to see a twenty- to thirty-foot wide chasm running longer than the length of the structure right where the boreholes had been. The lights were still swinging wildly. The fissure under the grating was eight feet wide in some places. There was still a sound of ice cracking way down deep in the abyss. Everyone stood then but suddenly realized the grating was bending. They quickly jumped to the outside of the grating. No one uttered a sound. At that same moment, the lights went out.

Chapter Twenty-Nine

There was chaos as everyone started talking at once. It was pitch-black, and the workers were afraid to move in the dark for fear of falling into a crevasse. The entire earthquake probably lasted only a few minutes, but it felt like an hour.

Matt shouted, "Quiet! Everyone be quiet. I thought I heard someone calling for help."

Everyone was silent immediately. Then they all heard a faint, faraway voice screaming.

At first they couldn't tell where the voice was coming from. Then Matt determined the cry was from the far end, back up the slope toward the cafeteria.

They could not see anything in the pitch-blackness. Trying to stay calm, Matt inquired, "Does anyone have a flashlight?"

In the pandemonium, those who often carried flashlights had not remembered they even had a flashlight until Matt's words jarred their memory. Quickly one flashlight came on and then another. The light beams were moving back and forth in the direction of the voice, searching for the person calling for help.

Spotting some movement, they concentrated their flashlights on the side cafeteria wall. In the center of the beam of light, they saw a man's hand. Someone was holding onto the round leg of a metal storage rack with one hand, his body dangling above the chasm. The storage rack was attached to the outside wall of the cafeteria. The man was about ten feet back from the corner of the cafeteria wall.

"It looks like Basak!" someone yelled. "Hold on, Basak!"

Suddenly a third flashlight came on, and a young Turkish worker thrust it into Matt's hand. "Take mine, Mr. Matt."

After shining the light at Ann's feet to make sure she was standing on solid ice, he started running up the grating toward the man with Jim on his heels. Matt shouted as he ran, "Everyone, be careful where you step! Someone with a flashlight, find me a coil of rope. Look in that metal locker by the cafeteria door! More flashlights are in there too."

The first man who had turned his flashlight on held the light on the terrified man as Matt made his way to the edge of the chasm.

When Matt and Jim reached the side wall of the cafeteria, they saw it was going to be very difficult to rescue Basak. The edge of the deep crevasse paralleled the side of the cafeteria wall. Even if they could get the rope over to him, he couldn't catch it with one hand and put a loop over his head and down around his waist without slipping and falling to his death. Matt quickly concluded they couldn't throw him a rope from there effectively.

One of the workers had found rope and more flashlights. Jim got ahead of Matt when he stopped to get the rope. Jim, who now had a flashlight, shined the light on Basak, who was holding onto the ice-cold vertical leg of the storage rack with only his right hand. He was terrified and frantically trying to pull himself up. He was a big man and overweight, and, consequently, couldn't reach high enough to get a grip on anything else with his left hand. The other leg of the shelving was too far to his left. The bottom shelf was too high for him to reach. His left hand was flailing wildly, attempting to grab anything else. This hand was numb from holding onto the narrow ice ledge earlier. Tiring now, he again grabbed the shiny slick leg with one hand above the other. Everyone knew he couldn't hold on much longer.

Jim said to Matt, "I'll go get him. This guy is heavy, and you know I can still lift more than you can in the weight room."

Quickly he grabbed the rope and handed one end to two men, who took a loop around a heavy pump motor and held on. Jim then tied a loop around his waist, leaving about twelve extra feet of rope, and tied another loop in the loose end. As Jim edged his way out to the man, keeping his feet on the narrow ledge of ice between the chasm and the wall of the cafeteria, the two men let out the line. Jim crept out toward the man trying to reach the shelving, which was screwed to the wall of the cafeteria, without falling himself. The chasm was very deep and with the lights out Jim couldn't see the bottom. Basak was just below him.

As Jim got closer, he suddenly realized there was nothing under the front vertical shelving legs. The edge of the ice at that point cut back under the cafeteria wall. A footpad screwed into the bottom of the leg was all that kept Basak's hands from sliding down and off the slick, chrome leg.

Jim was holding onto the shelving to support himself when all at once the top row of sheet metal screws securing the rack to the cafeteria wall pulled out with three loud pops. The vertical legs started to bend, and the shelving leaned out over the abyss. Now, only three lower screws were holding the shelving to the wall, and they were starting to release. Time was running out.

Holding on to the precarious shelving with his right hand, Jim dangled the other end of the rope with the loop above Basak's left hand. Terrified beyond reason, he caught and jerked the rope, almost pulling Jim off the ledge. When he finally understood what Jim wanted him to do, he worked his hand through the loop, and, with help from Jim, he finally maneuvered the rope around his waist.

Still holding onto the shelving and hoping the lower screws would continue to hold, Jim tried to calm the panicked man while quickly taking up the slack.

They weren't going to die now, but if the shelving let go, the weight would pull Jim off the ledge. They would both have one heck of a wild ride and would probably be badly injured.

With all the flashlights concentrated on the rescue attempt, the men were pressing forward to see what was happening. Matt had to keep warning them to stay well back from the unstable edge of the ice.

Jim took up more slack in the rope by putting a loop over his shoulders. His boots with cleats gripped the narrow ice ledge. Slowly, with the man's hands gripping the ice edge and Jim holding most of his weight and leaning back against the wall, they crept the ten feet to the corner. Matt and another man pulled Jim and Basak to safety. Both men collapsed on the ice, exhausted. Matt and some of the men helped them move back from the edge.

Chapter Thirty

After the rescue, Matt instructed Muhammad and Adem, "Go outside. Make sure the security guard is all right. Then check the generators for damage and the diesel tanks for fuel leaks, but don't restart them until you hear from me."

They departed with a walkie-talkie.

Matt also directed the cooks to inspect the kitchen for gas leaks and anything electrical that could start a fire or shock someone when the generators were started.

"Ann, do you have a flashlight?"

"Yes, Matt."

"Can you take the stewards and walk carefully through the sleeping quarters, lounge area, latrine area, and showers?"

"No problem."

"Ann, go slowly and be careful, especially when you cross the grating. When you get in the covered walkway and the domes, watch for weak spots in the floor. Shine your lights up at the aluminum structure. Unplug anything that could cause an electrical short when the generators come on. Do you have your walkie-talkie?"

"Yes, and I have a green light on the battery."

"Good." Matt gave her a quick hug, not worried what the men standing near might think. Matt grinned, and Ann headed for the sleeping quarters with two workers. They all had flashlights.

Within thirty minutes, all reports were in. The kitchen had no gas leaks. The security guard was okay. Ann had reported the damage she found to Matt. Both structures were a mess. Furniture was tipped over, and lamps were smashed on the floor. A vending machine was lying on its back with broken glass on the face. The portable toilets had moved around, but none had tipped over.

Muhammad checked the short wave. He called the helicopter pilot and the mechanic at the heliport on the walkie-talkie. They were safe, and there was no damage to the helicopter or the two snowmobiles or Bobcat. Muhammad rushed back to join Matt to check the damage. No sense calling headquarters at Ankara until they knew the full extent of the damage.

All agreed it was safe, the generators were fired up, and the lights came back on.

Matt had already sent the cooks and kitchen workers to clean up the kitchen and cafeteria and make some coffee. Everyone else was sent to clean up the mess Ann had found. He and Muhammad made sure no one could go out on the ice or walk in the center of the grating.

All five — Matt, Jim, Ann, Muhammad, and Adem — were now surveying the chasm under the grating. There were still cracking sounds coming from the huge crevice through the boreholes.

Muhammad said the ice that fell had contacted water flowing under the glacier. He thought the cracking sound would stop soon, but it was not safe to go out there. The ice was very unstable. It could crack anywhere at any time.

Matt felt defeated — all of this time and money spent; all of the expensive heaters gone. The main structure was damaged, and the vertical supports on each end sagged into the abyss. The horizontal base tubing was badly bent on each end, and the fabric, stretched tight, was all that kept the structure standing.

The five went outside with flashlights to survey the chasm in the ice. It extended about ten meters beyond each end of the huge enclosure.

Much damage had occurred, but after Matt, Ann, Jim, and the engineers examined the inside and outside of the structure, they declared it safe enough for the people to enter. The bracing and fabric were still securely holding at each end. The strong fabric showed no sign of ripping.

Everyone except the core five had gone into the sleeping quarters as Matt and Muhammad had advised them to do. They were told, "Don't go out onto the ice, and if you come back into the main structure, walk on the outside of the grating, certainly not in the middle." Additional sections of grating had been brought in to cover critical walk areas, such as the entrance to the sleeping dome and the exit door on the end of the main structure.

Finally, Matt said, "I'm going out on the ice."

Mohammed and Jim tried to talk him out of it, but he simply said, "Please bring me a safety harness and a rope. I've got to see what it's going to take to get this operation started again."

Word quickly spread that Matt was going out on the ice, and quietly the entire crew came back out of the cafeteria and sleeping quarters.

Matt gave the end of the rope to Jim and two other husky men. They could see where the fissure had cut right through the center of the three boreholes, the weak spot in the ice. The men holding the rope stayed well back from the edge. Matt crept cautiously over to look into the huge, gaping canyon now in front of him in the ice. He did not trust the edge. It could break off under his weight, sending him plunging into the crevasse, even with the climbing rope attached. As he got to the edge, he looked down, trying to see the bottom. His eyes traveled down the face of the ice wall across from where he was. What he saw took his breath away.

About forty feet down, just below where the bottom of the boreholes had been, was the top edge of a long wooden wall. It was the outside wall of the ark. It extended some thirty feet straight down and, as far as he could see right and left. It was the most amazing sight he had ever seen. Strips of ice were still peeling off the wooden wall and falling in the abyss. As he turned around, the entire crew, including Ann, was facing him, anxiously waiting to hear what he could see.

"Can you see any of the equipment?" Jim asked.

"No," he shouted, "but I see something else! Don't rush over to this edge because it could break off, but I was just looking at one entire side of Noah's ark!"

Everyone stared at Matt in disbelief thinking he was kidding at first but soon realized he was serious. Wide-eyed, forgetting the danger and Matt's caution, some men started running to the edge. Matt quickly admonished them to stop as he slowly inched away from the precarious edge. In seconds the area was alive with singing and dancing as Matt, Jim, Ann, and the crew hugged each other. Some were even crying and others got down on their knees in prayer.

Matt noted the time to log in the book. It was 9:38 p.m.

Everyone was anxious to see the ark. Matt had the men bring over a large section of grating from up by the cafeteria. They extended it out and solidly anchored the narrow end away from the edge.

When Matt deemed it was safe, Ann was encouraged by the crew to be the next to see the ark. Secured with a safety harness and rope, she ventured out onto the ice grating. Overcome with emotion, she finally got to see what she had been dreaming about since she was twelve years old. She could hardly believe the actual ark was right below where she stood. Her eyes were fixed on the dark wood planking below her, imagining the men who attached that wood so long ago. The next to go out were Jim, Muhammad and Adem. After that, Matt allowed the rest of the crew to go two by two to the edge and view the ark. Matt insisted that each person be tied off with a rope attached to a safety harness. The film crew filmed everyone taking his or her turn seeing the ark. Then they filmed the amazing pictures that would soon be seen around the world, the side of Noah's ark now exposed in a wall of ice.

Digital cameras were snapping every time another person went out on the walkway. Ann hugged Matt and Jim again.

Matt, Jim, Ann, and Adem were helping the crew stay organized as they took turns. They had to caution the excited crew not to get careless and be sure those holding the ropes were ready in case someone fell into the crevasse.

Matt remarked, "What luck! The boreholes were centered directly over the vertical wall of the ark. This and the water flowing under the ice caused a weak area. That's why the ice cracked and fell away during the earthquake."

Matt, Ann, and Jim all stood and watched the excited men taking their turns viewing the ark. Some took turns over and over again. The film crew was filming it all.

Matt said, "This is amazing! Something I've dreamed about since I was a young boy."

Ann was still wiping the tears with her handkerchief.

Jim concurred. "What a sight! I was beginning to think we would never find it. I mean, I must admit, I knew it was there, but I was beginning to think it had collapsed, and the old wood had worked its way to the bottom."

Matt looked at Jim and chuckled. "I thought I was the only one thinking that. But isn't it a bit of a coincidence? An earthquake cracked the ice. I mean, what are the odds? A major earthquake right now? It's been over a hundred and seventy years since the last one."

"That's almost too coincidental," Jim said. "I think someone up above got tired of watching us search and not find it, even with all the clues that were given to us. Someone probably figured if we didn't get some help, we'd never be smart enough to find it." All three laughed.

"It was right under our noses all the time," Matt marveled.

"We just needed a little extra help," Ann said.

It was getting late. Everyone had gotten their fill of seeing the wall of the ark, and they were now drifting off to their sleeping quarters. Even Adem told them good night and left the ice.

Matt, Jim, and Ann went out the lower door to the outside. Standing at the end of the crevasse and looking back into the huge, gaping chasm under the lights of the structure, they could just make out a dark spot in the ice wall where the ark was buried. It was dark outside, but the moon hiding behind the clouds was bright. Every few minutes it would peek through the overcast and cast a halo around the clouds, lighting up the ice cap.

They discussed how to repair the damaged structure.

The three of them walked a few steps away from the structure and looked toward the valley below. A few twinkling lights could be seen each time the moon was covered by the clouds. A stiff breeze was beginning to blow, but it wasn't quite as cold as usual.

Matt moved closer to Ann, and she leaned against him. They all knew everything would now change on the mountain.

Matt said, "Soon this place will be crawling with officials from the Turkish government wanting to see the ark. I'll stall them a day or two. Right now it isn't safe. I'll call in a construction crew from Dogubayazit in the morning. We'll have to build a safer viewing platform on the ice with a handrail. We can't have the president of Turkey or any dignitaries falling into the abyss."

"No, that wouldn't be good." Jim chuckled. "I'll get Muhammad and Adem involved. They can get things organized in a hurry. They speak the language and have the contacts."

For several minutes, not a word was spoken. All three were lost in a wonderful feeling of accomplishment. They had never known such peace and satisfaction.

Chapter Thirty-One

A bdul was asleep when the radio operator woke him up.
"Wake up, sir. The message has come."
The man had turned on the bedside lamp. Abdul jerked awake when the radio operator touched him on the shoulder. He set up on the edge of his bed, sleep in his eyes, and his hair tousled about. He was in his khaki, sleeveless T-shirt and khaki boxer shorts. He was nervous and irritable. He had been dreading this call.

"Read the message," he growled.

The man's voice trembled as he read, "An earthquake has revealed the ark. The news is contained on the mountain. Message sent to Ankara that all is well and no damage sustained from the earthquake. Request your immediate arrival. Forty-one total count. No weapons except three security guards with pistols. I will identify myself when you arrive."

"That is the entire message, sir."

"Alert the pilot and the men I've selected. You know who they are. We will leave in fifteen minutes. That will be" — Abdul looked at his watch — "at ten-thirty sharp."

As the helicopter flew up the Ahora Gorge, Abdul, sitting in the front seat next to the pilot, looked through the windshield at the awesome sight of the moonlight on the rocks in the canyon below them and the helicopter spotlights on the massive, jagged rock wall in front of them. The size of it all dwarfed the helicopter.

The pilot coaxed the chopper higher and higher until the rocks stopped and the huge face of the glacier appeared. Within minutes, they reached the top of the glacier. The pilot turned off the lights as they cleared the rim. The moon shone brightly on the ice. They continued to climb at a steep angle, flying about twenty feet above the ice, continuing far up the glacier to the domed buildings high on the ice cap.

Everyone in the helicopter rode in silence. In the back of the helicopter were seven of Abdul's best men. Abdul referred to them as his soldiers. They were all trained to kill and all heavily armed. Some had Uzis, some large-magazine machine pistols. Even the pilot was a trained killer, fully armed. He would guard the helicopter and have it ready to fly when the mission was over.

This mission would be simple. Abdul had been informed earlier there were three guards, each working an eight-hour shift to allow for round-the-clock surveillance. They were the only ones on the mountain allowed to carry weapons, and they each carried only a Glock. The rest of the people were all archaeologists, engineers, filmmakers, cooks, or other workers, and none were armed. He had known this for weeks. The message he received tonight confirmed nothing had changed.

Finally Abdul spoke. "All right, everyone listen. I'll go over the plan one last time. First, you eliminate the security guards. Second, shoot out any yard lights. Third, round up everyone and bring them into the big dome. There are forty-one people at the site. Our contact will reveal himself. Have him take roll call. When you're sure everyone is present, kill them all. If they have been digging in the ice, there has to be a large hole somewhere by now. Drop all the bodies in the hole. In fact, bring them to the edge of the hole to shoot them — less blood on the ice to deal with.

"Fourth, get the explosives out of the helicopter and set them where I tell you. Fifth, set the detonators and on my orders get back in the chopper. Sixth, we will fly a safe distance away, and I will detonate the explosives. The explosion will blow up the ice, covering the bodies and the ark. If no one escapes to tell what actually happened, no one will ever know the ark was discovered. It will appear on the seismographs that a second, stronger quake occurred, opening the ice and swallowing all the workers.

"Then we will land again and examine what we've done. We want to be sure this all looks like the earthquake killed everyone, and we don't want any evidence the ark was ever found. And that will be the end of it! Do this right, and we will probably get a large bonus."

The men cheered and pumped their fists in the air.

As the chopper moved up the steep slope of the glacier, Abdul was again deep in thought. He was always a little afraid at the beginning of every operation like this, always worrying that something could go wrong and that he could be killed. He was careful to never let his fear show on his face. He would never show his men even a hint of the fear he sometimes felt.

Chapter Thirty-Two

att, Ann, and Jim reentered the large structure. Everyone had gone to bed. Matt glanced at his watch. It was 10:45 p.m.

"I was expecting Muhammad to be here by now," Matt said. "He left to write out a statement informing the Turkish government that we discovered the ark. That was almost forty-five minutes ago. I'll go see what's holding him up. We need to get that special message sent. Are you two ready to call it a night, or do you want to meet Muhammad and me in the cafeteria after we've sent the message? We'll probably be a few minutes. We have to also send a damage report about the earthquake, but I'm sure he has it ready to broadcast."

"I'm ready for some coffee," Ann said.

"We'll meet you," Jim added. "Hurry."

Matt headed for the communications room. He was anxious. In all the excitement, he hadn't realized Muhammad had been gone so long. He should've had the *communiqué* ready for Matt to sign and send at least a half hour ago.

Matt opened the door to the communications room. There was a tall bank of file cabinets in front of Muhammad's desk. The light was on over his desk. Matt called his name. There was no reply, so he turned to leave. He would have to see if Muhammad had gone to his quarters.

As Matt turned, something on the floor around the corner of the file cabinets caught his eye. The black rubber mat covering the floor had a strange-looking wet spot. The room was fairly dark except for the small light over the desk and the green glow coming from the radio dials illuminating the area.

Matt went back to the door and turned on the overhead fluorescent light. As he walked to the end of the file cabinets, a cold chill moved up his spine. He bent down. The slick wet spot was actually sticky, red blood.

Cautiously, Matt rose and walked around the end of the file cabinets that divided the room in two parts. There, still in his chair turned away from his desk facing Matt, sat Muhammad. His eyes were wide open, staring at Matt. His shirt and lap were covered in partially coagulated blood. Blood was still dripping from the gaping slice in his throat. There was a puddle on the floor, from which a small stream trickled to the end of the file cabinets.

Shocked at the sight of his friend dead in front of him, Matt glanced around the room to be sure the killer was not still there. There was a lot of blood on the desktop behind Muhammad, flooding the yellow tablet he had been writing on. It appeared he had been writing the communiqué for Matt to approve when someone came up behind him, slit his throat, and then turned the swivel chair around, positioning the body to face the two-way radio at the far side of the room, their only communication between the mountain and civilization.

Matt was in shock. *What maniac would do this?*

Even though the dials cast their eerie green light across the room, Matt suspected the radio had been disabled. He keyed the mike, but there was no sound. He then looked behind the radio. The broadcast cable had been cut.

He turned to leave. A crumpled piece of paper on the floor by the radio caught his eye. He quickly picked it up, spread it out on the desk beside the radio, and tried to decipher the Turkish words.

Thoughts were racing through Matt's mind. *Actually these are just scribbled notes, maybe an outline of what someone wanted to say. Could these be Muhammad's notes?*

He made out a few more words. *No, this is the message the killer sent out.*

Matt read out loud. "Earthquake revealed ark."

Further down the page were more words. *This is another message.* "Earthquake, no damage. Search continuing."

Matt knew now.

His pulse raced! Rotor blades. He could hear the unmistakable beat of a helicopter's rotor blades coming up from the Ahora Gorge. No one was expected to arrive today, certainly not at this time of night and not from that direction.

Matt was pretty sure the people in that helicopter were not going to be friendly. He shoved the message in his pocket, bounding out the door. Running toward the cafeteria, he mentally assessed the situation. *No one except the people up on this mountain know the ark has been found. The person or persons who murdered Muhammad and called in this helicopter are going to make sure no one else will ever hear about the great discovery. They will be extremists of some kind, and they will stop at nothing to keep the world from knowing the ark has been found.*

As the helicopter approached the domed buildings, Abdul snapped out of his thoughts and got ready for action. The moonlight was bright on the ice. He could see the helicopter pad was empty with no other helicopters on the complex. There were two snowmobiles parked in one corner. There were two yard lights; they would shoot them out. If anyone ran out of the building, they wouldn't be able to see well, but Abdul's men would be able to see them with night-vision goggles.

As they cleared the fence, the pilot turned on his landing lights and set the chopper down on the pad. He shut down the engine.

Matt could hear the chopper landing on the heliport. He had to find Ann and Jim before whoever had just landed rounded everyone up and shot them. Then he remembered, *We have no weapons*!

As he ran, his first thought was to warn everyone, but he knew the terrorists had to be coming in the main door by the helicopter landing pad right now. There wasn't enough time. If he tried to warn everyone by running around, shouting, "Terrorists! Run for your lives!" there would be mass panic, and they would probably all be shot in the melee. Also, what if he was wrong about the people on the chopper? What if he hadn't interpreted the words on the crumpled paper correctly? He didn't think he was wrong, but he wasn't going to take any chances. If he was right and these were terrorists, he felt the best chance for everyone to survive would be for him, Jim, and Ann to get outside the building now and not be rounded up with the rest of the people. Matt was hoping that whoever they were, they were not planning to kill anyone unless they killed everyone. If even one person escaped to tell what happened, their mission would all have been in vain. The world would know the ark was really here in the ice. They would just rebuild the next year, and they would find it again. Matt hoped he was right.

As Matt ran up the grating toward the cafeteria, he saw no one. Everyone was showering or had gone to bed. He hadn't seen one person yet. There were just empty tables in the cafeteria.

"No!" he shouted. Panicked, he knew he had been gone quite a while. Maybe Ann and Jim got tired of waiting and went to bed. *They have to be in here*, he thought. *They said they would wait for me in the cafeteria.*

Continuing his search, Matt ran back to the kitchen, and there were Ann and Jim by themselves at a table drinking coffee, laughing, and excitedly talking. He ran toward them barking the order, "Follow me quickly, now! Right now!"

As he got to the table, he grabbed Ann around the waist and pulled her backward off her chair. She started to protest until she saw the look of fear in Matt's eyes. She immediately got her feet under her and started following Matt toward the dishwashing and food prep area.

Jim sprang from the chair on his side of the table and followed Matt.

Matt directed, "Grab anything you can use as a weapon!"

He started looking for the carving knives. Matt grabbed a large knife, Jim snatched a couple of wicked-looking blades, and Ann picked up a meat cleaver. Matt slashed a hole through the heavy fabric material on the outside wall. They pushed through into the cold night air.

Abdul told his men, "Remain in your seats where you cannot be seen."

Two security guards came out of the shack from across the yard. They approached the side of the chopper, assuming someone was already coming to see the discovery. The pilot opened the door as if to speak to them, but before they could even open their mouths, he shot them. They both fell backward, round holes in their foreheads.

Next, the soldiers shot out the yard lights and quickly rushed the building. Within ten minutes, they had everyone out of the showers and their beds, standing in front of the crevasse in the ice with their hands in the air. Only two shots had been fired after they entered the building. Those two shots killed the third security guard, and the soldiers took his pistol. He didn't have a chance to fire a shot.

The dishwasher, who was the planted informant, immediately identified himself and joined the terrorists. He had a clipboard with a roster of every man who should be on the mountain. Before he even started checking off the names, he told Abdul three key people were missing: Dr. Matthew Lane, James Morgan, and Ann Tyler. Also absent were the helicopter pilot and his mechanic.

"Where are they?" Abdul demanded.

"The pilot and mechanic are at the lower heliport. They will be easy to get. Just go over on a snowmobile and shoot them. The three archaeologists should be in here. I don't know where they are."

"Well, let me explain something to you, 'Mr. Spy'." Abdul sneered with sarcasm. "We must kill everyone. No one can escape to explain what went on here. You understand me?"

"Yes, sir," the man stammered.

Shoving the man forward, Abdul snapped, "Go with these two, and find them." He dispatched two soldiers and the spy to start searching.

While Abdul waited, two men kept their guns trained on the workers, who still stood two deep in a line about twenty feet from the crevasse with their hands in the air, shivering from the cold and fear. Each of them knew that as soon as the bodies of Matt, Jim, and Ann were brought in, they would all be shot and their bodies pushed into the crevasse in the ice alongside Noah's ark.

"Where is the ark?" Abdul demanded.

Those in front of him pointed to the crevasse behind them. Roughly pushing the workers aside, Abdul grabbed the spotlight and slowly moved to the edge. His eyes followed the beam of light until he saw the wall of wood. The sight of the wooden wall startled him. Wide-eyed, he turned the spotlight right and left along the entire length as far as he could see each way. He was astonished at the sight!

It will be such a shame to bury it in the ice again, he thought. *But if I fail to accomplish what I was so well paid to do, I know what the consequences will be.* Seeing Noah's ark, Abdul wasn't very anxious to meet Allah after all he had done in his life.

Getting back to the task at hand, Abdul now knew where to set the explosives. A long line of explosives twenty feet back from the exposed wall of the ark should cause the ice to split and fall over the ark, concealing it forever as well as burying all the bodies.

Chapter Thirty-Three

"What's going on, partner?" Jim asked.

Before Matt could reply, the silence was broken by four shots being fired at the west end of the complex out by the helicopter pad, and the two yard lights went out. Matt's worst fears were now confirmed. These people were, indeed, terrorists. They probably had just shot some of the security guards.

As they quickly moved away from the slashed opening in the fabric, Matt told them about Muhammad and the radio.

"Oh no, not Muhammad," Ann gasped.

Matt handed Ann the crumpled paper. "Decipher this when we get in some light. I did the best I could. I think the helicopter that just landed is full of terrorists and the people who could help us think we survived the earthquake and now we're just fine up here. But believe me, we're not."

The only place for Matt, Jim, and Ann to get out of sight was a steel generator building. It was close to them. Two more shots echoed through the night as they darted inside. A huge diesel engine turning the generator took up most of the space and was running. The room had no lights, but Jim had a small penlight. He closed the door behind him, but there was no way to lock it.

Matt said, "We've got to get some weapons. Jim, you and Ann stay here. They must have shot the security guards out by the heliport. I'll go see if I can get the weapons the security guards were carrying. I'll be right back." He crept back out the only door.

Matt inched his way in the semidarkness toward the heliport. In the distance, he saw the glow of a cigarette. Someone was standing outside next to the helicopter. Matt could barely make out the two crumpled forms of the security guards near the terrorist's feet.

There were several oil drums close to the smallest dome building a few feet in front of him. He slowly crawled toward those drums without being seen. There were clouds in the sky, and a stiff breeze was blowing.

Searching the ice, Matt spotted a rock. He picked it up and hurled it over the helicopter. It made a loud noise as it hit the ice on the opposite side.

The terrorist immediately ran to the other side of the chopper, shouting something in Arabic.

Matt moved closer, keeping the oil drums between him and the helicopter. He found another rock as he went.

The terrorist returned to his post next to the helicopter, obviously scared and nervous now. He had a large-magazine, machine pistol in his hands, and he was searching the night for whatever danger was out there.

Matt was close enough now to see the bodies of the two security guards. One was lying face up, the other facedown. Matt could see the holster on the man lying face up, but he couldn't tell if it had a gun in it because the flap was closed.

A cold wind was blowing, but Matt was sweating. Peeking through a small crack between two oil drums, he knew he was running out of time. Finally a cloud covered the bright rays of the moon. He took one last look at the holster he hoped had a gun and threw the rock over the helicopter again. The terrorist ran to the other side and began shouting. Then he started shooting.

Matt ran as fast as he could toward the dead security guards. It was pitch-black now, and Matt almost stumbled over the bodies. He dropped to his knees and felt around and put his hand on the holster of the dead guard. He raised the flap, but the holster was empty. He felt under the body and all around, but there was no gun. He then felt the dead guard who had been face down. He rolled him over, and there in his holster was a pistol. Matt yanked the pistol out just as the moon came out and the terrorist rounded the tail of the chopper. Startled, he saw Matt, and for a split-second, they just stared at each other. Matt cocked his gun, aimed, and fired point-blank at the surprised terrorist. *Click.* The firing pin came down on an empty chamber.

The man started to grin as he pointed his gun at Matt. Two shots rang out from behind the oil drums. With an astonished, terrified look on his face, the terrorist dropped to his knees. He squeezed the trigger as he fell to his face, and the automatic shot off at least ten rounds over Matt's head and into the helicopter cockpit.

Matt was shaking as Jim and Ann stepped out into the moonlight from behind the oil drums.

"Thanks for saving my tail," Matt said as he ran to them.

"You owe me big time now, bro," Jim quipped. "But I guess I've finally had to kill someone." Jim was shaking as he kept staring at the dead terrorist by the chopper.

"How did you come by the semiautomatic?"

"It was a team effort between Ann and me," Jim excitedly whispered back. "A big guy with this gun came into the generator room. Ann was hiding in a dark corner, and I had climbed up on top of the radiator before he came in. As the barrel of his gun came toward Ann, a beam of moonlight through a louver shined on the barrel. Ann struck out with her cleaver where she thought the man's hand would be. I think she chopped his thumb off! I jumped down from the top of the engine, grabbed the gun, and hit him over the head with it. He was out cold. I didn't want to fire the gun to shoot him, so I found duct tape in the generator room and bound him up real tight."

"Unbelievable!" Matt glanced from Jim to Ann. "Well, we've got two down, and I don't know how many more to go, but we've got three guns now."

"Four," Ann whispered. "I found the other guard's pistol and the bullets to the pistol you tried to fire still in the bullet holders on his belt."

"Let's get back behind the oil drums. I'm sure some others will be along shortly," Matt said. "That helicopter is almost as big as the one in Iraq. There could have been ten people on that chopper."

"Well, if so, there's only eight now," Jim replied.

"I'm glad you're an optimist," Matt whispered.

Matt, Jim, and Ann waited behind the oil drums. It was hard to see. The moon kept going in and out of the cloud cover, and they had to peek around the drums to see anything. They kept glancing behind them in case someone came through the hole in the wall at the kitchen. Tension was mounting.

Ann thought she heard a noise behind her back where they came through the opening Matt had sliced in the tent. She listened carefully; then she heard it again. It sounded like two men, one whispering to the other. They were still out of sight but were arguing.

One said, "He didn't even give me a weapon. I shouldn't have to be out here. I did my job. Now you guys can do yours!"

The other man whispered, "Shut up, and keep moving!"

Ann recognized one voice, but she couldn't place who it was. She took a chance to move from behind her drum up to Matt and Jim. With hand signs, she gestured and pointed behind them and held up two fingers.

Matt nodded. He understood. He signaled to Jim to stay where he was to keep an eye on the west door. Then he motioned for Ann to get behind the group of drums behind Jim. Matt started working his way carefully back toward the main dome structure and the voices.

It was dark again now. The moon was partially hidden behind clouds, but Matt caught a glimpse of two men slowly moving toward him. He ducked back before they spotted him. One had an Uzi machine gun. The other man was smaller, and he was following along behind him, arguing.

Matt heard the man with the gun say in Turkish, "Shut up, and stay close behind me!"

There was nothing for Matt to hide behind. He dropped down flat on the ice close to the base of the curved fabric building and waited. He had no choice. It was him or them. Someone would die. Matt had his weapon aimed up at exactly where he expected the man in front to first appear. The terrorist had his night-vision goggles on. He was not looking down where Matt was lying. He didn't even see Matt until he saw the fire from the gun, not twenty feet in front of him and down on the ice.

A short burst from Matt's gun sent a dozen lead projectiles into him before he could aim his gun. Both the lead man and the spy who was with him were dead before they hit the ground.

Matt quickly checked for a pulse on both men, grabbed the Uzi, and ran back to Ann and Jim, who were still watching the west door. As he rounded the curve of the building, in a soft voice he said, "Don't shoot. It's me."

Ann had heard the shots and was almost hysterical when Matt returned. "Are you all right?" she asked with tears in her eyes.

"Yeah, I was lucky."

"I was so scared!"

Abdul tried to get his men to respond on the radio. He was growing impatient and very angry. He had heard the last shots over fifteen minutes ago, but the men he had sent out had not come back. They didn't respond to his calls. He also couldn't reach the pilot.

"You three!" He motioned to three of his men. "You go to the helicopter. Find out why the pilot is not answering and bring back the bodies of those we've killed. I want to see what these archaeologists look like, the ones who found Noah's ark."

"Shh," Jim cautioned. "I heard something at the door in front of us."

Quickly all their eyes were on the door, searching for any movement. Then the door started to open. Soon a man came through very slowly and cautiously, gun barrel first. After glancing around, he came out. He turned and fired several rounds into the drums. Ann gasped! The front drums were filled with hydraulic oil and engine oil, the heavy liquid keeping the bullets from coming out the back side. The oil started pouring out of the holes in the front of the drums, but Matt, Ann, and Jim didn't move.

The drums were situated so they could watch the man through the cracks between the barrels—at least until he moved out toward the helicopter. Then they had to sneak peeks around the edge of the drums, which was riskier.

In just a few seconds, out came two more men. They spoke in Arabic and in low tones. When the moon came out again, the three terrorists could see the pilot lying on the ground next to the two security guards. Without a pilot, the soldiers were very upset. They saw the bullet holes in the helicopter door. They all moved to the chopper, and one man opened the door. Ann heard him say, "No more radio."

Matt whispered to Jim, "We've got to take them out before they go back in … on my signal while the moon is still out." They both rose up slightly above the top of the drums and, with a loud burst of gunfire, shot the terrorists before they could shoot back. The man closest to Jim fired a burst as he went down, hitting Jim in the thigh.

Ann was shaking as she slowly stood up. All three terrorists were lying on the ground halfway between the entrance to the far west dome and the helicopter. Both Matt and Jim were visibly shaken. Neither had ever actually aimed a gun directly at a person and shot them before tonight. Now they had killed six men.

"You're hit!" Matt quickly looked at Jim's leg and saw he had only been grazed. He was bleeding but not much. They knew they didn't have much time to think about it. They rushed to the bodies to make sure everyone was actually dead. They were. Matt and Jim grabbed their weapons and two-way radios and ran back behind the drums.

Seconds later, the leader inside the building was screaming into the radio, demanding to know what had just happened and what was taking so long. There was no doubt about the fear and panic they could hear in his voice.

"We've got to be cautious and on our toes," Matt said. "So far we've just been extremely lucky."

"Let's hope our luck holds out," Jim answered breathlessly.

Chapter Thirty-Four

Abdul didn't know what to do next. He had sent five ruthless killers plus the spy out to bring in three unarmed archaeologists, one of whom was a woman, and they never came back or called in. What was going on? Surely the trained killers could find and bring in three unarmed civilians. He only had two soldiers left plus himself, and they were needed to guard these people on the ice.

Abdul was nervously pacing and screaming to his men. "This should all be over by now! All these witnesses should be dead! The explosives still in the chopper should be properly set for detonation, and we should be ready to lift off and push the detonator button! What has happened? Will someone tell me what has happened? Even the pilot has not called me! We've been hearing all this shooting, so where are my men?"

His soldiers and all the prisoners just looked at him. Obviously he was losing it.

Abdul tried to tell himself that any minute the soldiers would come back in with three archaeologists either dead or with their hands in the air. Maybe the radios just didn't work up here. Maybe he should start killing the prisoners now. No, he would wait a few more minutes. If even one of the archaeologists got away to tell the story, all the killing would be for nothing. No, he had to make sure there was no one alive to tell the world the ark had been discovered.

If only he could communicate with the archaeologists, he could threaten to kill everyone if they didn't surrender. But he couldn't communicate with anyone at all, and all his screaming into the radio and threatening to kill everyone got absolutely no response — even when he spoke in English.

Matt, Jim, and Ann were still hiding behind the drums, waiting to see if more men came out. They would like to tell the leader that his pilot and five men were dead and one was taken captive and try to talk him into surrendering. However, they knew if he heard their voices and knew they were still around and not already headed down the mountain, he would probably start killing the innocent people a few at a time until they agreed to give themselves up. They didn't dare get on the radio and speak to him.

Abdul knew he had to get himself under control. It had been over an hour since he sent the first two soldiers and the spy out. A half hour ago he'd sent three more out. He had not heard a word since. He had to know! Telling the cold and frightened prisoners to sit down on the grating, he left his last two soldiers to guard them. His instructions were, "Shoot anyone who stands up!"

He headed for any door that led out of the dome complex but not the door his last three men used. He knew they went out the same door by the helicopter-landing pad, the way they had all first entered the building. He would not go out that door. Instead, he went out the north door toward the gorge.

Abdul had one ace in the hole, something he was sure the three archaeologists would not have. Hanging around his neck was a pair of night-vision goggles.

They had to be out here. His men had thoroughly searched the inside when they arrived, and he was pretty sure with every man looking for them, they had not come back in.

He turned left when he exited the building. It was pitch-black out now, and the wind was blowing so hard he had to lean into it. With the goggles, he could see everything, but with a green haze. He kept moving west around the north side of the dome and then around the smallest dome.

All at once he saw them, and a cold chill went through his whole being. Three of his soldiers were lying dead on the ground between the door and his helicopter.

As he inched farther around the dome, he could see the chopper on the pad and the two dead security guards. Fear paralyzed him as he also spotted the unmistakable form of his pilot dead by the chopper.

He knew for sure now. Everyone he had sent out was probably dead, and the archaeologists more than likely had their weapons.

They were out here somewhere watching the helicopter, just waiting for someone else to come. He could never get to the helicopter, start it, and get it off the ground before he was killed.

One of the snowmobiles he had seen by the outer fence would be his only hope. All the way around the helicopter and along the fence was the only way to get to them. It was still pitch-black outside, and the wind was howling so probably his footsteps would not be heard.

This assignment had gone totally wrong. How could he have let this happen? These three people, who had somehow escaped, had to be much more capable than simple archaeologists. They had ambushed his well-trained men and taken their weapons. The entire operation was a lost cause. He would have to try to escape with his own life and then disappear if he wanted to stay alive.

Quietly he walked along the fence. He still couldn't see anyone, but he knew they were probably behind those fifty-five-gallon drums close to the entrance door.

There was no key in either snowmobile. A locked storage shed, where the gas was kept, stood next to the snowmobiles. Abdul was sure that's where the keys would be hanging, but he knew if he tried to get the door to the shed open, someone would hear him.

"We've got to see what's happening in there, and we have to get some help up here." Matt had formulated a plan. "Ann, can you take a snowmobile over to the point of the mountain where we store the helicopter and get on the radio in the helicopter and try to get us some help?"

"I'll try. Where are the snowmobile keys?"

"Hanging on a hook inside the shed door. The combination to the lock on the shed is three thousand. Be careful."

"You be careful," Ann whispered. "I'm scared to death for you guys."

Jim was closest to the west entrance door. He said, "I'm going in here, Matt."

Matt cautioned, "Move slowly and carefully, bro. I'm going back where we started. I'll go into the kitchen at the slice in the wall where we came out. Let's check our watches. I have about twelve forty-five in the morning. It won't start getting light for several hours. Check your ammo."

The three set their watches and checked their ammunition. Matt quickly checked Ann's gun, making sure it was loaded and that she knew how to fire it.

They all whispered "good luck," and Ann started out first. Cautiously leaving the protection of her oil drum, she stepped away from the structure out into the night. She could just make out the terrorists' chopper sitting motionless in the dark. She knew the bodies of the guards and one terrorist were close to it, and the other three were between the chopper and the entrance door to her right. She didn't want to use her light, but she also didn't want to trip over any dead bodies.

She walked carefully in the direction of where she remembered the snowmobiles were. It was so very dark. All at once she tripped over a rock, but she didn't fall. She was quite a distance out from the building, so she turned her penlight on just instantly to make sure there were no more rocks and to get her bearings. She had the gun Matt had given her hanging over her shoulder. She knew a little bit about guns but nothing about this automatic weapon. Matt had quickly shown her where the safety was, and she knew where the trigger was.

She was getting near the snowmobiles now. Most of the time it was pitch-black, but as the moonlight peaked in and out of the clouds, she could see the snowmobiles ahead. She was shivering with fear as she made her way to the shed. She turned the penlight on and held the cold steel in her mouth as she quickly dialed the combination. Turning the light off, she snapped the lock and opened the door. It creaked loudly, startling her.

Ann stepped inside, turning her light back on. There were three sets of keys. She remembered one was labeled black for the black snowmobile. The other was blue. She ignored the third set. Grabbing the key for the blue machine and turning the penlight off, she stepped back out, not taking the time to close the door. She moved cautiously to the snowmobiles. Positioning her body between the machine and the complex, she held the light close to where the key went in. Lightning fast, she turned the light on and then off. *Yes, it is the blue one.*

She heard one crunch of the footstep on the ice, and suddenly he was behind her. Grabbing and squeezing her throat from behind,

Abdul stuck the barrel of his gun in her ribs. Ann let out a garbled cry. He moved his hand over her mouth and took the gun off her shoulder and put it over his. *What is he going to do to me?*

She could feel his hot, foul breath on her neck. He spoke in a Turkish dialect. Shoving the barrel harder into her ribs, he said, "The keys, the keys."

She gave them to him.

"You're coming with me. We're going to ride off this mountain together, understand?"

She nodded.

As he dragged her back to the shed, he growled the order, "Don't say a word." Reaching into the dark, he felt for the other keys. He shoved both sets into his jacket pocket. Clutching her arm, he twisted it behind her and pushed her back to the snowmobile and forced her on it in front of him. He put the key in but sat there watching the complex for about a minute.

His left arm around her neck was choking her, and the gun barrel was bruising her ribs. "That really hurts," Ann managed to stammer in Turkish.

"Oh," he sneered. "You and I speak the same language. We are going to get along really well," and he shoved the gun barrel even harder.

She cried out in pain.

"Shut up!" he barked and squeezed her neck harder.

Another thirty seconds passed as he sat there while he watched the complex. They couldn't see anything but the outline of the buildings and a small light coming from where Matt had sliced the fabric.

All that ran through Ann's mind was, *I'm sorry, Matt. I tried to be so careful.* She was trembling.

"Stop shaking. You're going to drive this thing, and if you don't do it right, I'm going to kill you. You understand?"

She nodded.

"What?" he said. "I can't hear you."

"Yes," she mumbled.

Finally he turned the key, starting the engine. "Drive up to that gate really fast."

She did as she was told. The gate wasn't locked. Abdul pushed the gate open with his foot and had her gun the machine through the gate.

Jim got through the door and was making his way down the passageway. The rooms on both sides, where the showers and the toilets were, had no lights on. If anyone appeared in his line of sight, he knew he'd have to shoot first and ask questions later.

Matt had reached the opening in the fabric where dim light was coming through. Pausing outside, he could hear one man shouting to another in Turkish. The man was standing at the cafeteria door yelling to someone out on the ice in the main building. Matt could now understand enough Turkish language to determine the leader had left them to guard the crew, and they were afraid he wasn't coming back. One man shouted to the other man, "Abdul's not anywhere in the building. He's been gone a long time. Should we kill all these people and blow it up, or wait in case he comes back?"

Before the man could hear the reply, he was dead. Matt had come out of the kitchen. The man in the doorway heard him, turned his weapon back toward Matt, and fired a quick burst. The bullets hit all around Matt, but none connected. Matt fired as the man was still framed in the doorway and killed him.

Just then Matt heard the snowmobile start up and run across the yard. Matt sprinted back to the opening in the wall to be sure Ann got away safely. What he saw terrified him. The moon was out again, and Matt could see Ann on the snowmobile all right, but behind her sat a large man all dressed in black. They paused at the gate while the big man pushed the gate open. Then they barreled through the gate, heading down the snowmobile path.

Matt could not shoot and risk hitting Ann. He turned and ran out to the remaining snowmobile, praying as he ran that the terrorist hadn't taken the keys to it also. He must've been trying to find the keys when Ann came out. The door to the shed was open, and there, shining in the moonlight, was the key bar, but all the hook holders were empty. Matt's heart sunk. He frantically went to the snowmobile and looked in the ignition. No key.

His head was spinning; his mind was racing. Then he remembered. He had signed approval for plastic magnet key boxes. *Had they arrived? Could I be so lucky?*

He knelt down and felt around. Nothing. Then the other side. There it was, a small plastic box with a magnet attached. He slid open the top, and there was a key.

As Matt started out, he saw two headlights from snowmobiles coming up from the lower heliport. *That must be the pilot and the mechanic. Finally they are coming to investigate all the gunfire that has been going on since the helicopter landed.*

Abdul forced Ann to drive the snowmobile at top speed on the beaten path that led to the area where the pilot and mechanic kept the helicopter, Bobcat, and two snowmobiles. When she first saw the headlights coming toward them in the distance, an icy feeling went up her spine. She knew it was the mechanic and the pilot coming to see what was wrong.

Abdul was turned sideways, watching the gate to see if anyone was following them. Ann felt him tense up when he turned and saw the headlights about a quarter mile away coming straight at them and closing fast.

Abdul shouted in her ear, "Don't slow down! You keep gunning it!"

She felt the cold steel gun barrel pull away from her rib cage as Abdul aimed ahead at the fast approaching lights. Within a few more seconds, he would pull the trigger and start spraying bullets at the unsuspecting men coming toward them.

Fear laced with anger surged through her. She was not going to let him kill these innocent men. She had to do something quickly.

They were moving away from the smoother ice that sloped down to the gorge and were now parallel and just above the very jagged ice where she and Jim had fallen in the crevice. She couldn't turn right and head up hill. It was much too steep.

Suddenly, Ann turned left off the path and onto the very rough ice. She made the move so fast Abdul almost lost his gun just trying to hang on. Immediately they were airborne. The snowmobile landed hard and bounced down the craggy surface.

Abdul struck Ann on the side of her head with his gun barrel. "Slow down and get us off this rough ice, or I swear I will kill you!"

Matt watched the red taillights ricochet violently over the ice pack as Ann turned hard to the left, avoiding the two snowmobiles coming toward them. Matt cringed. *This is bad! This is really bad! They're going out over the ice where there are crevices hundreds of feet deep. That's the area were Jim and Ann fell in.*

Matt stopped and went back to the storage shed. Groping in the dark, he found what he was looking for — a large four-prong grappling hook. It was specifically designed with the hook points bent out to bite into the ice and had a long coil of rope attached. Jumping on his machine, Matt accelerated back out the gate with the hook hooked to the back of the seat and the rope in his lap.

Abdul had been forced to have Ann slow down to try to pick a path through the ice field. He was so enraged with anger at the stunt Ann had pulled that he was shaking. If he didn't need her now, she would be dead. With a bit of good luck and if he didn't get rattled, he could still get out of this mess. First he had to get off this rough, dangerous ice.

Abdul remembered that even though the glacier sloped sharply from the compound to the edge of the Ahora Gorge, the ice they had flown over in the helicopter had appeared to be much smoother. It was a long way from the fenced compound to the edge of the gorge. *No one will chase us at breakneck speed toward the edge. If the moon will just stay out so I can see, we may make it. A few hundred yards before the deep drop into the gorge, I'll have this witch slow way down and curve to the right so we don't go over the edge. Then we can follow the east rim of the gorge and get below the glacier and into the rocks. Then I can shoot her and climb down off the mountain. Some of the Kurdish people who live on these lower slopes will help me get back to civilization for a price.*

Abdul was on the smooth ice heading down the steep slope, but his pulse quickened and his heart sank when he saw the lights of the other snowmobile come out of the compound and follow them. *Whoever it is, he must have the throttle wide open because he's gaining on us. He must know I have a hostage, so he probably won't shoot.*

He forced Ann to go faster.

How did this guy chasing me get started out after me so fast? I have the other keys in my pocket. There must've been a second key somewhere. Just my lousy luck. This whole mission has been cursed from the start. Nothing has gone right. I've never had such bad luck.

Abdul made Ann go faster yet, but still the pursuer closed the gap. *Who is this crazy person following us? No one but a man as desperate as I am would be racing downhill at full speed toward the edge of this gorge. If anything happens to shut off the engine, we will never be able to negotiate the slow right turn. I have to kill this man now, or it will be too late. One miscalculation, and we will hurtle over the edge and plummet six thousand feet to the bottom.*

The snowmobile was straight behind him now. Abdul turned to his left side to fire, and the man moved right. Abdul fired a burst, but he was too far on the other side and missed. Matt kept zigzagging to avoid the gunfire as Abdul swiveled left and then right.

Ann wasn't about to sail over the edge at full throttle. When Abdul was turned far around and looking backward, she quickly turned the key off, swung her right leg to the left side, and turned the skis hard left. The machine started to turn left, but the momentum tipped it over onto its right side. Abdul was taken totally by surprise and dropped his gun. He was still on the seat, but his right leg was trapped under the snowmobile.

Still traveling toward the edge of the glacier at breakneck speed, Matt could see Ann in his headlight holding onto the overturned snowmobile. With a quick burst, Matt maneuvered closer in a last-ditch effort to rescue Ann.

Gripping the top handlebar of the snowmobile, Ann positioned herself to jump over to Matt's machine. As Matt extended his hand, she grabbed it and catapulted herself, landing half on and half off. With superhuman strength, he pulled her in front of him as he locked his arms around her.

Matt shut the engine off and slammed on the brakes to stop the belt. They slowed some, but he knew at this speed and incline they would never stop in time, if they stopped at all. Still going way too fast, they could never turn in a short enough arc to avoid going over the edge without turning over just like the other snowmobile.

Abdul still couldn't get the snowmobile off his leg. His pant leg and boot had been ground away, and the flesh was being scraped off clear to the bone. He screamed, "Help me, Allah! Please help me!" as he slid along on the ice behind the snowmobile.

They were still almost even with each other. Soon they would all sail over the edge together.

Matt yelled at Ann to steer and apply the brakes. Springing to action, he tied the rope to the back of the snowmobile and started paying out the grappling hook. It was bouncing so hard on the ice, Matt was afraid it might come back and hit Ann or him. He had to haul it back in and try something else.

Quickly he untied the rope from the snowmobile, took one large loop and put it over his head, brought the hook up through the loop, and cinched it tight around his waist. He took the loose end of the rope and tied it around Ann's waist and pulled it tight.

Then he screamed at Ann, "Hold tight to the rope! On the count of three, we're getting off! One … two … three!"

They jumped to the ice, hitting hard, tumbling and rolling. Both were trying to get on their stomachs with their heads up toward the slope. For a few seconds, they just slid down the ice right alongside the two snowmobiles. Finally, Matt got the grappling hook under his chest with a firm grip in each hand. He put all his weight onto the two bars down on the ice. Instantaneously, he slowed down. Then he felt Ann hit the end of the rope. He prayed that the knot around her waist would hold. He could do nothing now but hold tight and keep all his weight on the hooks. They were digging deep grooves in the ice, but they were slowing down fast. As Matt held tightly to the metal hook, he looked over his shoulder and saw Ann below him as she held on to the rope.

Abruptly, Matt and Ann stopped. At that same moment, they heard one last, long scream as Abdul and both snowmobiles went over the edge. They could hear him scream for a long time.

The only thing keeping them from sliding over the edge was the grappling hook, and it was barely dug into the hard ice. Ann was on her stomach, trying to dig her toes into the ice. She had both hands holding the rope still tied to her waist. The wind was blowing, and the ice was cold on her face.

The bright moon lit up Ann's surroundings as she looked at the ice below her. The edge was only a few feet below her boots. She could see where the ice ended, and the blackness of the Ahora Gorge began. She was scared beyond belief. Her body ached all over, especially her right side and her right ankle. Struggling, she tried harder to dig her toes into the ice, but it was frozen too hard.

The area she was lying on had been rounded by the wind. It was as if she were lying on the roof of a dome-shaped building. The only thing keeping her from sliding off was the rope around her waist that she was desperately holding on to. The ice was slick and smooth as glass. She tried to dig her fingers in to help pull herself away from the edge without pulling on the rope. The ice felt like cold steel, and she couldn't penetrate it. Matt was barely visible on the curve of the ice way above her. She tried yelling, and she knew he heard her because he answered, but she couldn't tell what he said. She wanted so badly to crawl up to him, to be beside him.

What if the terrorists had killed everyone? What had happened to Jim? Was he okay? Would he come to rescue them? What if no one came? How long can Matt bear down on that hook? Would the hook still grip the ice if he released his hold or shifted his weight? She didn't think so, not on the steep slope they were on and certainly not with her weight.

Matt was terrified for Ann. He could die out here if he had to, but not Ann. Matt remembered this was the second time they had been in a desperate situation on the same glacier. He could do nothing now but keep bearing down on the grappling hook and hold on. He prayed Jim had overcome the rest of the terrorists and would find them before he couldn't hold on any longer.

After what seemed like an eternity, Matt heard a helicopter. Excited, he saw it. It was slowly moving high up by the complex, a searchlight scanning the ice surface. As it came closer, another huge disappointment: it was the terrorists' helicopter. They were looking for whomever Matt had been chasing. Matt was devastated. What would happen to them now?

Within minutes, the light was shining on their position. He knew they had been spotted. The chopper moved toward them fast now and soon was hovering over them. Matt feared they would realize he was not one of them and would either shoot both of them or even be crueler and shoot him so they could watch Ann fall to her death. He waited, expecting to die at any moment.

Then he heard a voice he recognized. It was Jim. He was shouting at him to hold on. He would take Ann up first.

Matt watched as Jim struggled to get Ann in the sling. She was way too close to the edge. From what he could see, she was only feet from sliding into the gorge.

Finally Jim was gripping Matt's shoulders and getting the sling over his head. Five minutes later, they were all in the chopper, safe again. Hugs, tears, and cheers filled the cabin as the pilot flew back to the complex. Matt and Ann repeatedly thanked Jim, the mechanic, and the pilot for their rescue.

Then they were full of questions. "What happened? Are the terrorists still in the buildings? How did you get away?"

Animated, Jim described the events that had occurred. "When I got inside, I came face to face with the last terrorist. We totally surprised each other. I had my gun aimed at him, and he had his gun aimed at me. For a split second, either of us could have pulled the trigger. I really can't say why I didn't. I'm not afraid to admit that I was shaking like a leaf. I was terrified. We stood looking at each other a few seconds more. Then he laid his gun down and put his hands in the air. I was dumbfounded. The guy just surrendered to me."

"Wow," Matt said. "Good going, bro."

Jim beamed at the praise.

"Was that really the last terrorist?" Matt asked.

"Yes, except for the one that took Ann, the one we saw you chasing down the ice. When the pilot and mechanic arrived on the snowmobiles, we watched with binoculars as both snowmobiles went over the edge. We all feared the worst."

Before long, they landed at the heliport by the site. The pilot and mechanic were still shocked to see all the bodies lying in the area.

Matt said, "We'll fill in the details later."

Matt and Ann thanked the pilot and the mechanic again and started to exit the chopper. As Matt helped Ann out of the helicopter, he realized she was badly hurt. Gently, he carried her inside.

Adem had repaired the radio and had informed the authorities of all that had happened during the eventful night. When the helicopter arrived, he was still on the radio. When he saw them all come in, he jumped up and sighed with relief. Realizing Ann was hurt, he immediately got back on the radio to make sure the medical doctor came on the first helicopter.

Matt stayed close to Ann. He hoped her ankle was not broken, but he was more concerned about the sharp pains in her side and the cut on the side of her head. He knew the rope he had tied around her waist probably caused most of the damage when she was jerked so hard. As he tried to make her comfortable, he prayed she would be all right.

Everyone felt terrible that Muhammad and the security guards had been murdered. However, they all knew it could have been much worse. The intent of the terrorists had been to murder them all and to destroy the ark.

Chapter Thirty-Five

A few days later

"I just feel such a loss from the death of Muhammad and the three security guards." Ann had just finished sharing dinner at Ira and Paula Jensen's home.

"So many innocent men were murdered. It's dreadful," Paula sympathized. "But what a story! You guys should write a book."

"Speaking of stories," Ira inserted, "the broadcast will begin in just a few minutes, girls. Here, Ann, let me help you to the couch."

"Thanks Ira, I can make it. These crutches get me around pretty well. I really wanted to stay on the mountain, but Matt insisted I come back, so this time I let him win."

A knowing wink was exchanged between Ira and Paula.

"Letting me stay here to recuperate is so nice of you. I don't know how I can ever repay you."

"You just stay as long as you want. We love having you, Ann. You've been through so much. You need some time to heal before you go back up there," Paula said, fluffing the pillow under Ann's elevated leg. Since her life-or-death ordeal, Ira and Paula had been like surrogate parents to Ann.

"Come and sit down, Paula," Ira beckoned. "The program is starting."

Watching the two-hour television special about the discovery of Noah's ark was exhilarating. It seemed like just yesterday that they had found the ark.

When it was over, Ira excitedly quipped, "That was some special! Broadcast all over the world. After the news broke a few days ago that Noah's ark had been discovered on Mount Ararat, most people did not believe it. The broadcast tonight presented the facts. Just the building of the complex was a remarkable achievement. I must admit I was a bit dubious when Matt first outlined his ambitious plan to me. After seeing the film tonight, I can only applaud his creative imagination and sheer genius."

"Matt said it could be done, and he did it. I'm so proud of him!" Ann exclaimed. As soon as she blurted out the words of adoration, her cheeks flushed.

"But how did they film so much of the earthquake as it was happening?" Paula inquired, oblivious to Ann's embarrassment.

"I didn't know Esen had filmed it until just now. I'm as surprised as you are. Esen is our main cameraman and always has at least one camera with him, even in the cafeteria. He would sometimes film us telling stories after dinner. How he managed to film the earthquake with everything so chaotic, I don't know. As we saw tonight, even though the picture was shaking and sometimes at odd angles, he got most of it. He kept the camera running right up until the lights went out. It was horrific!"

"I'm sure it must've been," Paula consoled.

"The photographer must really love his work," Ira added. "He has marvelous footage of Matt throughout the entire project and some real great film of you and Jim, especially when you found the big beam last fall. The reaction of people, especially government leaders from so many different countries, has been astounding."

Paula commented, "I heard on the news that places of worship are overflowing even in non-Christian countries."

"I just hope it lasts," Ann wished.

"I'm sure it will last, and the best is yet to come."

"Yes," Ann said. "I've got to get well soon. I'm going to be there when Matt enters the ark. He called me this afternoon; they're allowed to use satellite phones now. They're busy adding length to the complex, so the whole ark is under cover. He's hired special contractors to chip away all the ice covering the entire top of the ark. He thinks they will be able to stand on the actual top deck of the ark in about two weeks. He is hoping I can be there. And I will be there!"

Chapter Thirty-Six

There were many new faces on the mountain that Ann didn't recognize. Those she did know greeted her warmly and were concerned about her injuries.

The men beamed as they introduced her to the new workers. Ann had earned their respect. They admired the fact that she had taken time to learn their language. This beautiful woman had worked incessantly without complaint on the project and even experienced the force of the earthquake alongside them, quickly administering first aid to those in need. They knew Ann was the one who had led Dr. Lane and Jim Morgan to the lost photographs of the ark. Paramount in their minds was the part she played in saving their lives by evading the terrorists and by helping Matt and Jim subdue them.

Ann was happy to see her old friends and chatted with everyone. She smiled and shook the hand of each new employee.

There was only a thin layer of ice now on the top of the ark. The workers were moving slowly and carefully so they would not damage the wood.

The ark was not level. It sloped several degrees down in the bow facing the Ahora Gorge and several degrees to port. Matt had noted that the huge main door on the port side was missing. Some old reports said it had been removed by Noah and used to build a shrine on the mountain near where the ark came to rest.

They soon came to the area of the top perimeter wall where the piece of the ark they found last fall had broken off. Matt and Jim chipped away the last of the ice from that spot. All the workers stopped briefly to watch. Matt, Jim, and Ann all put their hands on the heavy planking. It was exciting to at last touch the vessel.

The wood was very dense and looked dark brown in the bright sunlight. The engineers and two scientists were amazed at the condition of the wood. It was like the beam they had examined last fall — very dense, very hard, almost like rock. Each piece of wood showed marks from the axes that had shaped them so long ago.

Matt looked up at the photographers standing on the top ice filming the deep pit with the entire perimeter of wood outlining the huge vessel. *That will be quite a picture*, he thought.

The ark had not broken in two separate pieces as had been reported in earlier sightings. The surface of the perimeter wall was rough and split. Some dowels were missing, some heavy planking warped and twisted, but it was still intact.

When the bare wood of the main roof hatch was exposed, they excitedly tried to open it. But it wasn't going to open and reveal its secrets that easily. On one side, they could see the remnants of the old rusted hinges that were originally attached to the cover. Matt said, "Come on, everyone; let's try again."

Prying with steel crowbars, they finally got it open. Bright sunlight penetrated the dark void below. There was no ice inside the hatch. Everyone stayed clear for a few minutes on the advice of the two scientists to let any gas that might be toxic from centuries of decay escape.

Matt couldn't believe there was no ice in the top of the opening. He shined his flashlight down in. It was very dark inside. He saw a wooden deck below. He could see some old steps of the original ladder, badly warped and twisted. They couldn't be trusted. An aluminum extension ladder was lowered over the original steps to what appeared to be solid footing below.

Moving slowly and cautiously down the aluminum ladder with his bright flashlight, Matt went into the ark. As he descended, he was surprised that there was very little ice, only a patch here and there. He was astounded by the thickness of every support. Even the roof planking was over a foot thick. The deck he saw below looked solid. He shined his light on it before he put his weight on the floor. It felt strong.

All the wood above and the heavy walls were notched and dowelled. There was a heavy, musty smell inside. The wood was covered with a layer of dust. Under the dust was a shellac-like coating. The inside walls here were not as twisted as the exposed perimeter walls were.

Soon the rest of the inspection team — Jim, Ann, Adem, the two scientists, and two structural engineers — were all in the room with Matt, marveling at what they were witnessing.

Jim whispered, "Where's all the ice, Matt?"

"Exactly," Matt said.

He turned his light on some old shelves on one wall, now sagging. He said quietly, "I'd guess this room was a little crowded for eight people for so many months. They shined their lights around the room. Everyone was speechless, examining the interior of Noah's ark.

Matt broke the silence. "That's strange."

"What's strange?" Jim asked.

"It looks like there used to be some kind of a table here."

"Where?" Adem asked.

"See the six sawed-off stubs in the floor?" Matt was kneeling down with his flashlight. "The floor was actually built around them. I believe a heavy table was here. Each of these legs has been sawed off close to the floor ... sawed with a steel-tooth saw. I would guess sometime in the last couple hundred years someone took a large table out of the ark."

"It must have been fun getting it down off this mountain," Jim joked.

"They might have had to cut it into smaller sections," Adem remarked.

"I'd like to know who took it," Ann said angrily.

"Maybe the Russian expedition removed it," Matt theorized. "They had enough soldiers to get it down off the mountain and horses at the base camp to take it back to Russia. Maybe something was even carved on the top, possibly carved by Noah or his sons."

"It would be a great artifact to find," Jim added. "Maybe we can look for it someday."

In one corner were several clay pots and clay bowls. Most were broken, but some were still intact. They would be examined more carefully later.

In another corner was a pile of old wood. The pieces had been shaped, but they were badly cracked, twisted, and curved. Ann and one of the scientists knelt down close to it. Ann exclaimed, "It was a rocking chair!"

"A what?" Jim asked.

"Look at it. It was a rocking chair. Here are the rockers."

The scientist agreed with her.

"You're right. That's what it must have been. Too bad it hadn't been covered with pitch," Jim remarked. "Look how well it preserved the wood in the ark."

"They couldn't have sat on sticky pitch," Ann declared.

Matt heard them, but he was already through the doorway on the port side. It had a very heavy frame but never had a door in the frame. *Maybe a curtain*, Matt thought. He was walking on a horizontal walkway, careful with each step. He shined his flashlight all around in the dark. He soon realized why the ark had not collapsed, even without ice inside for support.

The walls were all vertical timbers. Hundreds of large diameter trees had been cut to the proper length, the branches cut off, the bark removed, and the two opposite sides smoothed and then stood up side by side. They were solidly anchored top and bottom, and horizontal braces kept them aligned. They were also covered with pitch on all four sides before they were put into place. They still appeared straight and strong. This ship was built to last.

Soon all eight of them were moving cautiously through this top deck, the highest deck in the vessel. The heavy-timber rooms were on both sides of the walkway in the center of the ship. The sound of their voices inside the vessel was strange. Matt described it as hollow sounding, but they could hear no echoes.

Matt had given strict orders; no more than the eight of them were to come in. He had promised, "If we feel it is safe, everyone will have a chance to go through the inside of the ark."

They continued cautiously. There were ramps leading to each deck below. "Look at this," Matt said. "The vertical walls are lined up so each wall is sitting on top of the heavy, thick deck and directly over the vertical wall below. The entire vessel is constructed like a giant honeycomb."

One of the structural engineers spoke up. "No wonder it lasted so long."

The engineers marveled at the design. They agreed that structurally it couldn't have been built any stronger. It was perfectly designed, and every interior deck, wall, and brace had been covered with pitch to preserve it.

They all stayed together. Ann stayed close to Matt. Shining their lights all around, they discussed each deck as they went.

There was some damage on the next deck down. They skirted weak areas in the wooden deck, and the structural engineers agreed they would need some steel jacks and shoring.

"Look, Matt, Jim!" Ann cried out, her light playing on two vertical hollow chutes extending from the deck above to the deck below. "They look like wooden chutes for water and feed, just like you guys predicted. You were right. I'm very impressed." She laughed, and everyone lightly applauded Jim and Matt.

They discovered some pieces on the deck that had been wooden wheels with iron fittings. The iron was mostly gone, but residue of the old rust was there. Jim, kneeling down beside one, exclaimed, "This used to be a pulley."

Matt said, "All this will have to be photographed and catalogued before any other people are allowed in."

Still on the second deck, there were many stacked small cages in some of the rooms. Some still had wooden bars. Other larger cages had been equipped with iron bars, but most of the old iron bars were just rust. The rust would crumble when touched, so they did not disturb them.

The eight explorers were still on the top and second decks when they spotted wooden boxes, pitchforks with only rust where tines had been, and twisted but still recognizable wooden shovels. Then they came across four piles of old rust that they determined had been hanging lanterns now fallen and lying on the deck. A few areas of old wood had rotted away where the animals had worn off the pitch. But all in all, it was fairly safe to walk if you were careful.

There were only three decks inside the ship, plus the keel below the bottom deck. They had walked through most of the top deck and the middle deck. This middle or second deck would have had the large door on the port side, but ice had formed in the ark where the door was missing.

Finally they got down to the bottom deck. Here they found larger rooms for large animals. The lower port side also contained a lot of ice. But on the higher, starboard side, there was no ice, and they spotted more vertical chutes. They came from the deck above, terminating just a few feet above this deck. There also were more remnants of old wooden vats, shovels, and pitchforks.

"Look at this!" Ann shouted excitedly. Wedged behind a vertical wooden chute in the lowest deck were two small wooden blocks.

Everyone hurried over to see what Ann had found. The blocks looked strange, but when she trained her light on them, it was apparent they were wood carvings. One was a lion, and one was an elephant. Only the bottom part of the trunk was broken off.

Matt looked higher behind the chute and found a carved doll with human features.

They would have to chip and melt the ice to see what other artifacts had been left by the family.

When Matt and Ann returned to the family quarters of the ark, they found themselves alone. The others were still on the lower decks. Ann was examining the rough vertical wall timbers. "Look, Matt," she said, astonished, "grooves have been cut in the wall here. What do you suppose they mean? They're just in this area close to where the table had been."

Matt came with his light and studied the marks. "They have been cut into the wood all right. In fact, I'll bet there is a mark for every day they lived in this ark."

"Of course," Ann said. "They're not divided in groups of five. They may be groups of seven, but no cross marks. I'm almost certain that's exactly what it is. We'll have to get better light to actually count them."

Then in a dark corner, Matt surprised Ann. He came up behind her and put his arms around her. It was cold in the ark, like a deep freeze. They were in their parkas, and both had on insulated khaki pants, but Ann felt Matt's warmth.

He whispered in her ear, "Can you believe all this, Ann? It's so astonishing. It almost seems unreal."

"It's beyond my wildest dreams."

For a couple of minutes, they just stood in the pitch-black enjoying being alone in Noah's ark.

Then Matt turned his flashlight on again. He had a mischievous grin on his face as he said, "How would you feel about being kissed in Noah's ark?"

"I'd love it."

"Do you think Noah would mind?"

"I think if Noah is watching, he would feel we each deserve a special kiss. After all, in our search we not only found his ark, but we also found each other."

Matt kissed Ann tenderly as they shared a special moment they would remember all the rest of their lives.

* * * * *

Finally, the photographers were sent in. The next day, the artifact collectors began to catalog and put everything in protective wrap. There was much speculation about which member of Noah's family might have carved the animals and the doll. They wondered who used the rocking chair. Was it needed to rock a newborn?

Within two weeks, the ice was completely removed, and the needed shoring was complete. Each day a handful of select personnel thoroughly examined every inch of the ark for more artifacts. Besides the three carvings, they found bits of grain, grass, straw, ancient mold, animal dung, bugs, mites, animal hair, animal skin, and many other microscopic items. These were sent to a lab for further analysis along with the clay pots and the clay bowls.

After all the artifacts had been removed so they wouldn't be damaged, Matt kept his promise. Every man who had worked on the mountain was given the opportunity to tour the ark and see photographs of the artifacts lying right where they were found.

When it was considered safe, religious leaders from all over the world were invited. Many came to see the ark. Finding the ark was declared the single most important artifact ever found in the world's history. It would have a profound effect on many future generations.

Chapter Thirty-Seven

A month later, Ann, Matt, and Jim arrived back in Washington. Matt and Jim had not seen a television set or heard the world news for months. They were amazed how the world seemed to have changed since the news was released about finding the ark. People were glued to their TVs every time the Turkish government released new photos.

The press mobbed them as they got off the plane at the airport. Shocked at their instant fame, they were pressed to be guests on many television programs. The news media were especially interested in interviewing Ann, since she had been the only woman on the mountain with all those men. With her usual grace and dignity, she handled the questions well, praising the Turkish workers and the Turkish government officials.

A lot of things were beginning to change for the better. Matt, Jim, and Ann believed it could be mostly attributed to the discovery of a common bond that all the people on the earth could believe in — the biblical ark of Noah.

The story about the terrorists on the mountain had apparently never been released to the news media. The Turkish government had thus far been successful in hiding the incident.

* * * * *

The following week, Ann was watching a documentary about the discovery of the ark with several friends. Matt was the program host. As she watched him on TV with her friends, she couldn't help but be filled with pride.

"Next spring the engineers will begin to disassemble the ark, one section at a time. With heavy-lift helicopters, small sections will be taken to the base of the mountain and stored in a protective environment. At the same time, construction will begin on a permanent display complex at the base of Mount Ararat in Dogubeyazit, Turkey. Removing the ark from the ice and relocating it in a new state-of-the-art building will be a tremendous engineering challenge," Matt was saying.

"I'm reminded of the challenge the engineers in Egypt faced in 1965 at Abu Simbel. The newly completed Aswan Dam on the Nile River would soon form a huge lake. Two ancient temples built by Ramses II would eventually be covered by the rising water, and the priceless archaeological treasures would be lost forever.

"In four years, both of these beautiful temples were cut out of the sandstone and relocated sixty-four meters higher up on the bank of the Nile. The problems the engineers faced in that project were nearly insurmountable, but they accomplished it, and it is a wonder to see.

"The ark relocation will perhaps be even more challenging, but I believe our engineers can do it.

"The structure they will build to display the ark will be enormous in size. The entire ark will be displayed in a gigantic glass-enclosed case. The public will be able to view the ark from several levels. Some areas of outside wall will be left open so portions of the interior will be visible from viewing platforms. All the artifacts that were in the ark will be displayed in sealed glass cases. There will be an auditorium where films of the entire ark project from start to finish can be seen. The government of Turkey has been very gracious and wants the ark to be available to anyone in the world who would like to see it. They have publicly stated that since the ark came to rest in Turkey, they will be the guardians of the treasure but the ark really belongs to all the people of the world."

After the broadcast was over, everyone hugged and thanked Ann for inviting them to view the TV special with her. She promised they would soon get to meet Matt in person, but she didn't tell them he was due to pick her up for their first real date in only a few hours. She told herself, *They will all get to meet him soon enough, but tonight he's going to belong to me!*

As she got dressed for the special occasion, her mind was flooded with so many thoughts and memories and also some anxiety. She and Matt had only had short moments of time together, no real time for conversation.

Ann had never allowed herself to become emotionally involved with a man before. She had lived happily with her father until he passed away. They had lived quite modestly, and she had no idea her father had much money. When he died and his will was read, he left everything in the form of a trust to Ann. She was overwhelmed when she learned what was in the trust; she had become a fairly wealthy woman. Most of this wealth had originally come from her grandfather Dimitri Surikova. After her father died, Ann continued to work because she loved her work, not because she had to work.

She kept her wealth a secret. Should she someday meet the right guy, Ann wanted to be sure the man of her dreams loved her, not her money. She had no way of knowing she would fall in love with a man who did not need her money.

It was a little awkward when Matt rang her doorbell at precisely seven that evening. Ann had selected a simple blue sheath dress with matching brocade coat. Her tanzanite jewelry accented her flawless complexion. Her hair was cascading down her back in auburn curls.

"Ann, you look absolutely stunning. What a lucky guy I am to be escorting such a beauty tonight!"

Ann felt like she was floating on a cloud as she took Matt's arm and walked to the car.

They talked about the TV special as Matt drove to a popular D.C. nightclub.

Before getting out of the car, Ann turned to Matt and said, "Wouldn't it be wonderful if my grandmother Jelena was still alive and could have witnessed the discovery of the ark? I think she would have been so happy and proud."

"I've got a feeling she did see it. And I know she is proud of you."

Ann smiled. "I hope she is. I loved her so much."

After dinner, Matt asked Ann if she would like to dance. He took her in his arms, and they glided across the dance floor. He was a marvelous dancer. Ann couldn't believe the orchestra was playing "The Way You Look Tonight."

It was the song from her dream.

When they left the club, Matt drove to his favorite park. The air smelled fresh and clean. The clouds were gone, and a huge yellow moon had just appeared on the horizon.

Matt and Ann joined several people walking through the grounds. Light from the street lamps illuminated the path as they walked hand-in-hand.

Soon they came to a quiet, secluded area. A flood of emotion engulfed Ann when Matthew gently pulled her close to him. She couldn't stop the rush of tears that came to her eyes. She turned her head to avoid his eyes for a moment and put her head to his cheek, closing her eyes as tears trickled down. All the pent-up feelings of these past months erupted at this tender moment. Safe in Matt's arms, Ann was in love.

Chapter Thirty-Eight

Jim was polishing off the plate of enchiladas as Matt and Ann sipped their Mexican coffee.

When they had arrived earlier, the owner of the restaurant, Carlos, recognized them immediately and shook each of their hands. "I've been seeing you on television all week. How wonderful to have discovered such a treasure. My family is so proud to have you come to our restaurant."

They graciously thanked Carlos.

After dinner, Matt waited for the right moment. "I just had a talk with Ira. Are you two ready for some more adventure?"

Both Jim and Ann perked up and answered yes in unison.

Matt smiled at their enthusiasm. Their response had been a foregone conclusion. "Great, because we are all three going to either Egypt or Israel or in the desert between."

"I've always wanted to go to both of those countries," Ann said. "If I can ride a camel, count me in."

"What does Ira want us to search for?" Jim asked.

"The ark of the covenant."

"You're kidding." Jim shook his head. "You mean the actual stone tablets that God gave to Moses on Mount Sinai?"

"Yes, the tablets that contain the original Ten Commandments. The stone tablets were kept for centuries in a very ornate, protective gold-covered box. Ira has purchased an ancient piece of parchment he believes will finally lead us to the actual ark of the covenant. The parchment is being examined in the lab now. They're not positive it is authentic yet, but Ira is very excited and optimistic."

"Not Ethiopia?" Jim asked. "Many people believe the ark of the covenant ended up in a church in Ethiopia."

"Yes, I know," Matt said, "but Ira doesn't believe it. He believes if the ark is really there, it would have been shown to the world by now. It is an artifact like Noah's ark, actual proof that the words in the Bible are true. The proof of its existence would have far-reaching effects in the world as we know it today. The people who claim to have it in their possession know this, and yet they have not shown it to the world. Therefore, Ira doesn't believe they really have the artifact. No, Ira said the area between Egypt and Israel, and we need to be prepared for traveling in the desert."

"But, Matt," Ann joked, "they have already found the ark of the covenant. I saw it in a movie a few years ago."

"Like you said," Matt retorted with a big smile, "that was a movie. This is the real thing, and it exists somewhere just waiting for us to find it and show it to the world."

"Let's just hope it doesn't have magical powers like the one in the movie," Jim laughed. "Anyway, I'm ready. When do we go?"

"In two weeks," Matt said.

"Good, that will give me time to explore a fascinating rock cliff in Mexico before we go. Do you guys want to come along?"

"Well we would, but Ira wants us to go to Thailand."

"Thailand? Why Thailand?"

"Someone who lives there believes the table from the Ark is in his family collection. He is willing to sell it if the price is right. Let's stay in touch and we can meet where Ira wants to start the search."

"Okay, but if you get in trouble down there, just give me a call."

"We will," Matt replied. "Just don't fall off that rock shelf."

It was starting to rain as they left the restaurant. When they got to the door, Jim said, "You guys will have to excuse me, but I've got a hot date. I promised I'd pick her up when she got off work, and if I don't hurry, I'll be late. Got to go." He was running out the door to his car before anyone could speak.

Matt and Ann left the restaurant and drove to Matt's house. As Matt pulled into the garage and closed the door, he proposed, "How about snuggling in front of a warm fire on a cold, rainy night?"

"As long as you get me home at a decent hour."

They both laughed.

The future and another adventure were on the horizon.

www.ingramcontent.com/pod-product-compliance
Lightning Source LLC
Chambersburg PA
CBHW070427120726
47910CB00003B/685